Be__

hidden talent rediscovered

Bello is a digital-only imprint of Pan Macmillan,
established to breathe new life into previously published,
classic books.

At Bello we believe in the timeless power of the imagination,
of a good story, narrative and entertainment, and we want to
use digital technology to ensure that many more readers
can enjoy these books into the future.

We publish in ebook and print-on-demand formats
to bring these wonderful books to new audiences.

www.panmacmillan.co.uk/bello

Richmal Crompton

Richmal Crompton (1890–1969) is best known for her thirty-eight books featuring William Brown, which were published between 1922 and 1970. Born in Lancashire, Crompton won a scholarship to Royal Holloway in London, where she trained as a schoolteacher, graduating in 1914, before turning to writing full-time. Alongside the *William* novels, Crompton wrote forty-one novels for adults, as well as nine collections of short stories.

Richmal Crompton

NARCISSA

First published 1948 by Macmillan

This edition published 2015 by Bello
an imprint of Pan Macmillan
20 New Wharf Road, London N1 9RR
Basingstoke and Oxford
Associated companies throughout the world

www.panmacmillan.co.uk/bello

ISBN 978-1-5098-1024-6 EPUB
ISBN 978-1-5098-1022-2 HB
ISBN 978-1-5098-1023-9 PB

Typeset by Ellipsis Digital Limited, Glasgow

Visit www.panmacmillan.com to read more about all our books
and to buy them. You will also find features, author interviews and
news of any author events, and you can sign up for e-newsletters
so that you're always first to hear about our new releases.

Chapter One

THERE were long curtains of plum-coloured damask at the schoolroom window and between them, on a small round table, covered by a white crochet mat, a bright-blue plant pot containing a begonia, which Aunt Fanny had brought in from the conservatory that morning. Aunt Fanny had also carried up the gilded bulrushes in the tall Chinese vase from the drawing-room and set them on the floor between the two bookcases. She wanted the room to look as nice as possible for the new governess. . . .

All day she had been feeling restless, excited and apprehensive by turns, unable to settle to anything. She hoped that she had made a wise choice. Miss Fairway had seemed so kind and capable at the interview, but it had only lasted for twenty minutes, and it would, of course, be quite easy to seem kind and capable for twenty minutes. Suppose that really she were unkind and inefficient. . . . One heard such distressing stories of unkind inefficient governesses. She tried to remember what she had said at the interview, but she could only remember how nervous she had felt beforehand and how reassured she had been by Miss Fairway's pleasant middle-aged face, neat grey bombazine dress and plain black cape and bonnet. She hoped that she had made it clear that Stella was an exceptional child and, like all exceptional children, required careful treatment. . . .

She let her gaze wander round the spacious comfortable room, with its thick carpet, solid furniture and heavy wall-paper, whose intricate botanical pattern was interrupted at frequent intervals by indifferent water-colours in massive gilt frames and chromo-lithographs of what Aunt Fanny thought of, simply and without the slightest interest or curiosity, as "foreign parts." The latter, together with the globe, bookcases and a small blackboard on an easel, were concessions to the "school" part of the room. Otherwise Aunt Fanny had tried to make it more like a sitting-room.

In Aunt Fanny's own childhood it had been the best spare bedroom—a post of honour for which its position on the first floor and its large window overlooking the garden clearly marked it out, and it was not without a secret feeling of guilt that she had altered the arrangement. Though she had been mistress of East Lodge for more than seven years, she could never make any change in it without that secret feeling of guilt, as if even now Papa might appear, eyes bloodshot, face purple, demanding with the familiar bellow of rage, how she *dared*. ... But surely even Papa would realise that Stella could not be expected to do her lessons in the little attic room that had served as a schoolroom for her and Adrian—tucked away under the roof, ice-cold in winter, stifling in summer. It had been all right for her and perhaps for Adrian, but not for Stella. ...

Her gaze rested finally on Stella herself, sitting at the big round table in the middle of the room, wearing a clean holland frock, with a starched white cambric pinafore, her feet, in long black stockings and strap-over shoes, perched on a wool-work footstool, her head, with its shining fringe and cascade of golden ringlets, bent over her cross-stitch work.

It gave Aunt Fanny a stab of joy so intense as to be almost pain to see Stella, happy, beloved, cared for, in this house where she herself had passed her childhood in a state of bemused terror—bullied by her father, neglected by the servants, despised by Adrian. The fact that Stella was happy and well cared for here seemed somehow to restore the balance. Though, of course, she knew that Stella was Adrian's little girl (poor Adrian! One must not think ill of the dead), she often seemed to become, in some strange way, the child that Aunt Fanny had been ... or else the child that Aunt Fanny had been became Stella—Aunt Fanny wasn't quite sure which. Anyway, to dress Stella daintily, to make much of her, to surround her with love and care, satisfied some thwarted vanity in Aunt Fanny herself, restored some remnants of her tattered self-respect. Though no one would have guessed it now, Aunt Fanny had not been unlike Stella when she was a little girl—she had had the same golden hair, blue eyes and skin of apple-blossom delicacy—and, looking at Stella, something in Aunt Fanny would say tremulously over the gulf of years, "It's all right now, darling. There's someone to take care of you now. . . ."

Stella glanced up and met Aunt Fanny's anxious gaze.

"Are you feeling nervous, darling?" said Aunt Fanny.

"No, thank you, Auntie," said Stella, and bent her head again over her work, drawing her needle out of the canvas and placing it carefully into the next hole.

Aunt Fanny felt, as often, put to shame by the child's serenity and industry.

"Dear, dear!" she said brightly. "Here I am wasting my time. . . ."

She took up her own needlework and sat down at the table by Stella. Her needlework consisted of one of the red flannel petticoats that she always presented to her protégées in the village at Christmas. Her hands were so unsteady, however, that after a few moments she laid the work down again.

"I expect you'll find your lessons much more interesting with Miss Fairway than you did with your poor old Auntie," she said with a sigh.

Stella threw her that bright clear unfaltering glance, and the childish lips parted in a reassuring smile.

"Indeed, I won't, Auntie," she said.

Aunt Fanny sighed again and, taking up her needlework, made an effort to go on with the feather-stitching round the hem. Her nervousness was changing to a blank and heavy depression. Ever since Stella was a baby, the two of them had shared this happy enclosed world of nursery and schoolroom, and now it was to be invaded by unknown—perhaps hostile—forces.

She had decided to engage a governess only after a bitter internal struggle. She had loved teaching Stella her letters, guiding the tiny hand in the "strokes and pot-hooks" that preceded the copybook, initiating her into the copybook itself, with its wealth of moral precept, helping her to read "The cat is on the mat," "The ass is on the grass," "The hen is in the pen," to do little sums in addition and subtraction with the aid of counters. But that had passed all too quickly and now ... Aunt Fanny had made up her mind from the beginning that only the best was good enough for her darling, and she had long ago realised that, as far as mental attainments went, she herself was not the best. Her spelling had always been erratic and she had always surreptitiously counted on her fingers. History and Geography she found fairly easy to teach. She set Stella a page to learn and then "heard" her by the simple process of repeating it sentence by sentence and leaving Stella to supply the last word.

Aunt Fanny. Madrid is the capital of——?

Stella. Spain.

Aunt Fanny. It is situated 2150 feet above——?

Stella. Sea level.

Or:

Aunt Fanny. Henry III, the eldest son of John, was nine years old at his father's——?

Stella. Death.

Aunt Fanny. His guardians were Gualo, papal legate, and William the Marshal, Earl of——?

Stella. Pembroke.

But there was no doubt that Stella learnt far more quickly than Aunt Fanny could teach her, that she asked questions that Aunt Fanny could not answer, and that of late she had seemed bored by the lessons.

About a fortnight ago, Aunt Fanny had discovered that Stella had copied out "All is not gold that gliters"—the day's "copy" set by Aunt Fanny—the required ten times, though perfectly aware that Aunt Fanny had misspelt the word glitters.

"I didn't think it mattered very much," Stella had said with an apologetic little smile, as if she herself had been at fault.

It was then that Aunt Fanny, reluctantly and with many secret tears, had decided that the time had come to hand over her precious charge to a better qualified instructress.

So now Miss Fairway was coming.

Oh dear, thought Aunt Fanny, holding up a needle and jabbing at it ineffectively with the end of an embroidery thread. I wonder ... I wish ... Suppose ... Perhaps ... For even Aunt Fanny's thoughts were jerky and disconnected.

"Shall I do it for you, Auntie?" said Stella.

"Thank you, dear," said Aunt Fanny.

Stella threaded the needle with a, quick deft movement and the two of them worked together in silence for a few moments. Aunt Fanny noticed despairingly that her feather-stitching was taking such an erratic uneven line that even the Poor must notice it and comment on it adversely. Oh well ... Oh dear. ...

Suddenly she decided that it would be much more fitting to receive the new governess alone in the drawing-room than in the schoolroom with Stella. She hadn't been sure about it from the beginning. ... She never was quite sure about anything.

She rose abruptly and gathered up her work.

"I think I'll go down to the drawing-room, dear," she said. "You can go into the garden if you like."

"Thank you, Auntie," said Stella, raising the serene blue eyes for a moment from her work. "I think I'll just finish this piece."

When Aunt Fanny was a little girl she had never been allowed to enter the drawing-room. She used to peep fearfully through the half-open door as she passed it on her way to the front door, and it had always seemed to her more like a palace than an ordinary room.

It still seemed to her like a palace. ... It was the largest room in the house, and had a deep bay window whose recess was filled by a tiered fern-stand of gilded wickerwork, holding in its intricately planned receptacles at least a dozen ferns and flowering plants. In the middle of the room was a "folding door," never closed, at which hung white lace curtains, tied back with broad blue ribbons. On the wall at the further end was a mirror covering the wall from floor to ceiling also draped with lace curtains, which reflected the bay window and suggested an archway leading into another similar room. On the massive marble mantelpiece was an elaborate "overmantel" containing innumerable little shelves interspersed with mirrors, each shelf supporting its array of knick-knacks. The carpet, of moss green boldly patterned with pink roses, was thick and luxurious.

Sometimes Aunt Fanny would stand in the middle of the room and look round—at the stuffed birds and wax flowers under their glass domes, the chiffoniers and cabinets and what-nots full of framed photographs, ornaments and "souvenirs," the curved tête-à-tête seat covered with yellow brocade, the occasional tables loaded with albums, the rosewood piano with its openwork front picked out in pink silk, the gilded fern-stand—and would find it difficult to believe that all these treasures were really hers.

But to Aunt Fanny the greatest treasure in the whole room was the oil painting of Stella that hung in the centre of the wall opposite the overmantel. It had been painted last year and the artist had captured perfectly the evanescent charm of childhood. Stella sat on a low stool, wearing a white frock with an apple-green sash. There was a picture book on her knees and she seemed to have just glanced up from it for a second. The blue eyes were grave and dreamy, the childish mouth exquisitely wistful in the shadow of the long golden curls. The next moment, one felt, the bright head would be bent over the book again, and the child would have returned to the world of dreams that she had never really left.

When Aunt Fanny was a little girl she had never had her portrait painted—not even a daguerreotype of her existed—but, looking from the portrait of Stella that dominated the drawing-room to the framed photographs of her that covered every available space on mantelpiece, piano and chiffonier, she was conscious of a vicarious glow of that warm contentment that, she imagined, came from memories of a happy childhood.

It was only after much searching of heart that Aunt Fanny had had gas installed in the downstairs room of East Lodge, and now, from the middle of the drawing-room ceiling, hung a chandelier supporting three gas brackets—so high that Mary, the housemaid, had to use a device rather like an extending toasting-fork with a long taper at the end to turn on the taps and light the "bat's wings" of flame behind the round shades of frosted glass. That had been one of the most decisive actions of Aunt Fanny's life, and she couldn't understand even now how she had ever had the temerity to carry it through. Half a dozen times she had nearly countermanded the whole thing. In the bedrooms candles were still used as a matter of course, and when Aunt Fanny was by herself in the evening (as she nearly always was) she used the silver oil-lamp with the red-silk frilled shade that had always been used in Papa's time. She felt in a confused sort of way that, by refraining from using the gas, she atoned for the enormity of having had it installed. "But you see, Papa," she kept explaining, often aloud, for she had the habit of talking aloud when alone, "everyone has gas now. . . . After all, it's 1887. . . ."

It was 1887.

On the Continent Germany, Austria and Italy had just signed the Triple Alliance, Bismarck had dissolved the Reichstag that had objected to his unprecedented expenditure on armaments, France and Russia were drawing closer together, Bulgaria was freeing herself from Russian control, and Prince Ferdinand of Saxe-Coburg had mounted the throne at Sofia. . . .

In London the Marlborough House set ruled Society and the old Queen was gathering her courage to face the ordeal of her Jubilee. . . . Alma Tadema, Landseer and Leighton seemed still to stand secure against the challenge of the Pre-Raphaelites. . . . Henry Irving and Ellen Terry filled the Lyceum, and all London flocked to see Mrs. Langtry in Pinero's latest play and to Brompton to see Colonel Cody's cowboys and Indians in the Wild West Show. . . . The Liberal Party was splitting over the question of Home Rule, Parnell was losing control over the extreme element of his countrymen, and the Colonial Conference, at which Australia had undertaken to pay for the maintenance of a British squadron on her coasts, had roused little general interest or enthusiasm. London itself was a medley of splendour and squalor, of extravagance and poverty. Swells, toffs and society beauties jostled beggars in rags and homeless children. Cobbled streets echoed to the sound of horses' hooves—carriages with powdered footmen beside the coachman on the box, dogcarts with "high steppers" and grooms perched up behind, victoria and barouche, brougham and landau, hansom cab and horse bus, pony trap and coster's cart—to the cries of street vendors and the strains of German bands. In the tall houses overworked kitchen-maids staggered up four or five flights of stairs carrying buckets of coal and cans of hot water. . . . When dusk fell, housemaids, with ankle-length aprons and streamered caps, drew down Venetian blinds and lit gas brackets beneath ever-darkening patches of ceiling. . . . Consumptives languished and died in sick rooms from which every breath of air was excluded by the careful family doctor, even the keyhole blocked with paper to prevent a draught. . . . Women strove to free themselves from the trammels of their sex or, failing that, to achieve the fashionable pyramidal shape, rising from full skirts, lifted provocatively to afford the fleeting glimpse of a daintily booted ankle, through bustle and padded bosom, to small neat heads and smaller bonnets.

Aunt Fanny cared for none of these things. She knew, of course, in a general way that the world was going from bad to worse, that Society was being invaded by vulgar American heiresses and still more vulgar South African millionaires, that gentlemen were beginning to smoke in the presence of ladies, even in public, that there were unwomanly women (only a very few, fortunately) who rode to hounds, went out with the guns and even, incredibly, played cricket. Of those other still more unwomanly women who supported what the dear Queen so rightly called "this mad wicked folly of Women's Rights" she did not allow herself even to think. But none of this seemed real to her, not in the way in which Stella and East Lodge and Miss Fairway were real. . . .

The hemstitching was becoming more and more erratic. Oh dear! She wished Miss Fairway would come. . . . She wished she wouldn't come. . . . She wished she would come. . . . She wished she wouldn't come. . . . She laid aside her needlework and went to the window, looking out at the garden over the semi-tropical barrier of the fern-stand's occupants.

The sight of old Hobbard, the gardener, mowing the lawn in his slow sturdy fashion, as if both he and the lawn were part of a world that would endure till Doomsday, reassured her. There was nothing to worry about. If Miss Fairway were not satisfactory, of course, she could dismiss her, though the thought of dismissing her made her heart flutter again with nervousness and apprehension. She never knew how to dismiss people. . . .

She fixed her pale short-sighted eyes on the green expanse of lawn that sloped down to a ha-ha dividing it from the park-like meadow beyond. On the lawn were star-shaped beds of geraniums, calceolarias and lobelias just as there had been in Papa's time. It was a pleasant rambling garden but, though Aunt Fanny had spent all her life in East Lodge, she remembered no romps on the lawn or games of Hide-and-Seek in the shrubbery and orchard. She only remembered how she had hidden in the stables from her father's anger, how she would run for refuge to the summer-house whenever he appeared at one of the windows of the house, how savagely he had punished her for breaking the stem of one of the tulips that still grew every spring in the star-shaped beds on the lawn. She was ashamed of remembering these things. It proved her, she thought, uncharitable and un-Christian. "Forgive your enemies," she quoted to herself, then was horrified that she should think of Papa as an enemy. . . .

But, though she had never played and romped in the garden, Stella did, flitting about among the trees, with bright eyes, rosy cheeks and flying ringlets. And, watching her, Aunt Fanny would feel a lump in her throat, would again become confused between the past and the present, seeing Stella as the little girl of forty years ago miraculously freed from un-happiness and fear.

"It's all right now, darling," she would say again. "Everything's all right now. . . ."

The sound of the crunching of the gravel on the drive outside made her heart leap and flutter.

It must be the carriage returning from the station with Miss Fairway.

Chapter Two

FOR several minutes after Aunt Fanny had left the schoolroom Stella still sat intent on her needlework—a cross-stitch kettle-holder that she was making for Aunt Fanny's birthday present. The pattern was a particularly pleasing one, a robin redbreast on a spray of green leaves against a pale-pink background.

Stella was a painstaking little girl and never minded how much time or trouble she gave to a task in order that the final result might satisfy her. She was leaving the red breast till the end because she thought that it was the most interesting part.

She worked slowly and carefully, only raising her head for a few seconds when she heard the sound of wheels on the gravel outside that told her the new governess had arrived. Then she finished off her thread neatly at the back, cut it short with the scissors, held out the work at arm's-length and considered it with grave absorption, head on one side.

The spray of leaves was finished. It looked very nice. She would start on the brown part of the robin this evening. She folded it up, put it away in her work-basket, which lay on the table in front of her, got down from her seat and went to the cupboard beneath the bookcase, where her toys were kept. She was a small, daintily built child, and her movements were quick and graceful. Choosing a gaily coloured rubber ball from her playthings, she went downstairs, stopping to pick up some skeins of embroidery thread that Aunt Fanny had dropped in her hurried flight from the schoolroom, and to put them neatly together on the hall chest, where Aunt Fanny would see them when she came out of the drawing-room.

She stepped from the dim hall into the golden warmth of the sun-drenched garden and stood for a moment, looking about her. Hobbard was still mowing the front lawn. She could see his broad gnome-like back bent over the mowing machine, his course followed by a shining ribbon-like strip of freshly mown grass.

There had been an occasion—a year or two ago—when Stella had been greatly distressed to see Hobbard's mowing machine approaching a cluster of daisies in the centre of the lawn. She had crouched over it, protecting it, and had wept bitterly when he had finally insisted on cutting it. Aunt Fanny had comforted her and explained to her that daisies, being, as she expressed it, "weeds by nature," could not be allowed to grow on a well-tended lawn, and after that Stella had carefully picked the daisies out of the grass cuttings and put them into water. Both her grief and the impulse to save the daisies from destruction had been genuine enough at the time, but she had continued to perform the little ceremony long after she had tired of it, because both Hobbard and Aunt Fanny seemed to expect it of her, and Aunt Fanny used to tell people about it.

She didn't want to do it this afternoon. She wanted to see the new governess. She went round to the side lawn and began to bounce her ball on the grass, running after it and catching it, throwing covert glances at the drawing-room window as she did so. She couldn't see Aunt Fanny, but the lace curtains and interstices of the fern-stand gave her occasional glimpses of a pleasant-faced middle-aged woman in a grey dress and black cape and bonnet, sitting very erect on an upright chair, her hands, in black cotton gloves, folded on her lap. That must be Miss Fairway. Stella was looking forward to having a governess. She loved Aunt Fanny and had enjoyed being taught by her, because Aunt Fanny was always so kind and so pleased by the progress she made, but there was no doubt that the lessons had of late been growing very dull. Aunt Fanny became so confused when you asked her questions and would get a different answer to a sum each time she did it. Throwing her ball to the end of the lawn and running to retrieve it, Stella caught a glimpse of Aunt Fanny's face. It was flushed, as it always was in moments of emotion, and she was talking quickly and earnestly. . . . Stella threw her ball among the lavender bushes that grew just beneath the drawing-room window and ran after it, crouching down among the bushes, looking for it. (It had lodged itself conveniently in the centre of the thickest bush, so that she need not find it till she wanted to.) Through the open window she could hear everything that Aunt Fanny and the governess were saying. . . .

"She is my brother's child," said Aunt Fanny.

(Her thoughts went to Adrian. . . . He had suffered, like her, from their father's tyranny but, strangely, it had not formed a bond between them. There had been enough of his father in him to make him delight in tormenting his sister and drawing their father's anger upon her. Aunt Fanny had pitied the gentle timid girl he had married and, despite her natural distress, had felt secretly guiltily relieved for Violet's sake when he was killed by a fall from his horse a year after the marriage.)

"Stella was born a month after his death," she went on, "and her mother died a week later."

("I'm coming, Adrian," Violet had said in that anxious propitiatory voice in which she always answered her husband's summons, and to Aunt Fanny, "You'll look after the baby, won't you?" . . . and, before any of them realised it, had slipped quietly away.)

For a few moments Stella could not hear what was said, then Aunt Fanny's voice was raised again on that rapt ecstatic note it always took when she was talking about Stella.

"She has an extraordinarily sweet nature. She cannot bear to see or hear of suffering." (For a moment Stella thought that the story of the daisies on the lawn was coming, but it didn't.) "And you will have no trouble with her work. She is so quick to learn that it is a question of keeping her back rather than forcing her on. She is very conscientious and absolutely straightforward."

Stella listened, gravely intent, without a trace of self-consciousness or embarrassment. It was as if they were discussing someone unconnected with herself, and she were carefully checking the points to make sure that they were correct. Sensitive . . . affectionate . . . clever . . . conscientious . . . straightforward. She accepted the fact that she was like that with no more conceit than if it had been a question of the size of her shoes or the material used for her underclothing.

"And I have always kept everything ugly from her," went on Aunt Fanny, lowering her voice slightly. "She's absolutely—innocent. I dismissed a housemaid only last year for talking to her about divorce."

Stella's mind went back to Ivy's dismissal, went further back to that sudden anger that had seized her when she overheard Ivy refer to her as a "sly little piece." There had been no pique or personal resentment in her anger. She felt as if Ivy had slandered—not herself but someone to whom she, Stella, owed devotion and loyalty. "Sly" . . . when everyone knew that she was straightforward, when Aunt Fanny told everyone everywhere that she was truthfulness itself. ("I've never known her tell a lie in her life," Aunt Fanny would say proudly.)

The next day was Ivy's "afternoon out," and Ivy said that she was going to visit her cousin, who had recently divorced her husband.

That night Aunt Fanny, coming to say goodnight to Stella as usual, found her sitting up and gazing into the distance, her eyes wide and puzzled.

"Auntie," she said, "what's divorce?"

In a way she wasn't acting. There were two Stellas—the one Aunt Fanny knew and was always describing to people, and another one who was sometimes the same as Aunt Fanny's Stella and sometimes different. This latter Stella was fully aware of the meaning of divorce, but the other was quite honestly ignorant of it. The other was just what Aunt Fanny thought she was, as dewily innocent of the darker side of life as she had been on the day when Aunt Fanny took her from her mother's arms. Sometimes she found Aunt Fanny's Stella rather a nuisance (as, for instance, when she had to keep on picking the daisies out of the grass cuttings), but it was just as real as the other one.

"Divorce, my love?" said Aunt Fanny, trembling.

It horrified her to think that even the shadow of the knowledge of evil had touched her darling.

Stella turned blue candid eyes on to her.

"Ivy was talking about it," she said.

Aunt Fanny's thin body stiffened and quivered, but she hid her indignation as best she could from her little niece, and her voice was almost steady as she said, "It's something that little girls cannot understand, my pet. Don't think of it again. I'm glad you told Auntie. You must always tell Auntie when people talk about things you don't understand, will you?"

"Yes, Auntie," said Stella.

"And now go to sleep, my precious."

"Yes, Auntie."

And Stella went to sleep, secure in the knowledge that Ivy would be packed off bag and baggage first thing the next morning. In a way she was sorry. She had liked Ivy—a jolly bouncing girl with a hearty laugh and a fine repertoire of popular songs—and she missed her very much at first. But she never for a moment regretted what she had done. She felt rather as a judge must feel whose duty it is to condemn a criminal for whom he has a personal liking. . . .

"I'm very careful indeed of her friends," Aunt Fanny was saying. "I don't think that one can be too careful—about everything—in the first years of a child's life, do you?"

Stella moved her position a little so that she could see the governess better. She had loosened her cape, showing the bodice of the grey bombazine dress, with the white cambric tucker at the neck, the collar held together by a large brooch consisting of a plait of grey hair wound round and round, covered by glass and encircled in gold. Perhaps it was her dead mother's, thought Stella with compassionate interest. . . . The pleasant kind face looked tired and worn. Perhaps her other pupils had been rough and rude and stupid and had worried her. She, Stella, wouldn't be like that. She would work hard and be polite and obedient and try to make her happy. A warm glow filled her heart. It was lovely to feel that you could make people happy. . . .

She drew back from the window as Mary entered the drawing-room, carrying the tea equipage, which she set on a low table covered by a cloth whose deep and intricate border of crochet work was one of the show pieces of Aunt Fanny's youth. Aunt Fanny began to busy herself in her usual ineffective fashion with the copper tea-kettle, making several attempts to light the little spirit flame underneath it, and in the end letting Miss Fairway do it for her. Aunt Fanny was secretly terrified of the tea-kettle. It always boiled over, and, however hard she blew, she never seemed able to blow out the little blue flame. This afternoon Miss Fairway did it all for her quickly and efficiently. Then Aunt Fanny made the tea and began to talk about Stella again.

"Yes . . . the portrait is an excellent likeness. . . . She resembles me as I was at her age." Aunt Fanny's diffidence and timidity had returned. Her voice trailed away uncertainly. "My mother died when I was a child. . . . I had a very unhappy childhood. . . . I decided that Stella should know nothing but love and happiness. . . . My father . . ."

But Stella wasn't interested in Aunt Fanny's childhood. She had heard too much about it. She did not for one moment believe that Aunt Fanny had been like her when she was a child, though she pretended to, in order not to hurt Aunt Fanny's feelings. She was always very careful not to hurt people's feelings. . . .

She found her ball in the middle of the lavender bush and stepped back onto the gravel path. She would have liked to go into the front garden again, but Hobbard was still mowing the lawn and might expect her to pick the daisies out of the grass heap, if she did. He was rather a silly old man and had adored "little Missie" from her babyhood. He told her that he saw elves and fairies in the garden when he came to work first thing in the morning, and once he had arranged a "fairy feast," consisting of acorn cups set round the top of a tree stump, for her to discover in the spinney. Stella, who had never really believed in fairies (though, of course, Aunt Fanny's Stella believed in them), found him very irritating sometimes.

She wandered down through the kitchen garden towards the

iron gates that led out into the lane at the back. A tramp was coming slowly down the lane. He was bent and dusty and hatless, his clothes were in rags, his boots tied on with string. His hair and long white beard were matted, his face deeply lined. He stopped at the gate to watch her, and she began to run about, playing with her ball as if she had not noticed him. She could see herself quite plainly through the old man's eyes. She shook her head a little as she ran to make her curls fly out behind.

"Missie!" he called in a low hoarse voice.

She stopped suddenly, turned a startled glance onto him, then went slowly down towards the gate. Now that she was close to him, she saw that he looked old and ill and tired. She stood watching him gravely, while something in her waited expectantly for the wave of pity and distress. . . . When it came it was quite satisfactory in its effect. It seemed to engulf her whole spirit, turning the sunny garden black before her eyes.

"Poor old man!" she said compassionately. "Would you like to come in and rest?"

She was sure that Aunt Fanny wouldn't mind her inviting him in to rest, because Aunt Fanny knew how terribly it hurt her to see people unhappy, knew that she *had* to try to help.

He shook his head.

"No, thank you kindly, missie, but if you could get me a drink of water . . .?"

"Of course," she said, turning to run back to the house. When she reached the hall she paused for a moment outside the drawing-room door. She could hear Aunt Fanny's voice . . . then Miss Fairway's . . . "Stella . . . Stella . . . Stella . . ." No, she mustn't interrupt them. And it would be useless to go to the kitchen and ask Cook or Mary. They hated poor people unless they were nice and clean, and this poor old man certainly wasn't nice and clean. Coming to a sudden decision, she went upstairs to her bedroom and filled her glass from the carafe of water, then went to the schoolroom. A dessert plate on the side table held her peach—beautifully round and soft and golden-pink. She was allowed one peach a day. Generally she had it with her supper, but Aunt

Fanny never minded if she ate it before supper. She looked at it longingly. She loved peaches . . . but the poor old man needed it more than she did. Probably he had never had a peach in his life before. She took it from her plate, was tempted to put it back, resisted the temptation, and went out into the garden again, carrying the glass of water in one hand and the peach in the other. At the greenhouse door she stopped. Perhaps it was rather silly to let him drink out of her glass. He *was* dirty. . . . On the greenhouse shelf was the chipped enamel mug that Hobbard used for the cold tea he always brought with him in a tin can. That would do. A poor old man would like it better than the glass. She filled it at the tap from which Hobbard filled his watering-can and took it down to the old man.

"Here's the water," she said, smiling at him.

He took the mug through the gate in a shaky dirt-engrained hand and drained it zestfully. Then she held out the peach.

"And I've brought you a peach," she said.

His face looked just as she had hoped it would look—surprised, delighted, bewildered.

"God bless you for your kindness, missie," he said.

There, of course, she realised the little scene must end, so she smiled at him again and turned away to run down the path, through the kitchen garden, stopping at the end to wave to him. He was standing there watching her, the peach still in his hand, his toothless gums showing in a grin of bemused delight.

She ran back to the house. She would miss her peach at supper-time, but she had made the old man happy, and it was better to give other people pleasure than to have it oneself. She wouldn't tell even Aunt Fanny about giving him the peach. One shouldn't tell other people about the kind things one did. It was enough to know oneself. To know oneself gave one a lovely warm feeling inside. . . .

Aunt Fanny called her from the drawing-room as she was crossing the hall.

"Oh, there you are, dear. Come in. . . . This is Miss Fairway who is going to teach you."

Stella entered the drawing-room and held out her hand to the newcomer.

"How do you do?" she said.

Miss Fairway looked at her with interest, and her spirits rose. This was a refreshing change from the dreary garrulous old aunt. The portrait had prepared her for the child's exquisite colouring and the look of tender innocence that should (though it frequently does not) characterise childhood, but it had barely done justice to its subject. The blue eyes met hers with frank friendliness, the lips were parted in a half-shy smile of welcome. There was a poise, a lack of self-consciousness, about the fairylike little figure that was oddly appealing. No, the aunt hadn't, after all, overrated her charms. . . . She was going to enjoy this place. A lifetime spent in in-structing the young had taught Miss Fairway how few children can properly be described as lovable . . . but this child she loved already.

"Now we'll go and see the schoolroom," said Aunt Fanny.

She was feeling expansively happy. Miss Fairway seemed fully as kind and capable as she had seemed at the interview, and it was clear that she liked Stella, and that Stella liked her. Dear little Stella, so affectionate and sensitive! The thought that anyone might be unkind to her darling brought a hot suffocating feeling to Aunt Fanny's throat. She meant to keep a careful eye on her even now. She must not betray her trust.

Stella followed them upstairs to the schoolroom.

"This is the schoolroom," said Aunt Fanny.

She looked round the room with satisfaction. The begonia and the vase of gilded bulrushes certainly were happy touches, lending an air of elegance to the otherwise sombre room. She would leave them there for the present. Her eyes went to the side table.

"You've had your peach, have you, my pet?" she said.

"Yes, Auntie," nodded Stella. "I took it this afternoon."

Again the temptation to tell Aunt Fanny about giving it to the poor old man assailed her . . . but she resisted it. It was enough to know oneself. . . . Then, as her mind went over the afternoon, a chill fell on her spirit. It was a series of delightful pictures—all except one. And that one was not delightful at all. It was the picture of a little girl crouching among the lavender bushes under the drawing-room window, listening. . . . She tried to cover it over with the other pictures—the little girl playing in the garden, the little girl giving her peach to the poor old man, the little girl welcoming the new governess—but that picture of the little girl crouching beneath the drawing-room window, listening, refused to be hidden. Even the final picture of a penitent little girl, really and truly sorry, failed to blot it out.

"Yes, it's a pleasant room," Aunt Fanny was saying. "We have always enjoyed our lessons here, have we not, my love?"

"Yes," said Stella, looking from Aunt Fanny to the governess with a smile. She smiled at Aunt Fanny to assure her that she had enjoyed her lessons with her in the past, and at the governess to assure her that she was going to enjoy her lessons with her in the future. She didn't want either of them to feel hurt.

"And now," said Aunt Fanny to Miss Fairway, "I'm sure that you would like to see your room and unpack."

A few minutes later Aunt Fanny, having shown the governess her bedroom, came down to the drawing-room. Stella stood by the window. There was something forlorn and disconsolate about the small figure. She was the penitent little girl.

"What's the matter, darling?" said Aunt Fanny, concerned.

"I want to tell you something," said Stella. The corners of the wistful mouth drooped. The blue eyes held a world of childish unhappiness.

Aunt Fanny paled.

"You're not feeling ill, my pet, are you?" she said.

"No," said Stella," but—I've done something naughty. My ball went on the bed just outside the drawing-room window and I went on the bed to get it. I forgot that you said I must ask you or Hobbard to get my ball when it went on the beds, in case I did some damage to the plants. I didn't do any damage, but—I went on the bed when you'd told me not to."

Aunt Fanny's eyes were misty with emotion.

"My darling," she murmured.

"It's made me so unhappy," went on Stella in a small unsteady voice, "to think that I'd done something you'd told me not to."

"My love," said Aunt Fanny, "you are a very good little girl to tell me and we will neither of us think of it again. You must always tell Auntie—won't you?—when you've done anything you're ashamed of. That's Auntie's good little girl!"

A few moments later Stella was running happily out onto the lawn. Hobbard had finished mowing it and had taken the grass cuttings away, so it was quite safe. . . . She was glad that she had confessed to Aunt Fanny. The ugly picture was destroyed. She could hardly remember now even what it had looked like. Only the other pictures remained . . . the little girl playing in the garden . . . the little girl giving her peach to the poor old man . . . the little girl welcoming the governess. . . . The little girl confessing a fault to Aunt Fanny had taken its place at the end of the gallery, but the ugly one had quite disappeared.

Chapter Three

MY DEAR COUSIN (wrote Miss Fairway),

I will now fulfil the promise I made of acquainting you as soon as possible with the Particulars of my new Situation. I am indeed Fortunate. The house is a commodious gentleman's Residence set in pleasant rural Surroundings on the outskirts of a village, Runeham by name, and I am treated with every Consideration. My employer is perhaps—if I may say so without disrespect—somewhat Lacking in Poise and Wisdom, but my Pupil is everything that Could be Desired. In appearance she is quite a little Beauty and is possessed of Intelligence far above the Average. I have never met a child so Quick to Learn and Understand. It is indeed a Relief to be rid of that Sensation of pushing a heavy weight uphill that I have had to Contend with in teaching Certain former Pupils. When my employer informed me that the child was "sensitive," I Feared that she might be one of those children who Weep and make Scenes, but it is not so at all. Her "Sensitiveness" takes the form of Understanding at once when one is Tired or wishes to be Left Alone. It is indeed unusual to find such tact and Sympathy in a child. It is unusual, too, for a Pupil to pay such Graceful Attentions to a Governess as bringing in Posies from the garden to arrange in a Vase in her Bedroom.

I hope that I have not drawn the Picture of a Little Prig, for the child is far from being that. She is full of Gaiety and Good humour and can romp as whole-heartedly as any child I have known. She has, moreover, a Delightful Imagination and invents games which we sometimes play together throughout the day, each taking some imaginary Character. ... You will Declare that the child has Bewitched me, and in a way this is True.

From the Beginning she welcomed me as Friend and Playfellow as well as Instructress, and that is something Novel and Gratifying for a governess. During this fine Summer weather we have had our Lessons out of doors, and the Lessons have, I fear, often Deteriorated into little Talks about flowers or birds or other natural Phenomena. It is, I suppose, the combined Effect of the Fine weather and the beautiful Garden and my Exceptional Pupil that has given me a strange feeling of Unreality, which I have never Experienced before. I hope that it does not mean I shall Wake up one Morning to find myself still Governess to those Unruly Smiths! No doubt it will Pass as I become more accustomed to my Enviable Situation. The child, I must add, has decided Talent. She paints Charming little Studies of flowers and leaves and has a more Sensitive Touch on the Instrument than any child I have ever taught, as well as an exceptionally Quick Memory.

I am writing this in the Schoolroom, while my pupil is Resting in her Bedroom. She rests for half an hour every day after luncheon, but today she is resting for an hour, as some Children are coming to tea and she sees so few People outside the Household (my Employer is Particular about that and, I think, Wisely) that it is a great Occasion for her. It is probably the fact that she sees so Few People that has kept her so Unspoilt. One of the children who are coming to tea is Hugh Carlswell, the son of Sir Miles Carlswell of Runeham Hall. He is about three years older than my pupil and is a very Handsome Child. He has the air of a little Prince just as my pupil has the air of a little Princess. They make such a Charming Couple that one cannot resist looking into the Future and discreetly Speculating. ... He is a somewhat slow and serious child and one can see how much he admires my little pupil's Quick Intelligence and Flashes of charming Fancy. Though he is at present an only child, his mother is expecting an Interesting Event shortly, to which, I need hardly say, the whole Neighbourhood is looking Forward with Sympathetic Concern. The other guests are Biddy Lytton, the Vicar's daughter, and Doreen Blake, daughter of Nicholas Blake,

22

the novelist—a cousin, who is Staying with her and whom I have not yet met. There are very few children in the Neighbourhood who are Suitable Companions for my little pupil. The village Schoolmaster, Mr. Sanders, has a son about her age, but, though he is Well-spoken and Well-mannered, the mother is quite Common and so, of course, we cannot allow Stella to Associate with him. This is Difficult, as the child has no idea at all of Social Differences. We met the boy—Paul Sanders—in the village this morning and it was a very Delicate Task to make her understand why it was Impossible to ask him to join her little Gathering this afternoon. She is full of a sort of Overflowing Affection for Everyone around her, which is very Affecting and Beautiful.

Well, I must now go and prepare my little hostess to receive her Guests. I suppose that I shall in time become Accustomed to this Fortunate Situation and that the Sense of Unreality I told you of will Disappear.

I remain,

Your affectionate Cousin,

LUCIA FAIRWAY

Hugh Carlswell was the first of the guests to arrive. He was a tall fair child, with serious blue eyes and the look, as Mr. Lytton, the Vicar, put it, of a young Viking. He carried his slender figure with a careless air of breeding, almost of arrogance, as though the spirit of his forebears, who had exercised lordship over Runeham and the surrounding villages for so many generations, still lived in him. Many of them had held high offices of State, but the present baronet, Sir Miles Carlswell, though a staunch Tory, contented himself with the life of landlord and sportsman and the leadership of local affairs. He and Lady Carlswell still reigned in almost feudal fashion at Runeham, dispensing charity with open hands, fulfilling every obligation of their position punctiliously according to their lights—kind-hearted, generous, intolerant.

Aunt Fanny was awaiting the guests in the drawing-room, wearing her best dress of prune-coloured surah, with high neck, tightly buttoned bodice and an over-dress draped up onto the bustle behind.

She was engaged on an elaborate piece of Berlin wool work (the red flannel petticoat was, of course, reserved for more private occasions), and Stella sat on a stool near, her small bright head bent over her cross-stitch, her curls shading her face. She had reached the red breast now and was working rather slowly because she was enjoying it. . . . She wore a white muslin frock with blue shoulder ribbons to match her blue sash, long black stockings and buttoned boots.

Aunt Fanny rose when Hugh was announced, dropping her wools all over the carpet. That broke the constraint of the meeting between the two children, and Stella laughed as they scrambled about the floor picking up the skeins of wool, while Hugh, who seldom laughed, smiled his slow grave smile.

"I'm so sorry, my dears," said Aunt Fanny, dropping the wools again as quickly as they were picked up. "So very sorry. . . . Thank you *so* much. . . . And now, Stella dear, perhaps you will take Hugh into the garden till Biddy and her cousin arrive."

The two children went out into the garden, and Aunt Fanny went upstairs to the schoolroom, where Miss Fairway was superintending the preparations for tea. There were to be jellies and sugar biscuits and a chocolate iced cake, which Mary had just brought up from the kitchen.

"We were wondering whether to put the cake or the begonia in the centre of the table, Miss Markham," said Miss Fairway. "Which would you prefer?"

"The cake," said Aunt Fanny, plunging at a decision and immediately regretting it. "No, perhaps not. . . . Perhaps the begonia. . . . It looks so nice. . . . So does the cake. . . . What do you think, Miss Fairway?"

"On the whole, the cake," said Miss Fairway. "The begonia, I think, shows off to excellent advantage where it is and might make the table appear overcrowded."

"Yes, the cake," said Aunt Fanny, trying to sound as if the decision were hers. "Certainly the cake."

"This is my garden," said Stella.

The two children stopped by the small square garden outlined in stones and shells. Virginia stock grew in it and marigolds and snapdragons and mignonette and some rows of radishes.

"Hobbard says that they're too crowded together," said Stella, "but I always want to have as many as I can. I love flowers so, don't you?"

He nodded, in silence, his eyes fixed on her. She looked up quickly and met his gaze.

"What are you thinking of?"

"I'm thinking of the time when you found a rabbit in a trap and brought it home."

The small flower-like face seemed to stiffen in sudden pain.

"It was so *cruel* !" she said. "I don't know how people can be as cruel as that."

"They do a tremendous amount of harm, you know, rabbits," he said gently.

"I don't care," she retorted. "I'd rather let them do all the harm they wanted to than be *cruel. . . .*"

He nodded again gravely—not in agreement, for he looked on rabbits as vermin, but because it was right and fit that she should feel like that. She belonged to a world set high above the ugliness of life. He knew very few girls. In Runeham itself there were only Stella and Biddy Lytton, who was plain and unattractive. He seldom met Stella (as a rule he came to tea to East Lodge once during the holidays, and Stella went to tea once to the Hall), but he had admired her ever since he could remember, and he thought about her a good deal during the term time at school. She was part of those vague aspirations towards a nobler life that swept over him at Evensong in the school chapel when the lights were lit and the organ poured forth its rich mellow notes. With her he was always conscious of a deep sense of unworthiness, a strange humility.

"It died, after all," she was saying sadly. "I stayed up with it nearly all night. Aunt Fanny let me because I was so unhappy. I can't bear to think of it even now."

"Don't think of it," he counselled tenderly.

"I'll try not to," said Stella with a tremulous smile.

She had, indeed, completely forgotten the incident till he reminded her of it, but at the memory she experienced again—mingled with a certain obscure satisfaction—all the old grief and indignation.

They were walking now beside the long herbaceous border.

"Do flowers seem like people to you?" she asked. "They do to me. That one looks wise and important. And that one looks friendly. And that one looks proud. And that one a little lonely. Those two always seem to be talking to each other. And this one looks kind and rather tired."

He listened and watched her, entranced. Her quick play of fancy made him feel slow and clumsy, but he loved to feel slow and clumsy beside her. Only with her did he experience this willing abasement of humility, the delight in something that he considered as far above him as the sun itself. . . .

She stooped down to pull out a weed, her bright curls falling over her shoulders, then stood upright.

"I saw you riding past with your father this morning."

"Oh, yes. . . ."

He did not say that he had scanned house and garden for a glimpse of her without success.

"I was in my bedroom."

"Oh . . ." He didn't know which room her bedroom was and was too shy to ask.

"We were going to Tagget's farm," he went on. "He can't pay his rent again. He's had a bad year. . . . Follett wanted us to turn him out, but I'm glad my father isn't going to. The old man's hardworking. He's just had bad luck. . . . Then we had to go round to Benson's. He keeps his place in a shocking state. I don't think he's touched his hedges for over a year. He's letting everything go. He's taken to drinking. I'm afraid we shall have to get rid of him."

His young face was set and earnest. He took his responsibilities as heir to Runeham Hall very seriously. He sometimes lay awake at night pondering over the problems his father had discussed with him. He was desperately anxious that the estate should be well administered, the tenants fairly treated.

The cloud over his face deepened as he continued :

26

"My father wants to turn out Fletcher, at Deep Deen farm, because he's a Radical. He says he won't have any radical tenants. He's just found out that he voted for Piggot at the last election." His brows drew together in a frown of perplexity. "I don't like it. It doesn't seem fair. If he's a good tenant that's all that ought to matter to us, but my father doesn't see it like that. . . . I'm sorry for the man. His wife, you know. . . ."

Stella thought of Mrs. Fletcher—a gaunt wolf-like woman who seldom came out before dusk because part of her face was eaten away by disease. She remembered how angry Aunt Fanny had been when Stella met her in full daylight in the village. The echo of Aunt Fanny's disgust was in her voice and on her small set face as she said,

"Yes, I know. It's absolutely *horrible*."

He looked at her in sudden surprise, and with her quick perceptions she saw that she had blundered. He hadn't expected that angry disgust. It was the wrong reaction. There was even the dawning severity of condemnation on his young face. He worshipped her as long as she remained his ideal, but he would depose her quickly enough if she fell short of it. She recovered herself instantly.

"I meant horrible that they haven't been able to cure her," she explained hastily. "It's so *wicked* that they haven't been able to do anything to help her. *Poor* woman! I'm so *sorry* for her."

Her voice wasn't quite steady and her eyes were dewy with tears. She was quite sincere, because, after all, when you looked at it like that, when you imagined what you yourself would feel if half your face was eaten away so that people couldn't bear to look at you, you were so sorry for her that it was all you could do not to cry.

There was a short silence, then she went on, "I ought to go and see if Biddy's come."

She was glad of an excuse to go in. Her face still wore that look of tender pity that was her tribute to Mrs. Fletcher's affliction, but inwardly she was furious with Hugh for doubting her, for even suspecting that she didn't feel as sorry as he did about Mrs. Fletcher—or sorrier, because everyone knew that she couldn't bear anyone to be ill or unhappy. . . . He had blurred and distorted the picture of herself that she liked to carry with her, and she always found it hard to forgive people who did that. She had to forgive Hugh, of course, because his admiration was necessary to her, but she wanted to get away from him and from the place where it had happened as quickly as possible.

Biddy and Doreen had just arrived and were shaking hands with Aunt Fanny and Miss Fairway in the drawing-room. Biddy was a plain little girl with red hair and colourless eyelashes, unbecomingly dressed in a pink sateen frock and stiff brown straw hat trimmed with green ribbons. Her round freckled good-humoured face was alight with affection as she flung herself on Stella.

"Oh Stella darling, it's *lovely* to see you again. I've been so excited that I just didn't know what I was doing. . . . This is Doreen. She's staying with us for part of the holidays."

Doreen was smaller and thinner than Biddy. She had large dark eyes in a pale pointed face, and straight dark hair.

Stella was holding out her hand with a little smile of welcome.

"I'm so glad you could come," she was saying.

Biddy watched her admiringly. She herself, she knew, could never hope to attain the perfection of graciousness that seemed to have been Stella's ever since she was a baby. She did not resent this, or any other of Stella's perfections; was, rather, humbly grateful for her friendship. She wrote to Stella every week from school and kept her photograph on the locker by her bed. She glanced at Doreen half anxiously, half triumphantly. Doreen must realise now that everything she had told her about Stella was true. But it was difficult to know what Doreen was thinking. She was greeting Stella gravely and without a smile, fixing dark eyes on her with a directness that Stella secretly found a little disconcerting. ("I'm not going to like her," Stella was saying to herself. "I didn't think I should.")

Hugh was introduced to the newcomer and then Miss Fairway came down from the schoolroom.

"Tea's ready," she said brightly. "Anyone ready for tea?"

Paul Sanders arrived as soon as tea was over, bringing a note from his father about the prizes for needlework that Aunt Fanny always gave to the village school children.

Ever since he had known that he was to bring the note to East Lodge he had been torn between elation and despair. He longed to see and speak to Stella, but he knew that even if he saw her he would be too paralysed by shyness to speak. On the whole he hoped that he would just have a glimpse of her without her seeing him. It would be enough just to have a glimpse of her. . . .

"It's Paul," cried Stella, catching sight of him as he stood at the side door, waiting for the answer to his note. "Oh, Auntie, do let him come and play with us."

"But, my pet . . ." protested Aunt Fanny, dismayed.

It was delightful to think that her pet was so innocent of worldly wisdom, but—Hugh Carlswell and Paul Sanders!

"It's so *unkind* not to," pleaded Stella. The others had gone into the drawing-room and were looking in turn into a stereoscope, in which Miss Fairway was showing them views of Pompeii. "He's seen us. He must have seen us come downstairs. I shall feel *miserable* if you just send him away. It will hurt his feelings. It will spoil everything for me. . . ."

"Well then, my darling," agreed Aunt Fanny, who couldn't bear to spoil everything for her darling, or to rub off anything of the bloom of her innocence.

Stella went to the side door, where Paul was still waiting.

"You can stay and play with us, Paul," she said. "Auntie says so."

He stared at her. He was not a bad-looking boy, though his dark eyes seemed too large for his thin pale face, but his wrists protruded several inches from the frayed cuffs of his shabby suit, and so shy and awkward was his manner that the general impression he gave was that of an ill-favoured hobbledehoy.

"I—I—couldn't," he stammered.

"But you *must*," smiled Stella.

She pulled him down the passage and into the drawing-room. He followed, lowering his head, looking up through his thick untidy fringe like a captured animal, frightened and defiant.

"This is Paul," said Stella, addressing her guests. "You all know him, don't you? We're going to play Hide-and-Seek in the garden. . . . Let Paul hide first."

"No, no," disclaimed Paul in sudden terror. "No. . . ."

"Well, I'll hide with you, shall I?" she said. "Paul and I will hide together, and the rest of you look for us. . . . Come on, Paul."

She threw a quick smile at the others, a smile that took them all into the conspiracy for making the newcomer feel at ease.

"Count forty and then come," she said, and pulled Paul after her out of the house and across the lawn to the kitchen garden.

"They won't find us here for ages," she said as she led him to a corner of the greenhouse behind the stove. "Come and sit down."

He sat down at some distance from her, staring at her in an ecstasy of adoration.

"You—you'll get your dress dirty, won't you?" was all he could find to say.

"Oh, ho," she said, glancing down at it carelessly. "Anyway, it won't matter if I do. I'm so glad you've come, Paul. I wanted to ask you to tea with the others."

She was happy to be with him. It gave her a safe, anchored sort of feeling. She thought again of that sudden question in Hugh's eyes, that shadow—faint but definite—of condemnation. It had made her unsure of herself. To be with Paul restored her self-confidence. There would never be that question in Paul's eyes, never even a shadow of condemnation. With Paul whatever she did or said was right, just because she did or said it. She watched him compassionately. . . . He looked hungry, she thought, hungry and neglected and afraid. Stella had often heard the problem of his parents discussed. People said that both father and son were quite presentable, but that the mother was impossible. There were very few children in the neighbourhood, and had Mrs. Sanders been in the slightest degree presentable, many mothers would have let their children play with Paul, who was "quite a nice little boy," but, of course, one could not be on terms of anything approaching familiarity with a woman of that type.

"You're so—kind," he said.

His voice was hoarse with emotion. He felt that it must be a dream. He could not actually be sitting here alone with Stella, whom he had worshipped ever since he could remember. He had pictured scenes like this, of course, but had never connected them with real life. He was separated from her, he knew, by a wide social gulf. Often in his imagination he went away from Runeham, won glory in some high position (the details of which were vague) and returned as her equal.

"I can't believe I'm really here," he said naïvely.

Her heart welled over with pity.

"I wanted to ask you properly with the others," she said, "but Aunt Fanny wouldn't let me."

He looked at her for a few minutes in silence, and his eyes seemed to grow larger, darker. His long sensitive mouth quivered.

"It's because of—my mother, isn't it?" he said.

She was taken aback by his directness, thrown momentarily off her poise.

"You can't help it," she said. "It's not your fault. It's mean to——"

"They don't understand," he burst out passionately. "No one understands. . . . I don't want them to, except you. . . . I want *you* to understand. My mother's wonderful. She's the most wonderful person in the world. I know she speaks badly and does things wrong, but things like that oughtn't to matter. . . ."

"Of course they oughtn't," murmured Stella sympathetically.

She was piqued that he wasn't talking about her, as she had expected him to, and at the same time gratified. He was talking to her—some instinct told her—as he could never have talked to anyone else.

"I'll tell you," he went on, "because I want you to know—I don't care about other people—but my mother's wonderful. It's—Father. He drinks. People don't know that. . . . He's supposed to have bad headaches, you know, when he stays in bed, and they manage the school without him, but really that's when he's been drinking. People are sorry for him and think he's better than she is, but he's unkind to her, and she—slaves for him and keeps everything going and never lets anyone—guess about him. She's worth a hundred of the people who look down on her."

"I'm so sorry," said Stella. She moved her hand till it lay on his. His was thin and bony and a little grubby. "I'm so terribly sorry. . . ."

The sympathy in her voice brought a lump to his throat and he could only stare at her, fighting back his tears. The relief of telling her the secret, together with her kindness, sent a wave of weakness through him.

"I've never told anyone before," he said. "I knew you'd understand. . . . You're—different from anyone else in the world."

Secretly Stella agreed with this view, but she gave a deprecatory little smile as she said, "I'm not. Of *course* I'm not. I'm——" She wondered whether to give a list of faults so that he could contradict her, and decided not to. She could hear the voices of the others as they entered the kitchen garden to look for them. "Well, I'm just ordinary," she ended still with that deprecatory little smile.

"I'm working for a scholarship, to Southwood Grammar School," he said. His thin pale face looked desperately earnest. "Then if I get it I shall have a chance of going on to college. I shall have to work hard, of course. . . ."

He looked at her without seeing her, gazing into a future in which he was no longer separated from her by this impassable gulf, in which he had something to offer her almost, if not quite, worthy of her bright perfection.

She stirred uneasily, fearing that his thoughts had wandered to a world in which she had no part.

"What are you going to be when you grow up?" she asked.

"I don't know," he answered slowly. "I'd like to be a doctor, but that takes a lot of money. Perhaps I shall be a schoolmaster, but——"

He left the sentence unfinished. He meant that he did not mean to be a village schoolmaster, like his father. That would not bring him any nearer her.

She searched for something that would dispel that far-away look from his eyes.

"You must do all you can to help your mother," she said.

It was as if a light had suddenly been lit in his sombre face.

"I will," he said, "and I shan't mind about things so much now that—you know. You're so kind."

She shook back her curls.

"I won't tell anyone, ever," she said. "It shall be a secret between us. And I'll get Aunt Fanny to let you come to tea properly sometimes. . . . I'm so glad you came today."

His heart was so full of love and gratitude that it was like a physical pain. There followed a short silence, during which he saved her from death by fire, drowning, a runaway horse and at the hands of a tribe of savages.

" I'll work hard," he said huskily. "I'll——"

The voices drew nearer and Biddy burst suddenly in at the door.

"They're here!" she cried and leapt upon them. "They're here! I've found them!"

The other two followed more slowly.

Hugh looked aloof but not resentful or superior. He considered Hide-and-Seek a childish game and did not in any case enjoy parties. It was his duty as a representative of the Carlswells of Runeham Hall to take part in social activities, and he did so, with an air of grave courtesy, of schooled politeness. Stella, of course, made this party different from an ordinary party, but he had seen very little of her. . . . He fully approved her action in going to hide with Paul Sanders, who was so obviously an outsider, ill-at-ease and awkward. It was a gracious act, worthy of her. . . . He had been intensely bored by Biddy Lytton and her cousin, but he had played his part conscientiously, inspecting with care every place that might have concealed the "hiders." Coming back from the greenhouse, he walked with Paul, talking to him as his father would have talked to Paul's father—with a kindly assumption of equality, ignoring, as he could well afford to because it was so obvious, the gulf that lay between them. He took the shortness and curtness of Paul's responses to be the result of natural diffidence, and increased the kindliness of his own manner in order to put him more at his ease. Hatred surged through Paul like an overmastering flood. . . .

It was just as the party was breaking up that Biddy found the dead bird in the spinney.

"Oh look!" she cried. "A dead bird. . . . It's a chaffinch. Isn't it pretty?"

The children crowded round. The little body lay behind a tuft of grass under the oak tree, the soft pink breast unruffled, the head lying inertly on one side.

"*Oh!*" gasped Stella, stepping back and covering her face with her hands. "Oh, poor little thing!"

Hugh threw a reproachful glance at Biddy.

"We'll bury it," he said. "Where can we get a trowel?"

"There's one in the tool-shed," said Biddy.

"I'm sorry," said Stella, with a rather pallid smile. "I didn't mean to make a fuss. It was just—seeing it like that suddenly. . . ."

"I know," said Hugh. All the chivalry in him leapt to arms at sight of her distress. "Go to the summer-house with Biddy while Paul and I bury it."

He fetched a trowel and began to dig a hole under the oak tree. Paul watched him. Just as the confidence and ease of the other boy's movements made him ashamed of his own awkwardness, so the immaculate tailoring of Hugh's well-fitting Eton suit made him ashamed of his own suit of worn patched serge.

The three girls went past the herbaceous border to the summer-house.

"What a lovely colour!" said Doreen, stopping by a Canterbury bell.

"I know it was silly of me to make such a fuss," said Stella.

Doreen turned and looked at her for a few moments, then said, "But you'd seen that dead bird before. When Hugh was hiding and you went to look behind that tree in the spinney, you saw it."

Stella's eyes widened and a blank look came into the small lovely face.

"Seen it before?" she said. "I don't know what you mean. Of course I hadn't seen it before. I know I'd looked behind that tree just near it, but I didn't see it. It wouldn't have upset me like that if I'd seen it before, would it?"

"I don't know," said Doreen.

There was a curious silence. The two children stood staring at each other, appraising, challenging. Biddy, aware of a strange tension in the atmosphere, looked helplessly from one to the other.

Just then Hugh and Paul returned.

"We made it a nice grave," said Hugh, "under the oak tree."

"I'll put some flowers on," said Stella. Her little face was sad and wistful. "He was so pretty. He must have been so happy singing in the sunshine."

"Don't worry about him, darling," said Biddy affectionately.

"I ought to go now," said Hugh. "Thanks so much for having me. I'll go and find your aunt and say goodbye to her."

Paul, listening to this unselfconscious leave-taking, was overwhelmed by shyness and despair. He could never be like that. Never. However long he lived. However many scholarships he won. . . . He wished he hadn't come here. It made the difference between him and these people unbearable. Even the memory of Stella's kindness shared the general blackness of his outlook. She had only been kind to him because she pitied him for being—different.

He muttered a sulky "goodbye" and, turning abruptly on. his heel, walked away from them down the drive. Hugh stared after him, his young brows drawn into a frown.

"I say!" he protested. "The fellow's got rather odd manners."

But Stella only smiled.

"He can't help it, Hugh," she said.

She was tempted for a moment to tell him about Paul's father, but remembered in time that she had promised not to. Besides, it was rather exciting to feel that she knew something that other people didn't know.

"We ought to go, too, Doreen," said Biddy, drawing a deep sigh of contentment.

It had been such a lovely afternoon.

"Isn't she *sweet?*" said Biddy enthusiastically as the two little girls walked back to the Vicarage. "Isn't she just as sweet as I told you she was?"

"She's terribly pretty," said Doreen slowly.

"I don't mean only that," said Biddy. "She's so kind. . . . Wasn't she lovely to Paul Sanders, just because he's—well, he's quite a common boy and hadn't been asked there?"

"Y-yes," agreed Doreen judicially, "but she was—being her person."

Biddy stared at her.

"What on *earth* do you mean?"

"I'm not quite sure, but she's got a person—a lot of people have, you know—and she—well, she *does* her person."

"Do you mean that you think she's really different from what she seems?" asked Biddy. Her small round face was pink with indignation at the idea.

Doreen was silent again. She considered the question thoughtfully, impersonally.

"No. . . . I daresay she's the same as her person quite often, but she likes watching herself being it."

"I think you're *hateful*," burst out Biddy indignantly. "You were hateful all afternoon. You were hateful when she was so upset about that bird."

"She *had* seen it before, you know," said Doreen quietly. "When she went to look behind that tree I saw her stoop and look at something just in that clump of grass. I didn't think anything about it at the time but—it couldn't have been anything but the bird."

Biddy's face was set and angry.

"So you think she *pretended* to feel all that?"

No, no, I don't," protested Doreen. "She felt it all the first time, probably, but no one was there to see. So when the others were there she just—did it again."

"I just don't understand what you mean, said Biddy helplessly. "Everyone loves her. She's always absolutely sweet and kind to everyone."

"I'm sure she is," agreed Doreen.

Chapter Four

MISS FAIRWAY stood looking down at the windswept sodden garden. The rain drove against the schoolroom window in sudden gusts with a sound like the scampering of tiny feet. The runnels of water on the glass turned everything outside to a blurred expanse of grey. In the garden all the plants that had not been securely staked lay beaten down in the mud.

The weather had broken over-night, and the long weeks of unclouded sunshine had given place to this lowering sky and heavy downpour.

The fire burnt brightly in the grate, but still the air struck damp and chilly. Miss Fairway had put a little black woollen shawl over her shoulders, and she drew it closer with a shiver as she turned away from the window.

Time had passed quickly and happily since her arrival at East Lodge. Her mind went back over the long sunny days . . . lessons in the garden . . . walks in the wood . . . arranging pressed flowers at the schoolroom table . . . reading aloud . . . games of make-believe.

"My pupil is so Good and Charming," she had written to her cousin, "that she is Spoiling me for Ordinary Children."

But, with the passing of the halcyon summer weather, a spell seemed to have been broken. Miss Fairway felt like someone who has awakened from an enchantment. It really *had* been an enchantment, she told herself. The child had bewitched her, with her charm, her grace, her whole delightful personality. Certainly she had at times been aware of a slight sense of strain, but she had put that down to the fact that she had never before had to do with a child so affectionate and considerate and anxious to please. The golden warmth of the sunshine, the fragrant beauty of garden and countryside had, of course, contributed to the spell. For, looking back now in the cold light of this dull rain-sodden day, Miss Fairway realised for the first time that in spite of her pupil's apparent readiness to do everything her governess wished, they had in fact done only what the pupil wished, discerned suddenly a hundred little ruses and subterfuges by which the child had put off unpleasant duties, had done only those lessons she enjoyed, had, while apparently settling down to some lesson she disliked, adroitly led their activities back to some more congenial field. A sense of shame seized Miss Fairway. She had failed in her duty. Without meaning to, without even knowing that she was doing so, she had committed the supreme crime of "giving in" to a pupil. Now that she realised it, she must be firm.

She felt no resentment against Stella. It was, after all, only to be expected that she should have used her natural weapons to gain her ends. It was Miss Fairway herself who had been to blame. She should have been on the alert to see what was happening, to counter the childish tactics by tactics of her own. She braced herself with a little shiver, drawing her shawl again more closely over her shoulders. Today she would make a fresh start. The training of such a gifted pupil was a great responsibility. She must not fail in it.

She took out of a drawer in the table the little black silk apron that she always wore for lessons and tied it round her waist. Then she set out the lesson books. They would begin with English History. Stella disliked learning dates and had learnt none at all since Miss Fairway came to East Lodge. Somehow she had always managed to induce her to mount one of her favourite hobby-horses (the British Empire, or the Greatness of Mr. Gladstone, or Our Beloved Queen), and kept her there with childish cunning till the end of the lesson. Today Stella must learn dates . . . Arithmetic, too. . . . It was annoying, as she looked back over the past weeks, to discover how many Arithmetic lessons had gradually and imperceptibly lapsed into pleasant little discussions on flowers or birds or trees. . . . Of course, being out of doors had helped the process. It would be easier to be firm indoors. . . . She must be firm. . . . Her professional conscience was roused. . . . With children one must master or be mastered.

She went to the top of the stairs and rang a little bell.

"Stella, dear!" she called.

After breakfast, Stella always went into the garden for half an hour if it was fine, or if not, stayed in the morning-room with Aunt Fanny.

She came slowly upstairs at the sound of the bell. She wore a dress of grey merino, trimmed with rows of blue braid, and a clean pinafore. Her face looked less eager and happy than usual, as if the dullness of the weather had quenched her spirits, and for a moment Miss Fairway was tempted to put off the beginning of the process of being firm till a finer day. Then she took herself in hand. That sort of thing was fatal, as she knew by experience.

"We'll begin with History this morning, dear," she said brightly. "I want you to learn some dates."

"Dates!" said Stella with a little grimace. It was a roguish, pleading, almost mischievous little grimace. It made Miss Fairway a conspirator against herself. . . . With an effort Miss Fairway resisted the temptation to surrender.

"Yes, dear. We've neglected them long enough. I Want you to learn this column. You know, you have a very good memory." (Odd, the instinct one had to placate the child, especially when one remembered how sweet-tempered she had always shown herself.) "See how quickly you can learn them."

Stella leant back in her chair, her eyes fixed un-seeingly on the page of dates, her fair curls shading her face. Then she looked at her governess, who sat very upright on her chair at work on one of those strange calico garments freely adorned with red braid that Aunt Fanny sent out at regular intervals to the Mission field.

"They'll be terribly pleased to get that, won't they, Miss Fairway?"

"Yes, dear," said Miss Fairway.

Stella fixed her blue eyes dreamily on the distance.

"It must be so *dreadful* for them not knowing anything about

God," she said. "I don't know how they can *bear* it. ... What's the place like where that's going, Miss Fairway?"

On any of the preceding days, out in the sunny garden, with the birds singing around them, Miss Fairway would have been drawn into the trap.

Today she said, "Never mind about that, dear. Get on with your dates."

A look as near sulkiness as Miss Fairway had ever seen on it came into the small exquisite face. ... Stella felt listless and depressed. It wasn't only that she couldn't lure Miss Fairway away from the hated page of dates. It was something much deeper and more complicated than that. She had been very happy with Miss Fairway all these weeks, and she had quite honestly looked upon her happiness as enjoyment of the new companionship, pleasure in those delightful lessons in the garden, those walks in the woods, those games of make-believe. Actually it had been the happiness of the artist at work upon a painting ... adding a touch here, a touch there ... intent on giving shape and colour and form to his ideal. And now the picture was finished. ... She had no doubt now that Miss Fairway saw her exactly as Aunt Fanny saw her, as she saw herself—and that sense of depression and futility that so often assails the artist at the completion of a piece of creative work assailed her. She looked from Miss Fairway, who seemed this morning more than usually dull and plain and disagreeable, to the pouring rain outside, from the pouring rain outside to the column of dates in front of her ... and her depression increased. Beneath the depression there was in her mind a faint vague replica of what was in her governess's. She must be firm. ... One must master or be mastered. She raised her face from her book.

"What makes the rain, Miss Fairway?" she said. "I've never quite understood."

"We'll talk about that some other time, dear," said Miss Fairway.

She realised afresh how the child had led her by the nose all these weeks, how docilely she had followed all the red herrings she had chosen to draw over dates and spelling lists and long-division sums. She must be *very* firm.

Stella dropped her head suddenly onto her hands.

"I've got rather a headache, Miss Fairway," she said.

These were familiar tactics. Miss Fairway felt quite at home with them. She knew all the signs of infantile indisposition, and not one could be seen on the healthy little face confronting her. And yet—it offered her the chance of retreat in good order, and, despite her recent resolution, Miss Fairway was tempted to take it. If the child said she had a headache, surely she was justified in believing her ... and they could have one of those pleasant mornings of reading aloud, making up stories, drawing and painting, which Miss Fairway enjoyed almost as much as her pupil. She might even salve her conscience by setting Stella one of those little "pieces" that Stella memorised so quickly and recited with such charm and expression. But the very fact that yielding would have been so easy made her decide not to yield. For the tenth time that morning she told herself that she must be firm. ...

"Now you know quite well, dear, that you haven't got a headache. You mustn't speak again till you've learnt your dates."

Stella bent her head low over her book. Beneath the bright curtain of curls, the little face was set in tense unchildlike lines. When, however, at the end of quarter of an hour Miss Fairway said, "Do you know it, dear?" she responded with her usual eager half-smile.

"Yes, Miss Fairway," she said.

She was all the ill-treated children she had ever heard or read of ... but forgiving her oppressors, repaying good for evil, opposing sunny sweetness to tyranny and injustice.

Miss Fairway felt—as she was meant to feel—that she had been rather unfair. Stella was no ordinary child. She must go carefully, humbly. ...

"That's *very* good, dear," she said, when Stella had repeated the dates correctly, "and now we'll do Geography."

Miss Fairway taught Geography well and Stella enjoyed it. This morning Miss Fairway made the subject even more interesting than usual. But as she talked, described, narrated anecdotes, showed Stella pictures, a vague apprehension weighed down on her. The next lesson was Arithmetic, and she had decided to make Stella do the long-division sums that she had been evading all these weeks.

"Now, dear," she said when the Geography lesson was finished, "I'm going to set you three long-division sums. I'm sure you'll be able to do them. Do your best, anyway. I'll leave you for half an hour and go downstairs to do the flowers."

It was partly cowardice that made Miss Fairway choose this moment for "doing the flowers." She didn't quite trust herself to resist Stella's wiles. She had won the battle of the dates . . . but only just. Odd how she shrank from facing the issue. Was it fear of hurting the childish pride and sensitiveness, or was it—the thought burst into Miss Fairway's mind like an explosion—fear of the child herself? Fear of a mite like that! Miss Fairway dismissed the idea as preposterous.

It was too wet to pick any flowers, but she could change the water and cut the stems of the ones she had "done" yesterday. She took as long over it as she could, then went back to the schoolroom.

Stella sat at the table, putting the finishing touches to a drawing of a couple of elves floating in a water-lily on a pond.

"Look, Miss Fairway," she said. "They're going over to the island where the fairy queen lives. The fairy queen's having a party. . . . They've got their very best hats on. Their very best hats are nasturtiums. . . . They only wear buttercups every day."

Miss Fairway looked at it in silence for a few moments. It was a spirited little drawing—full of talent and originality. It was the sort of thing that Stella enjoyed doing and did well. She must have worked hard at it.

"Where are your sums, Stella?" said Miss Fairway.

Stella gave a rueful little smile, then pouted deliciously.

"I *hate* sums," she said. "I couldn't do them without you to help me."

"You haven't tried," said Miss Fairway, looking at the paper on which she had set the sums. "You've done nothing at all."

"I know. I couldn't without you to help me," repeated Stella.

"Now, listen, Stella," said Miss Fairway severely. "You've been a very naughty disobedient little girl. I told you to do those sums, and you haven't even attempted them. You're self-willed and obstinate and you shirk everything that you can't do well. Don't you know that it's only conceited little girls who refuse to do things they can't do well? It is very stupid indeed to behave like that, and you'll never learn anything at all unless you try to improve. Now set to work on those sums at once, and for a punishment you shall do sums all morning tomorrow."

Miss Fairway felt a sudden sense of exhilaration and with it a new affection for her pupil. To have given her a good talking-to like this had broken the curious spell that seemed to have been laid on her. She was, after all, only an ordinary little girl, to be scolded, punished, forgiven. This return to normality and the sense of relief that accompanied it seemed to reveal some nightmare quality in the cloudless serenity of the last few weeks—a quality of which she had been wholly unaware at the time. She glanced at Stella.

Stella sat with her head bent over her sums and her elbows outspread so that Miss Fairway could not see whether she was really doing them or not. Better leave her alone for a bit now . . . let her get over it. . . . She wasn't crying, anyway.

Stella was staring down unseeingly at the paper on which her sums were set. She was so angry that there was a sort of mist between her and the paper and she couldn't see the figures. It was the same blinding but strangely impersonal anger that had seized her when she heard Ivy call her a "sly little piece," when that hateful friend of Biddy's said that she had seen the dead bird before. It was as though she had to stand by and watch something beautiful being wantonly, cruelly despoiled. "Naughty" . . . "disobedient" . . . "conceited" . . . "stupid." She hated both the outrage and the perpetrator of it.

"Well, Stella," said Miss Fairway about quarter of an hour later, "how are you getting on?"

Stella raised from her work a small mask of penitence.

"I've nearly finished them," she said. "I'm—very sorry I was naughty, Miss Fairway."

"That's all right, dear," said Miss Fairway. "We won't either of us think of it again."

But Miss Fairway was wrong about that.

When Aunt Fanny went downstairs that night on her way to dinner, she paused outside Stella's bedroom as usual, listening for the deep regular breathing that generally met her ears and told her that her darling was safely asleep. Instead she heard the sound of stifled sobbing. Aghast, she opened the door and went in. It was so seldom that Stella cried. . . .

"Darling," she said, "what's the matter?"

There was no answer. All she could see was a tangle of fair curls on the pillow and a small heap under the bedclothes that shook spasmodically as the child evidently tried to check her sobs.

In a flash Aunt Fanny was across the room, gathering the little figure into her arms.

"What is it, my pet?" she said again. "Tell Auntie."

"I can't." The child seemed to be making a superhuman effort to control herself. "I didn't want you to hear. Don't tell her I cried. Please don't tell her. . . ."

"Whom, darling?"

"Miss Fairway. Don't let her know . . . She'll be so angry with me."

Aunt Fanny's heart began to beat with loud suffocating throbs as she faced the monstrous implication.

"Darling . . . is she unkind to you?"

"Yes," sobbed Stella. "But don't tell her I told you. Promise you won't. . . . I'm so—frightened."

By now Stella's emotion was more real than assumed. The memory of that look of severity on Miss Fairway's pleasant face as she delivered her little lecture had changed to an expression of savage ferocity, and Stella felt all the terror that the spectacle would in reality have caused her.

"She'll be so angry if she knows you know."

"Oh, my love," moaned Aunt Fanny, rocking the small sobbing form in her arms. "How remiss I have been! How blind, how careless! I should never have trusted her or anyone. . . . How long has it been going on?"

It was difficult to make much of what the child said—she was still sobbing so violently—but it must, of course, have been going on for some time. And everything had seemed to be running so smoothly. How cunning—as well as cruel—the wretch must have been! Aunt Fanny reproached herself bitterly. The very thing against which she had tried to guard had happened. She had sworn that Stella should never know the unhappiness she herself had known in her childhood, and she had failed in her trust.

"She shall be sent away, my pet. She shall be sent away at once."

Stella's terror seemed to increase. "Don't tell her I told you. Don't let me see her. . . ."

"You shall, never see her again, my love," Aunt Fanny assured her brokenly.

Miss Fairway stared in amazement at the thin gaunt accusing figure. Aunt Fanny was so angry that everything about her seemed to quiver. The very fringe trimming of her black silk overdress, drawn up behind with a large bow onto the bustle, seemed to dance with rage. The yellowed sinewy neck, revealed by the discrete lace-edged V opening, worked convulsively. For a moment Miss Fairway could not understand what she was talking about. When she did understand, she couldn't believe it.

"But, Miss Markham," she protested, "I don't know what you mean. You're surely not accusing me of being unkind to Stella?"

"Indeed I am!" said Aunt Fanny. "You've been inhumanly cruel to the poor little thing."

"Me?" gasped Miss Fairway. "Inhumanly cruel? *Me?*"

"Yes, you, you wicked woman!" quavered Aunt Fanny. Her heart was hammering in her chest. She felt that she was avenging not only Stella, but the ill-used child who had been herself. She was, as she had once dreamed of doing, denouncing and sending about their business those careless hirelings who had made her own childhood so unhappy. She had them at her mercy at long last. . . .

"Yes, you, you wicked woman! You enjoy making a child's life a burden to her. It's nothing to you that her memories of childhood will be memories of fear and unhappiness. Stella's so terrified of you that I had to promise that she should never see you again. I won't be responsible for the child's reason if she does. I'll pay you your salary tonight, and you must go tomorrow morning."

Miss Fairway's first thought had been that the whole thing was a fantastic dream, her second that Miss Markham must be mentally deranged.

"Has Stella told you that I've been unkind to her?" she said at last.

"She's told me everything," quavered Aunt Fanny. "I suppose you thought that you had terrified the child so that she would not dare to. You nearly had done, too."

"There must be some absurd misunderstanding," said Miss Fairway. "Will you let me see her, please?"

"Never!" said Aunt Fanny dramatically. "The child will sleep in my bedroom tonight, and if you attempt to communicate with her in any way, or if you do not leave the house tomorrow morning, I shall send for the police."

Miss Fairway looked at the weak, faded, still rather pretty face, the thin hollow cheeks blotched crimson, the eyes feverish with anger. . . . Could Miss Markham really have gone mad since tea-time? She had been quite sane at tea-time. No, she decided, her employer was still quite sane. What, then, could have happened?

She thought of Stella, so sweet and docile and affectionate . . . and suddenly she realised that, though she had believed herself supremely happy in this house all these weeks, there was nothing she so much wanted as to get away from it, nothing she so much longed for as a rough, noisy, naughty, normal child. . . .

"I will leave the house tonight," she said quietly.

Chapter Five

"It's simply lovely to have you again, Doreen," said Biddy happily.

She took a delaine dress, gaily patterned in pink and green, from the wardrobe and slipped it over her head. Her next words were inaudible, then her round smiling face emerged, and she pulled the dress into position about her.

"Do me up behind, darling, will you?"

Doreen buttoned the dress, which seemed too tight in some places, and too loose in others. Biddy made all her dresses herself by the simple process of cutting the material to the shape of paper patterns and stitching the pieces together. The results had to accommodate themselves to the dumpy little figure as best they could, for, beyond assigning them their official positions as "best," "second best" and "everyday," Biddy gave them no further thought.

Doreen had arrived at the Vicarage that morning in time for the annual Vicarage garden party, which was to take place in the afternoon, and the two girls were now changing for it.

Doreen, who was in half-mourning for her father, had put on a dress that she had bought in Paris—stiff mauve and white striped silk, with the fashionable leg-of-mutton sleeves, tight waist and bell-shaped sweeping skirt. The brim of her hat—white straw trimmed with mauve ribbons—dipped over her forehead and rose at the sides to show the dark wings of her hair.

Doreen had developed from a lanky child, with eyes too big for her small pale face, into a strikingly beautiful young woman. Her lankiness had given place to a perfectly proportioned slenderness, her pallor held the transparent glow of health, and her dark eyes and hair, together with her graceful carriage, gave her an air of distinction that was the more marked because of her lack of self-consciousness.

Biddy had altered little since their childhood. She had the same freckled face, carroty hair and short ungainly figure. She was still eager and clumsy and untidy and ingenuous and loyal and affectionate.

"I can't tell you how excited I've been about your coming," she said as she carelessly wound her thick straight unwieldy hair into a lop-sided "bun." "I hardly slept a wink last night, I was so excited."

"I've been looking forward to it, too," said Doreen, who had taken her seat on the bed and was watching Biddy with an affectionate, faintly amused smile.

"It doesn't mean the same to you as it does to me," said Biddy. "You've had a marvellous time in Switzerland all these years. You wouldn't even come and spend the holidays with us."

"Daddy wouldn't let me," said Doreen. "He hated my even going away to school, and he wouldn't spare a day of my holidays. I think that time I came to stay here—how long ago was it?"

"About ten years."

"Well, that was the last time I stayed away from home anywhere."

"Y-yes," said Biddy with a little sigh, "but with your father being a famous writer you knew lots and lots of interesting people."

"Oh, Daddy always liked to have the house full," said Doreen with a reminiscent smile. "We never knew how he found time to write."

"Do you miss him—terribly?" said Biddy wistfully.

"Not as much as Mother does," said Doreen. "I thought last year when Daddy died that she was going to die, too. Just because she couldn't go on living without him. . . . I got her to come to London, because I thought it would give her more of a chance of getting over it, and I'm glad I did. She's gradually beginning to enjoy life again, though she wouldn't admit it for worlds."

Biddy, who was hunting for a handkerchief in a drawer where scarves, gloves, veils, hair nets and oddments of underclothing were tumbled together in wild confusion, paused and stood looking dreamily in front of her.

"Just think, Doreen . . . all the years you've been meeting famous people from all over the world, I've never met anyone but just the handful of people who live in Runeham. I don't think there's been a single change of any kind. Some of the very old people have died, of course, but that's all. You'll find just the same people as were here ten years ago. I don't suppose you remember one of them, do you?"

Doreen wrinkled delicately arched brows.

"I don't know. . . . Tell me about them and perhaps it will all come back."

"Well . . ." Biddy found a handkerchief underneath a pile of petticoat bodices and tucked it into her pocket. "There's Stella."

"Stella?"

"Stella Markham. She lives with her aunt. We went to tea at her house."

"Oh, I remember." The dark eyes narrowed as they gazed back into the past. "There were two little boys there too. . . ."

"Yes," said Biddy eagerly. "Paul Sanders and Hugh Carlswell. Paul's doing frightfully well now. He got a scholarship to Southwood Grammar School and then last year he got one to Oxford. He's awfully clever. And quite presentable nowadays. He's still very quiet and shy, but he's good-looking and he has a good accent and nice manners. His father died two years ago and he lives with his mother. She's pretty awful, but people put up with her. Well, there aren't so many presentable young men about that one can afford to look too closely at their mothers."

"And the other?" smiled Doreen.

"Hugh? Oh, he's just what you'd expect him to be if you remember him. Very handsome, of course, and very conscientious. He's just left Cambridge and he's learning the estate work. He's running the home farm by himself on modern lines and he doesn't care how much work he puts in. He does far more for the tenants than the agent really approves of. He's a sort of young king about here."

"Whatever the quantity of young men," said Doreen with her faint smile, "you seem fortunate in the quality."

"Yes," admitted Biddy, "I suppose we are."

"Or is it, Biddy," said Doreen in affectionate teasing, "that all your geese are swans?"

"I don't know," smiled Biddy, "but Hugh really *is* a darling. His only drawback is that he takes life a little too seriously. That may be partly because of Pamela."

"Pamela?"

"Oh, she wasn't born till after you'd gone back, of course. She's Hugh's little sister. Didn't I tell you about her in my letters?"

"You don't write letters, Biddy. You send an occasional comment on the weather and a list of what's coming out in the garden, that's all."

"But I'm sure I told you about Pamela. She's the loveliest child, and it was only very gradually that they realised she wasn't—developing. She's nine years old now but she's just like a child of three, and I don't suppose she'll ever develop any more. The odd thing is that they adore her. She's sweet, too, but, of course, it's dreadful."

"I know," agreed Doreen, frowning. "I've come across cases like that. It's all right generally while the parents are alive, but what's to happen when they die?"

"There'll be Hugh," said Biddy. "He worships her. In a way I think he loves her even more than he'd have loved her if she'd been normal. He feels protective and responsible. . . . And she worships him. She cries when he goes out of the house."

"Hugh will marry some day. What then?"

"Hugh will only marry someone who'll love Pamela. I know that."

Doreen threw her a quick glance. Probably every girl for miles around dreamed secretly of marrying Hugh Carlswell.

"What did you say was the name of the little girl where we went to tea?"

"Stella Markham."

"Oh yes. I remember. There was an aunt and a rather nice governess."

Biddy's face hardened.

"She was a *fiend*, Doreen. No one knew it at the time—not even the aunt—but she was absolutely brutal to poor little Stella, and Stella was so terrified of her that she daren't tell anyone. Miss Markham found her crying in bed one night, and it all came out and she sent the governess packing then and there."

Doreen drew her delicate brows together again.

"Odd. . . . I remember the governess quite well. I don't set up as a judge of character, but I shouldn't have imagined she had it in her to be unkind to anyone. What did she do to the child?"

"Oh, Stella can't bear to talk of if even now. She says it's just like a bad dream. The dreadful part was that we heard the woman had got another post afterwards with quite respectable people. Miss Markham wrote telling them what had happened, and they not only didn't dismiss the woman but they never even answered the letter. Some people are criminally careless about their children."

"H'm," grunted Doreen reflectively. "It's a curious story. How has Stella turned out? But, of course, she's one of your geese, so I'll take for granted that she's a swan."

Biddy's plain good-natured little face broke into a smile.

"You're as much a tease as ever, Doreen. . . . Well," triumphantly, "even you will have to agree that I was right about Stella."

"I shall be quite willing to. I don't think I disliked her, did I?"

"You weren't nice about her."

"Wasn't I? What happened after the governess went? Did they get another?"

"Miss Markham taught her again at first, but she wasn't strong and had to give it up. Then she got a darling old thing called Miss Farthing (Stella nicknamed her "Penny") who was a great success. Stella's really clever, you know. She draws and paints and plays the piano almost as well as a professional. She's so quick to learn that she didn't want the ordinary sort of governess pushing her on. She just wanted someone to help her."

"Life seems to have been almost too good to the young lady," commented Doreen.

Biddy turned an earnest face to her friend.

"Oh, it hasn't, Doreen. Her aunt's been bedridden now for three years and Stella's nursed her day and night. She hardly ever goes out. She's supposed to be coming to the party this afternoon, but if her aunt is the least bit worse or seems to want her to stay, she won't come. She's too conscientious. I'm always telling her so."

"I'm sure you are."

"You're teasing me again," grinned Biddy.

"No, I'm not. I'm quite prepared to find her all you say."

The clock downstairs in the hall struck the hour.

"Oh dear!" said Biddy. "I don't know why I'm always on the minutes. Perhaps it's because I'm always losing things." She inspected her face disapprovingly in the mirror. "I wish I weren't the *plain* sort of red-haired person. It would be so lovely to be the other sort. I used to try to think of it as auburn, but I never really could. . . . You *will* like Stella—won't you, Doreen?—because I'm so terribly fond of you both. . . ." She plunged into the wardrobe and brought out a garden hat of speckled straw, which she rammed onto her head with one hand while she closed the wardrobe door with the other. "I'm ready now, if you are."

Aunt Fanny lay back on her pillows and closed her eyes. She was alone for the moment. Stella was changing her dress for the Vicarage garden party. She felt very tired. . . . Odd to spend all one's days in bed and yet always feel tired. It was nice to be alone. One could relax when one was alone. . . . She was glad that Stella was going to the Vicarage garden party. The poor child had so little pleasure nowadays. . . . It weighed on Aunt Fanny's conscience intolerably to think that she had turned her bright clever Stella into a sick-room drudge. She hadn't really wanted to. Over and over again she had begged Stella to let her get a professional nurse, but Stella would never agree to it.

"No, Auntie," she would say, "I'm going to look after you myself. It's little enough to do for you after all you've done for me."

Though Aunt Fanny loved being nursed by Stella, sometimes she couldn't help feeling that it would have been rather nice to have a nurse whose ministrations one could take for granted because one was paying for them, and to whom one need not feel perpetually grateful. She *did* feel perpetually grateful to Stella. Everyone said how splendid she was. Everyone agreed it was a tragedy for her to have to waste her youth nursing an old woman.

"They don't understand," Stella would say. "They say that I'm cooped up here all day and don't get any pleasure. They don't understand that it *is* pleasure to me to look after you, darling."

But Aunt Fanny felt guilty none the less. Sometimes the child looked so pale and tired.

When Stella said, "I just couldn't bear to think of you being looked after by paid nurses . . . hirelings," Aunt Fanny knew that it was perverse and ungrateful of her to feel, sometimes—just sometimes—that she'd like to be looked after by hirelings. She thought of the future with a sinking heart. People with her particular trouble often lived for years. Would Stella insist on nursing her year after year, wasting her youth? She didn't want to take advantage of the child's unselfishness. She had tried to make Stella understand that. But Stella was so sensitive. The last time she had raised the point Stella had been so hurt that she had cried.

"But, Auntie," she had protested between her sobs, "tell me what I do wrong. I do my best. Honestly, I do my best. Why don't you want me to go on nursing you? I couldn't just go about enjoying myself and thinking of you lying here lonely . . . I *couldn't* enjoy myself. . . . I know it's my duty to look after you. It would kill me not to. . . . Do tell me what I do wrong. I'll try to improve."

It had taken Aunt Fanny almost an hour to soothe and comfort her, to assure her that she was better than the best nurse, that it was joy and life to have her in the sick-room. . . . Aunt Fanny had felt utterly worn out by the end of the little scene and had had the worst heart attack she had had for weeks. Between her gasps of agony she had continued to assure Stella that no one else would have known how to deal with it, that no one else could have given her courage to endure the pain.

"And now, darling," Stella had said firmly when it was over, "you must never again even think of having anyone but me to look after you. If I hadn't happened to be there when the attack came on, I don't know what would have happened. I have the knowledge and I have the experience and I have *love*, which paid nurses haven't."

"Darling!" Aunt Fanny had murmured faintly, her brow still damp with perspiration.

She blamed herself severely for upsetting Stella. Stella, of course, had always been unduly sensitive. Careless words—words to which an ordinary person would not have given a second thought—could bruise and hurt that tender spirit irremediably.

Sometimes when, in her childhood, Aunt Fanny had criticised her for some slight fault, she had had to stay up half the night with the child, comforting her, eating her words, assuring her over and over again that she hadn't meant it, that she was a clumsy silly old woman, and that her darling was perfect.

Even now she had to be very careful, to weigh her words beforehand, lest Stella should misunderstand and be hurt. It made things rather difficult sometimes. Though she would not have admitted it even to herself, she was looking forward to this afternoon when Stella would be at the Vicarage garden party. There was a bell by her bedside, and, if she wanted anything, she would ring for Mary. . . . Mary was comfortable and homely and middle-aged and matter-of-fact. She need not try to control the symptoms of her illness so as not to distress or shock her, as she instinctively did with Stella. It would be a blessed respite and relaxation. . . . Aunt Fanny didn't put it that way even to herself. Determinedly she assigned the cause of the relief, of which she couldn't help being conscious, to the fact that Stella was to have an afternoon's pleasure, a holiday at long last from the sick-room.

The door opened and Stella entered. The prettiness of childhood had not, as it so often does, faded with adolescence. Her face had a beauty of bone and structure, quite apart from the delicate colouring of childhood, which it had retained. She stood at the foot of the bed, drawing on white kid gloves and smiling down at

Aunt Fanny. She wore a dress of white broderie Anglaise, with stiff shoulder frills over long tight sleeves, and a sash of pale-blue ribbon whose ends hung down almost to the bottom of the dress. Her white broad-brimmed hat, too, was trimmed with pale-blue ribbon.

"How nice you look, darling!" murmured Aunt Fanny. "Be sure you have a nice time. Who will be there, do you think?"

"The usual people. The only stranger will be that friend of Biddy's, Doreen Blake. She was quite a little girl when she was here last. She came to tea with Biddy. Do you remember her?"

Aunt Fanny sent her mind back across the years. She could only see Stella, her wonder child. The brightness of that vision threw everything else into an indistinguishable shade.

"No, I don't remember," she said.

"I didn't care for her very much," said Stella. "A sulky unpleasant little thing. . . . She may have improved, of course. Biddy was very fond of her. . . ."

"Will Paul be there?"

"No, he hasn't come down from college yet."

"I suppose Hugh will be there."

"Yes . . . I believe so. Lady Carlswell, too, if she can leave Pamela."

"Poor woman!" sighed Aunt Fanny, and then suddenly wondered how many people were saying the same thing about herself and Stella. ("Stella will be there if she can leave her aunt."

"Poor girl!")

"Don't hurry back, darling," she said. "Stay as long as you can. I shall be quite all right."

"Are you sure?" said Stella anxiously. "I don't like leaving you, you know."

"Oh, darling!" protested Aunt Fanny, "I shall be *quite* all right. I shall have a nice rest and a nice read. Mary will get me anything I want. I shall have a nice cosy peaceful afternoon. . . ."

Her voice trailed away nervously. Stella was looking at her gravely . . . in silence. Had she hurt her angel? Had she—horrible thought—given her the idea that she *wanted* to be left alone?

"I shall miss you, of course, my pet," she said hastily. "You know that. I shall be thinking of you all the time and wishing you were here. I shall be lonely without you, as I always am when my darling's away. I shall be counting the minutes." She stopped again. Stella was slowly stripping off the white gloves. Her nervousness deepened to panic. "What are you doing, my love?" she said breathlessly.

"I'm not going to leave you," said Stella in a firm quiet voice.

"But, Stella," protested Aunt Fanny quaveringly, "I didn't mean that—I didn't. Oh, darling, you must go. I want you to go. Do believe me. I want you to go. I only meant that—of course, I'd miss you, but I'd be quite happy. I——"

Stella was looking down at her with a grave smile. "I know, dear," she said soothingly. "Now don't worry or fret any more. It'll only make your heart bad. . . . Just lie back and rest. I shouldn't have a moment's pleasure knowing that you were missing me and counting the minutes till I got back. I'd be much happier staying with you. Really, darling, I should. You know how I love being with you, and the thought of you being lonely would hurt me so much all the time that I should be miserable. I'll just go and take my dress off."

"Stella . . ."

But Stella had gone from the room, closing the door behind her.

Aunt Fanny lay, her mind a welter of confused emotion . . . pride in and admiration of the child's wonderful unselfishness, shame at having caused her to miss her party and—pushed well down out of sight till it was just a vague unidentifiable depression—disappointment at the loss of her peaceful effortless afternoon. It would be lovely to have Stella, she told herself. How good the child was! How wrong and clumsy of her to have said that she would be lonely without her and that she would be counting the minutes! She ought to have remembered how sensitive Stella was. . . . Her agitation had made her heart beat violently and brought that suffocating pain to the region of her chest. If Stella had gone to the party she would have rung the bell for Mary to get her tablets from the drawer in the little table by her bed, but she didn't want to disturb Stella, to give her unnecessary trouble as well as depriving her of her afternoon's pleasure.

Quite often the pain passed if she lay quite still. . . . Yes, it was passing now. . . . It would be lovely to have darling Stella with her all afternoon.

Stella came back into the room. She had changed into a plain high-necked dress of dark blue alpaca, with a frilled fichu of white silk that fell softly from her shoulders and was tucked into her belt. Her hair—parted simply in the middle and taken back into a knot—lay in deep natural waves over her well-shaped head. Small shining tendrils escaped the knot and clustered about the nape of her neck.

"Now, darling," she said to Aunt Fanny, "everything's all right. I've written a note for Betsy to take round to the Vicarage."

"I'm so sorry. . . ."

"You mustn't think of it again," said Stella. "It's time for your rest now. You're looking a little tired. I'll sit here and read, as quiet as a mouse. Try to sleep, if you can."

She sat down in the armchair facing the window, a book on her knee. Aunt Fanny could see that she wasn't reading the book. She was gazing out of the window. . . . A curious fancy seized Aunt Fanny. She seemed to feel waves of anger and resentment emanating from the slight graceful figure. It was impossible, of course—she had never known Stella angry or sulky in her life—but she had to put it to the test, to know the worst. The thought that Stella was angry with her was unbearable.

"Have you got an interesting book, dear?" she said timidly.

The face that Stella turned to her was one of unclouded sweetness.

"Yes, thank you, Auntie."

Aunt Fanny lay back against her pillows with a sigh of relief. It was all right. . . . And yet, as soon as the figure had turned round, the hot stifling suggestion of anger and resentment seemed to fill the room once more. . . . Aunt Fanny's heart began to beat unevenly. . . . How stupid she was to imagine that Stella could ever be angry with her! It must be imagination but—she had to put it to the test again.

"Are you comfortable, dear?" she said. "Wouldn't you like another cushion?"

It was so long before Stella turned to answer that at first Aunt Fanny thought that she could not have heard. When she did turn round, her face wore the gentle loving smile that Aunt Fanny had longed to see.

"No, thank you, darling. I'm quite comfortable. Can't you sleep?"

"No, dear. I somehow feel quite wakeful this afternoon."

"Shall I read to you?"

"Yes, thank you, darling. That would be very nice."

Aunt Fanny tried to speak with enthusiasm.

If Stella hadn't been there she could have had a nice little nap, but that strange delusion (she knew it was a delusion) of anger kept her awake. If Stella turned round to read to her she could see her face, and the delusion might vanish. She loved to hear Stella's voice reading aloud, though she found it difficult to concentrate nowadays.

Stella moved her chair nearer the bedside. Aunt Fanny's eyes dwelt tenderly on the pure young profile, the lovely line of chin and throat, the perfect texture of the satin-smooth skin. Her little Stella . . . her baby . . .

Stella had a musical, well-modulated voice and read aloud admirably. She used to read aloud to Miss Farthing every evening as Miss Farthing sat with her needlework, and Miss Farthing frequently said that she had never known a child read more beautifully. She was reading Mrs. Henry Wood's *The Channings*, and Aunt Fanny listened with pleasure till—it was one of her bad days—gradually the pain in her chest started again. She wanted to ask Stella to get her tablets. She told herself that Stella was only reading aloud to entertain her, Aunt Fanny, and so could easily be asked to stop, but—It was as if there were some invisible audience, listening enthralled, who would be annoyed and irritated if Aunt Fanny interrupted. Aunt Fanny happened to be present at the performance, but had really no connection with it. . . . At last she could endure it no longer.

"Stella, darling," she said faintly, "I'm so sorry but—could you get me my tablets?"

Stella put down her book and looked at the grey sunken face with loving compunction.

"Of course, darling," she said. "Why didn't you ask me before?"

Aunt Fanny had fallen asleep, and Stella had slipped down to the morning-room to write to Paul. She sat down at the little writing-table by the window and took out of the drawer the last letter she had received from him.

There were four pages of it written in his small neat scholar-like hand. "You don't mind my writing all this to you, do you? I couldn't write it to anyone else, but you're so sympathetic, so utterly unselfish. It's apt to make other people selfish, you know. I expect that everyone you know unloads all their trouble onto you, don't they?" The rest of the letter consisted chiefly of descriptions of books he had read, of walks he had taken, of his friends and their doings, but there ran through it all a tacit admission that he was writing more fully, more confidentially to her than he could have written to anyone else. He was silent and reserved in personal intercourse, but even there she was aware always of his deep unquestioning devotion.

"Sometimes," he wrote, "the thought that I pour everything out to you—things I could never tell anyone else—makes me turn hot and cold, and then I seem to see you—so lovely, so unutterably kind and good—and I know that it's all right. It's just as if one were talking to one's guardian angel."

Stella laid down the letter and sat gazing into the distance. . . . "So lovely, so unutterably kind and good . . . one's guardian angel."

The compliments, she knew, would have made some girls feel elated and triumphant, but they only made her feel humble, as if a heavy weight of responsibility had been fastened upon her. When people thought of you like that, it meant that you had to exert every effort to become worthy of it, to go on trying, never to be satisfied with yourself. . . .

She had just taken up her pen and written "Dear Paul," when Hugh Carlswell was announced. He had come straight from the Vicarage garden party, and wore his frock-coat, silk hat and the conventional buttonhole. Despite his formal attire, he still had the look of a young Viking—a look emphasised by his regular features and soft wavy moustache.

He greeted her with punctilious courtesy.

"I just came round to make sure that your aunt was no worse," he said. "Everyone was disappointed that you were not at the Vicarage. I was—especially disappointed."

She gave him her faint wistful smile. "Were you?" she said. "That was nice of you. No, Auntie isn't worse. Actually, I think she's a little better. I was prepared to come till the very last minute. I'd even got my hat on, and then——"

"Yes?"

She put her hand to her head. "Shall we go out into the garden? I've got rather a headache. It's with being in Aunt's room all day, I suppose. She's asleep now, so I've just slipped down to write a letter."

His eyes rested on her in grave concern.

"You're worn out," he said indignantly. "Someone ought to speak to her about it. I've a good mind to do it myself."

"Oh, Hugh!" she cried, aghast. "You mustn't. I'd never forgive you—or myself. It would kill her. I didn't mean to grumble."

"You never grumble. But she's a selfish exacting old woman."

"Hugh, she isn't," she pleaded. "She doesn't even *ask* me to stay with her—at least not very often. But I know she wants me. I know that she's miserable and lonely when I'm not with her and—well, that's enough to keep me with her."

He looked at her with a softening of his rather stern young face.

"It would be—with you," he said.

"No, no," she disclaimed. "There's nothing noble about it. Please don't think there is. It's probably very silly of me, but—it's just the way I'm made."

"I know it is," he said softly.

She opened the french windows and stood there a moment, drawing in the fresh air.

"Isn't it lovely! It's the first time I've been out today. You must come and see Hobbard's carnations. He's so proud of them. He gets a little disheartened because there's no one to see his things nowadays. I can't have people here with Aunt so ill. . . . You've no idea what a thrill a visitor is! It was nice of you to come."

They walked together over the soft velvety turf.

"It would have done you good to come to the party," he said. "What happened?"

"Oh." She made a little deprecating gesture. "I suppose I could have come really. . . . I had my hat on all ready and—well, Auntie begged me not to. She said she'd be lonely and miserable without me. I couldn't have gone after that, Hugh, could I?"

"I suppose not," he said grudgingly, "but it's outrageous. Why doesn't she get a proper nurse? It's wearing you out."

"I think one week of an ordinary nurse would kill her," said Stella. "She can't bear me out of her sight. It's rather naughty of her"—she smiled indulgently as at the tricks of a beloved child—"but she can work up a heart attack at will if she thinks I'm going to leave her. . . . Perhaps I'm specially tired today because she made me read aloud to her for so long. She loves it, and, of course, she doesn't realise how tiring it is. She gets upset when I stop."

"Stella," he burst out, "you can't go on like this."

She drew up her slight figure with an air of gallant courage. "I can," she said. She smiled at him. "It sounds priggish, but if a thing's your duty you can do it."

"Is it your duty?" he asked.

"Yes," she said simply.

They sat down on the wooden seat beneath the chestnut tree at the end of the lawn.

The westering sun raked the garden, throwing long shadows on the grass . . . deepening the blue of her eyes, and turning the silky waves of her hair to spun gold.

His eyes rested on her as if he drew life and refreshment from the sight. She looked so calm and pure and gentle, sitting there motionless in the shadow of the tree. She seemed to him the epitome of all that was noble in womanhood.

The austerity of her costume and of her smoothly parted hair made him turn in disgust from the memory of the frills and furbelows of the chattering women guests at the party.

"What was the party like?" she said suddenly. "Who was there?"

"Oh, the usual lot. You know them all by heart."

"What did they do?"

"Played croquet and asked each other if they'd read *Rupert of Hentzau*."

She smiled.

"Was that friend of Biddy's there? I've forgotten her name."

She watched him closely as he answered, "Miss Blake? Yes, she was there . . ." and was relieved that he spoke so casually.

"She came to tea here when she was a child. Do you remember?"

He wrinkled his brows,

"No . . . I don't think I do."

"She was a darling. I liked her so much."

His eyes smiled at her.

"You have a way of liking people, haven't you?"

"Have I? I don't know. I think I'm very lucky. Except for one horrible governess people have always been kind to me."

"Some people wouldn't call you lucky," he said. "Lots of girls of your age would think they were very unlucky if they had to spend their lives looking after a fractious old aunt."

"I think I'm lucky to be of use to someone. . . . Was your mother at the party, Hugh?"

His face grew grave again.

"No, she couldn't go. Pam was worse. That new man hasn't done her any good. Mother heard that he'd performed some wonderful cures, but he only worried and frightened the poor little thing. I hope they'll leave her alone now. . . . She's quite happy and—in lots of ways, you know, Stella, she's quite intelligent. The other day . . ."

She listened, chilled by his interest in the child. She couldn't understand this deep affection for someone who was little less than a monstrosity. But she was quick, as ever, to take her cue.

"I know, Hugh. I do understand. And you must try to understand about me. You couldn't bear to hurt or disappoint Pamela, and I feel the same about Auntie."

When he took his leave she went down to the gate with him, then walked slowly back to the house.

She and Hugh had drawn more closely together that afternoon than they could possibly have done if they had met casually as guests at the Vicarage garden party. She had been bitterly disappointed at not being able to go to the party (what Aunt Fanny said had, of course, made it quite impossible for her to go), but she had had a much happier afternoon than if she had gone. She remembered with a faint smile how when she was a little girl Aunt Fanny used to say, "If you just do your duty, dear, you'll be happy." It sounded so priggish, but, after all, it was true. . . .

Chapter Six

Sɪʀ Mɪʟᴇs and Lady Carlswell generally gave a garden party at the end of the summer. It marked the close of the local summer festivities, as the Vicarage garden party marked the opening of them. The Hall, of course, did things on a grander scale than the Vicarage. There was a marquee on the lawn in case of rain or, if fine, an elaborate buffet on the terrace beneath the clipped yew hedge, a band came down from London to play waltzes and military marches, and an army of footmen carried trays of ices and strawberries and cream among the guests. The guests, too, were more distinguished than the Vicarage garden party guests, including members of all the neighbouring county families, with a discreet selection of local people.

Even to the villagers the event was something of a gala. They gathered at doors and windows to watch the procession of carriages that went by, to comment on the various turn-outs, to admire the sleek high-stepping horses, the liveried grooms and footmen, the flounced parasols and beflowered hats of the occupants.

Sir Miles and Lady Carlswell received their guests standing on the top of the terrace steps. Sir Miles—a tall thick-set man with a red weather-beaten face, kindly blue eyes and luxuriant white moustaches—greeted each with unaffected heartiness. He was intensely proud of his home and family and took an ingenuous delight in showing them off to the world. In contrast, Lady Carlswell performed her duty as hostess with an air of schooled graciousness. She, too, was devoted to her home and family, but such social activities were to her merely a part of her duty as mistress of Runeham Hall. She performed them punctiliously and with an air of resolutely concealed boredom. She was a stately handsome woman—almost as tall as her tall husband—and till Pamela's birth had looked younger than her years. Since Pamela's birth she had aged considerably. Her once blue-black hair was flecked with grey, her dark eyes had lost something of their fire, the lines of her finely-moulded mouth had tightened. Yet her whole face would light up with tenderness when her eyes rested on Pamela. She held her by the hand now—a fair-haired blue-eyed child with long shining ringlets, dressed in a frock of daintily embroidered cambric and a frilled cambric hat. She stood by her mother, looking up at the guests with solemn blue eyes in which only a slight suggestion of vacancy betrayed the confusion of the small brain behind. Suddenly she let go of her mother's hand and ran down the terrace steps and across the lawn to Hugh, who was mingling with the guests but keeping an eye on the side of the house round which Stella must come. She had promised to escape the jealous tyranny of her aunt today, unless her aunt were really worse, in which case she would send a message.

Pamela made indistinguishable sounds, and he bent down attentively to listen. Few people outside the family could understand what Pamela said. He identified the sound as "pitty flowers" and answered "Yes, darling, aren't they pretty?" and she smiled happily and clung more tightly to his hand. Looking back towards the terrace, he met his mother's eyes. Wherever Lady Carlswell was, whatever she was doing, she was always aware of Pamela, was ready always to go to her at the least sign of distress. Hugh would ordinarily have sent her a reassuring smile over the child's head, but, instead, he turned away in sudden embarrassment.

He had taken for granted that his mother would be delighted when he told her that he wanted to marry Stella. She possessed—he would have thought—every quality that his mother could wish for in her daughter-in-law. His mother disliked "modern" girls and there was certainly nothing of the modern girl about Stella. Stella was old-fashioned, quiet, modest, self-effacing and—exquisitely lovely. He had broached the subject to his mother last night in her bedroom, confident of her approval and sympathy.

When he had finished speaking she had looked at him for a few moments in silence, then said, "Oh, *Hugh*!" in a tone of undisguised dismay.

He had been so amazed that at first he could not speak.

"What do you mean?" he had said at last.

She had given him a faint unhappy smile.

"Don't be angry with me, Hugh. She's never seemed—*real* to me somehow."

"Just because she's so quiet and shy!" he burst out. "Surely you know how good and unselfish she is."

She put her hand onto his and pressed it. She couldn't bear the hurt look on his handsome young face.

"I suppose that I wouldn't really think anyone good enough for you, darling. It's a way mothers have, you know. . . . Do you love her very much?"

"Yes."

She sighed.

"Then I suppose you must marry her."

"You'll try to love her?" he pleaded.

"I'll try to," she promised.

He still felt aggrieved and hurt by the memory of the interview.

He had chosen the one girl of all the girls around whom his mother should have welcomed as the ideal future mistress of Runeham Hall, and it was monstrously unjust that she should have taken the attitude she had taken. She had nothing against Stella. "Not real." . . . Just because she was so shy and retiring, so unlike the girls he had so often heard his mother condemn. . . . He felt bitterly disappointed. Oh, but his mother had only to learn to know her, he assured himself. She would love her soon enough then. . . .

Pamela was speaking urgently and pointing to a bed of heliotrope. He stooped down and picked one of the flowers, putting it into her hand. She smiled up at him again—her vague but radiantly sweet smile.

She was a placid sunny-tempered child between the sudden fits of rage or distress that seized her at intervals for no apparent reason. She had, too, an odd unexpected gift of mimicry, though she hated to be laughed at.

He straightened his tall figure and—suddenly his heart quickened. Stella was coming along the terrace round the side of the house.

Aunt Fanny had given her her outfit for the party, sending to London for it. The dress was of white china silk falling in soft folds from the slender waist to the ground and forming a short train behind. The hem was embroidered with pink rosebuds, a cluster of roses was tucked into the belt of broad black velvet, and the white leghorn hat was trimmed with black velvet ribbons and roses. One strand of the black velvet ribbon went from side to side of the shady brim, under her chin, bending down the straw to make a sort of bonnet.

He met her at the foot of the terrace steps.

"You've come . . ." he said breathlessly, taking her hand in his.

His face wore that look of poignant defenceless happiness that proclaimed his secret to all who cared to look.

"Yes, I've come," she said softly. "I said I would. . . . Auntie's much better today."

She bent down with a gesture of radiant tenderness to kiss Pamela. "Well, darling . . ."

If anything had been needed to complete his happiness, that gesture completed it.

She looked around her. Lady Carlswell had left her post at the top of the terrace steps.

"I'm afraid I'm rather late. Where's your mother?"

"On the front lawn."

She took the child's other hand in hers, and they went slowly through the crowd of guests to the front lawn. Pamela walked between them, smiling up at Stella with her sweet vague smile. The other guests watched them with barely concealed interest, looking from Hugh's radiant face to the girl's demure loveliness.

Professional know-alls hastened to display a suddenly acquired wisdom.

"Oh yes. . . . I've seen *that* coming for some time."

Lady Carlswell, standing in the centre of a crowd, dressed in grey silk, with a grey feathered bonnet tied under her chin, holding up a grey frilled parasol, stepped forward to greet the newcomer. She wanted to make up to Hugh for the lack of enthusiasm with which she had received his confidence last night. If it had to be, she must, of course, try to accept it with a good grace. The girl was pretty, well behaved and of a good enough family. She didn't know why she had never taken to her. Perhaps marriage would give her that something she lacked—Lady Carlswell still couldn't think what it was. Certainly the boy might have chosen much worse. ... She drew Stella to her and kissed her lightly on the cheek, then, glancing at Hugh, was rewarded by his sudden flush of pleasure.

"So glad you could come, my dear," she said. "How's your aunt?"

"Much better, thank you," said Stella.

"Get her some tea, Hugh," said Lady Carlswell in dismissal.

It sounded a little abrupt, but she couldn't think of anything else to say to the girl. Odd to have a daughter-in-law to whom one could never think of anything to say but "How's your aunt?" And, of course, one couldn't go on saying that after marriage. ... Anyway, Hugh couldn't be cross with her. She'd kissed her. ... Her skin had felt like cool satin. No wonder that Hugh was in love with her, she thought with a sigh.

Hugh and Stella, with the child between them, crossed the lawn to where Sir Miles stood with a little group of friends discussing the conviction and imprisonment of Captain Alfred Dreyfus, whose cause was being violently championed in England.

"This Zola fellow," Sir Miles was saying. "Don't know much about him as a writer, but he's shown 'em up with a vengeance. By Gad, sir, we don't let things like that happen in England."

He greeted Stella with old-fashioned gallantry. His wife had told him that Hugh meant to propose to her and he approved the choice. Well-bred, well-behaved, dutiful—just the sort of girl to keep that good-looking boy of his out of mischief. Hugh had shown no signs so far of getting into mischief, but Sir Miles believed that every man needed a good woman to keep him out of mischief.

"Stay with Papa, will you, dear?" said Hugh to Pamela.

Docilely she let go of his hand and took the large hairy one that Sir Miles held out to her.

"That's right. ... Stay and look after Papa," he said, smiling down on her affectionately. "Papa's little sweetheart, eh?"

Hugh and Stella moved on across the crowded lawn.

"Will you come to the rose garden?" said Hugh.

Biddy and Doreen sat on a green-painted iron garden seat, its back forming an elegantly designed imitation of giant ferns, and watched the gaily dressed crowds that passed and repassed. ... Flower-laden hats ... frilled parasols ... floating feather boas ... tautly stretched veils ... tiny waists ... skirts that swept the ground or foamed into trains lifted by daintily gloved hands to display filmy white petticoat flounces beneath. From the band-stand came the slow sensuous strains of "The Blue Danube." Between the two sat Miss Templeton, the head mistress of the Runeham Hill School, a select educational establishment for the daughters of gentlefolk that topped the hill just outside the village. Miss Templeton—a small decisive-looking woman, with a long mouth and eyes that could brim with laughter or snap with anger equally effectively—was always invited to the annual garden party at the Hall together with her senior pupils, and she looked upon the occasion as part of the pupils' education. She saw to it that they were as fashionably dressed as anyone there, and she saw to it, too, that they met as many young men as possible. Unlike most head mistresses of her day, Miss Templeton considered the meeting with personable young men an important part in a young lady's education.

"It's got to be that or flirting with the gardener and writing notes to the groom," she would say in her precise voice. "I've even known it run to eloping with the second footman."

Biddy had been one of her pupils, and Miss Templeton was a frequent visitor at the Vicarage. At school Biddy had stood in awe of her. It was only since leaving that she had discovered the fund of humour and kindliness and sheer good sense that underlay the awe-inspiring manner. She was delighted to find that Doreen and Miss Templeton liked each other.

They were discussing the Woman's Movement, in which Doreen had become interested since her return to England.

"Why my gardener, who can barely read and is in any case always willing to sell his vote for a pint of beer, should have a voice in the conduct of his country's affairs, while a reasonably intelligent and educated woman like myself should have none, has always been a mystery to me," said Miss Templeton. "Officially I am supposed to frown upon the movement as unwomanly, whatever that may mean. Privately it has my deepest sympathy. Even the militants. After all, men got the vote by rioting." Her eyes swept the garden in a quick keen scrutiny. "Bella Monkton has secured an extremely attractive young man. It's improved her looks already. Her mother wrote to say that she needed a tonic. I think that this will serve the purpose just as well."

The Vicar and his wife came up to greet Miss Templeton. Mr. Lytton was short and tubby, with twinkling eyes and a round merry face. He was a man of small intellectual attainments but of such sincere kindliness and good-humour that he was popular with all classes of his parishioners. Essentially childlike himself, he was happiest when among children, and small groups of them would generally be seen accompanying him on his walks. He loved to tease them and joke with them, and they knew that the bulging pockets of his shabby coat could be counted on to produce sweets or nuts or apples. . . . His Sunday school was a riotously noisy affair, strongly disapproved of by disciplinarians.

Mrs. Lytton, as short and stout as her husband, was completely immersed in household and parish duties. Her reason told her that there was a larger, more important world than the one she knew, but she never quite believed it. Her horizon was bounded on all sides by her house, her parish, her husband and Biddy, and she was supremely happy within it. . . . Her husband had always seemed more her child even than Biddy, and on the rare occasions when he was depressed she would play a game of draughts with him and let him win—a proceeding which seldom failed to restore his spirits. Since Biddy grew up she had joined the conspiracy, and the Vicar was, as it were, a beloved child with two devoted mothers.

They stood rather in awe of Doreen, with her beauty and air of sophistication, her casual references to places and events of which they knew nothing . . . but it thrilled and delighted them to have her staying with them. They were incapable of that resentment of the unfamiliar that is the hallmark of small minds.

They greeted Miss Templeton with eager unaffected pleasure. The Vicar, who had once painfully attained to a bowing acquaintance with the New Testament in Greek and had now forgotten everything he ever knew of it, respected her classical attainments, and Mrs. Lytton admired the efficiency with which she ran her school. They chatted together for a few moments, then Miss Templeton said, "Will you do something for me?"

"Certainly," beamed the Vicar.

"I want you to go and take Bella Monkton's young man from her and give him to Priscilla Carlow. Bella's had that one long enough and poor Priscilla has none and is looking very bored. Find another for Bella, of course."

The two trotted off happily together. . . . Miss Templeton watched them as they secured a tall young man with flowing moustaches and beautifully waved auburn locks, introduced him to Bella, then carried off Bella's young man to Priscilla, who at once brightened and glowed into prettiness. . . . The Vicar and his wife turned to smile at Miss Templeton, like a couple of children pleased at having executed an errand successfully, then went to talk to their parishioners.

"Aren't they sweet?" said Doreen.

Biddy threw her a grateful glance.

"I was so afraid that you'd find them narrow," she said.

"No, they're not narrow," said Doreen. "They're beautifully simple and they have that instinctive wisdom that only simple people have. It makes the other sort of wisdom—the sort that one acquires—seem a bit second-rate in comparison."

Stella and Hugh passed them on the way to the rose garden. Stella's face looked pale under the shade of the leghorn hat. The white dress swept the ground with its hem of rosebuds. She threw them her faint sweet smile as she passed. . . .

"Isn't she beautiful!" said Biddy fervently.

"An interesting child," said Miss Templeton judicially. "Talented and—well, interesting. If her aunt had sent her to me I might have made something of her. . . . That's Molly Peter's sixth ice. She has a very delicate stomach. I'd better warn Matron to be prepared for a broken night."

"I don't quite know what you mean by 'interesting,' " said Biddy, throwing her ex-head mistress an affectionate teasing glance. "The truth is you can't bear to admit that there's any good in anyone who hasn't been to Runeham Hill School."

"Perhaps that is so," agreed Miss Templeton.

"You can't deny that she's been wonderful to her aunt," persisted Biddy.

"I quite admit it," said Miss Templeton. "Bella Monkton is managing her new young man extremely well. He is evidently inclined to be amorous. Excellent practice for her. . . . I can't think of any one of my own girls who would have devoted herself to an elderly relative as Stella has done to her aunt—if that is any comfort to you. . . . Colonel Bellfield has taken the Laidlow twins into the summer-house. A dangerous man, but fortunately the twins are inseparable, and he can't very well seduce the two together."

"Have you heard Stella play lately?" challenged Biddy.

"No."

"Well, she plays almost as well as a professional. Everyone says so."

"I admitted that she was talented," said Miss Templeton dryly.

Biddy laughed.

"I know you're trying to tease me," she said. "There's Mother beckoning to me. I ought to go and talk to people."

Doreen half rose to go with her, but Miss Templeton put out a hand and said, "Stay with me."

They watched Biddy make her way through the crowd. Mrs. Lytton was talking to the People's Churchwarden, a retired grocer of substance, who was inclined to be difficult, and she was in need of reinforcements.

"Poor Biddy!" said Doreen. "She's adored Stella since she was a little girl, and she can't understand why everyone else doesn't adore her, too. I evidently hurt her many years ago by talking about Stella's 'person.' I said that she was kind and sweet only because her 'person' made her be, which sounds rather silly. I don't quite know what I meant."

Miss Templeton drew her brows together thoughtfully.

"I think I do. Let's call it an 'eidolon' instead of a 'person.' It sounds more scientific, though, of course, it isn't. . . . I've just been re-reading Meredith's *Egoist*. Do you remember where he says that the egoist's hatred of the world is caused by fear on behalf of his 'naked eidolon'? 'There the poor little naked creature ran, for any mouth to blow on, and, frost-nipped and bruised, it cried to him and he was of no avail.' "

"Oh, but surely Stella isn't like that," objected Doreen.

"No. Hers is a different kind of eidolon, but it absorbs her as completely. It sets her impossible standards, puts her to uncongenial tasks. . . . She enjoys it at first, because, of course, there is a certain excitement in watching one's self being noble, but the perpetual disharmony between what she wants to do and what her eidolon forces her to do is rather wearing."

"What will happen to her?" said Doreen.

Miss Templeton shrugged.

"It depends how strong a hold her eidolon has on her. I've known girls like Stella marry and settle down into placid wives and mothers and completely lose that particular eidolon. If that doesn't happen—well, it can take rather unpleasant forms."

"What forms?" asked Doreen.

"Have you noticed that I'm making myself very unpopular by monopolising you like this?" said Miss Templeton. "You're extremely good-looking, my dear, and I've received black looks from several personable young men in the last half-hour. . . . There! I thought so! Authority has been asked to interfere and put a stop to the horrible and unnatural situation—a pretty young woman wasting her time talking to a plain elderly one."

Lady Carlswell was making her way to them across the lawn with a tall whiskered young man in tow.

"May I introduce Captain Garth? Miss Blake . . . Captain Garth. Miss Templeton, a friend of mine is most anxious to meet you. She has a young daughter and has been asking me about your school."

"But, Stella," protested Hugh, "you can't mean it."

The two sat on a wooden seat in a recess at the end of the rose garden, enclosed by a hedge of roses and presided over by an armless marble nymph brought from Italy by Sir Miles's grandfather.

The distant strains of the band floated sleepily through the summer air. Sounds of voices and laughter came from the lawns and shady walks. Stella sat with her head turned aside, her body tense, her lovely mouth set. . . . Her refusal of him had taken them both by surprise. Though he had told himself that she was a thousand times too good for him, that he would never be worthy of her, however hard he tried, somehow he had never really doubted that she would accept him. . . . When he looked forward into the future and saw himself in his father's place it had always been Stella whom he saw in his mother's—Stella moving gracefully about the old house, sitting next him in church in the high family pew, playing her part by his side in the social life of the county, supporting him in his plans for the betterment of his tenants' lot.

And Stella—she did not often look beyond the day's duties, for the picture of herself performing them gracefully and conscientiously generally filled her horizon, but, if she looked forward to any future, it was to a future as Hugh's wife. He had been faithful in his allegiance to her from boyhood, and she had never met anyone whom she would have preferred as a husband. Perhaps something in her echoed his own contention that he was not worthy of her, perhaps sometimes she thought that the wider world beyond Runeham might have something better to offer her, but if she had been told yesterday that Hugh was going to propose today, she would have taken for granted that she would accept him. It was Hugh's fault that she had not done so. Hugh had said too much. Inarticulate as a rule, he had on this occasion been carried away by his own eloquence. He had begun to explain why he loved her, and, having begun, he found it difficult to stop. She was so kind, so good, so beautiful, so utterly perfect. No other girl would have devoted herself, as she had done, to her aunt through the long years of her illness. He enlarged upon this theme ... repeated comments he had heard on it. .... Stella listened enthralled, and when he stopped she had to add the final touch to make the picture complete.

"I can't marry you while Auntie's alive, Hugh. It would be deserting my post."

His face paled.

"But, Stella ... you can't mean it."

"I do mean it, Hugh."

"You mean—you don't love me?"

Her eyes met his levelly.

"Yes, Hugh, I love you."

"Then——" He made a movement to take her in his arms. She drew away from him, putting out a hand to stop him.

"Don't, Hugh. ..."

"I'm sorry," he said contritely. "Listen to me, Stella. I know how—conscientious you are. I know that your duty always comes first. That's one of the things I love you for. But—surely, if you got a nurse—oh, any amount of nurses ... I'd be so glad and proud to undertake the care of her financially."

"Hugh, darling," she said in a low steady voice, "you don't understand. It isn't a question of money. It isn't a question of getting a nurse. It's that—it's my job. I've got to do it. She depends on me. She's unhappy whenever I'm not there. Oh Hugh, when I think of all she did for me when I was a child, I can't leave her to hirelings now."

He was silent for a few moments. She had let him take her hand and he held it, looking down at it, his young face set in lines of strain.

"Darling," he said at last, "couldn't we have her with us here? Then you could look after her, and——"

"No," she said firmly. The blue eyes gazed steadfastly in front of her, as if she saw visions that were hidden from him, heard voices he could not hear. "I couldn't do my duty to either of you, if I agreed to that. I'd be—torn in two," She turned her earnest gaze on to him. "Hugh, darling, I do understand how you feel. I—love you as much as you love me, but I can't buy my happiness at the expense of someone else's—and that is what it would be doing. I know it sounds stupid and old-fashioned and priggish, but the knowledge that I'd failed in my duty would poison my happiness. It would come between us. It would kill our love." He made a movement as if to protest but she silenced him by a gesture and continued: "Oh, do believe it, Hugh. Happiness isn't—snatching what you want just because you want it. It isn't worth having without suffering and sacrifice. The only real happiness comes from—living up to one's ideals, trying, however hard it is, to do the thing that one knows to be right. Hugh, I know it won't be easy, because we love each other, but that very love ought to help us not to cheapen it by choosing the easy way. You remember how Matthew Arnold says,

> Tasks in hours of insight willed
> Must be through days of gloom fulfilled . . .?

You must help me, not make things more difficult for me. . . ."

He bent his head and kissed the hand he held in his.

"You're so *good*," he said brokenly.

"Don't, Hugh. . . . I'm not good. It's only that—I must do my duty, as I see it. And please, don't let us discuss it any more. My mind's made up. I shan't alter it. Let's go back to the lawn. You ought to be talking to people."

Heavy depression swept over her as she drove home in the victoria. . . . Her thoughts turned to the life she would lead as Hugh's wife. . . . She saw herself, as Hugh had seen her, moving gracefully about the old house, sitting next him in church in the high family pew, playing her part by his side in the social life of the county. . . . What opportunities it would afford her of doing good and helping people! Perhaps she had been wrong in deciding to stay with Aunt Fanny. . . . She imagined herself telling Hugh that she had made a mistake and would marry him, after all . . . but turned from the picture with a mental shudder. No, she couldn't do that. It wasn't—herself. And she *had* decided rightly. She couldn't desert Auntie. Hugh had understood. He had realised that, though every other girl in the world might have neglected her duty in order to marry him, she would not do so. The only comfort was that the episode had made the pedestal on which Hugh had set her higher even than it had been before. There had been something almost of worship in the movement with which Hugh had bent his head over her hand. She had been right. She knew that she had been right. But the depression remained. . . . She felt like an artist compelled against his will to continue adding touches to a picture that is already finished, while a new one clamours to be begun.

Aunt Fanny turned as she entered the room. Her welcoming smile was anxious and propitiatory. That strange unreasonable fear of Stella that she looked on now as part of her illness held her in its grips.

"Had a nice time, darling?" she said nervously.

"Yes, thank you."

Stella took off the leghorn hat and held it by the black velvet ribbon. In her white dress and roses she was the spirit of youth incarnate. She seemed to shine through the gloom of the darkened room, as she stood there, fixing her eyes on the shrivelled old woman in the bed.

"There's something I want to tell you, Auntie," she went on.

"Yes, darling . . . what?" said Aunt Fanny.

"Hugh asked me to marry him."

Joy and thanksgiving flooded Aunt Fanny's heart. Her little Stella . . . her baby . . . wife to the man who above all others would make her happy. Aunt Fanny remembered how years ago she had dreamed this dream, and now—it had come true.

"Oh, my darling," she said, "I'm so glad."

Stella sat down on the bed and looked at Aunt Fanny with a smile that was both sad and tender.

"But I couldn't leave you, Auntie. . . . I told him that."

Ice-cold fingers seemed to close round Aunt Fanny's heart.

"But you could, dear," she said breathlessly. "I'd miss you, of course, but we could get a nurse. . . ."

The lovely young face was grave, austere. There was a far-away look in the blue eyes.

"I've always vowed that I'd never leave you to—hirelings, dear," she said. "I should never know a moment's peace of mind. I should always be afraid that you were lonely or neglected. I could never trust anyone but myself to look after you. . . . Darling, when I think of all you did for me when I was a child, how can you imagine for a second that I could desert you now—now when you need me more than you've ever needed me before?"

"But, Stella," panted Aunt Fanny, "listen to me, dear. Listen. . . . You wouldn't be far away. You could come and see me. . . ."

Stella shook her head.

"I couldn't do my duty to both you and Hugh. I explained that to him. Darling," she laid her hand affectionately on Aunt Fanny's, "you know that it takes all my time and energy looking after you. And it would take all my time and energy to be Hugh's wife. I couldn't do both. You ought to be flattered"—she smiled tremulously with a gallant attempt at raillery—"that I've chosen you."

"But Stella," said Aunt Fanny. Her face had taken a greyish hue. Her voice quavered unsteadily. She had a strange nightmare feeling that she was pleading for her life. "I'd be all right. . . . I wouldn't mind. . . . There are good nurses. . . ."

Again that slow resolute shaking of the lovely golden head.

"Darling, I couldn't bear it. I'd feel that I'd failed in my duty."

"Then—I could go to the Hall . . ." whispered Aunt Fanny. Terror surrounded her like a black mist, shutting out even Stella. "Just a room . . . a nurse . . . you could keep your eye on me . . . if . . ."

"No. . . . Hugh suggested that. It would be just the same. I should have to fail in my duty to one or the other of you and I couldn't bear it."

Aunt Fanny tried to say the thing that had to be said, but at first the words wouldn't come. The ice-cold fingers seemed to be at her throat now, choking her. . . . At last the words came, on a dry rasping note.

"But Stella, I might . . . it might be for years . . . years . . ."

"I know, dearest," answered Stella. Her voice was low and steady, "but I feel that—if I do what I know is my duty—that's all that matters."

Aunt Fanny looked up at the sweet earnest face, the lips touched with a tender reassuring smile . . . and seemed to see the face of a judge, stern, implacable, putting on a black cap.

Chapter Seven

"It was my fault," sobbed Stella. "If it hadn't been . . . if I hadn't . . ."

The rest of the sentence was lost in a tempest of sobs.

She lay outstretched on her bed, her coiled golden hair looking very bright, her figure very girlish and slender, in the heavy crepe mourning dress.

Biddy knelt by the bed, trying to console her.

"Darling, you mustn't think of that again. . . . No one but you would ever think of it at all. You've been so splendid. . . ."

"Splendid? . . . Oh, don't, Biddy. When it was all my fault."

"Listen, darling," pleaded Biddy, her own face wet with tears of sympathy. "Listen. You know what Daddy said. He said that in the case of nearly every death the person who cared most fancied that somehow it was their fault; that, if they'd done this, or not done that, the person wouldn't have died. And you've always had such a—such a supersensitive conscience. . . . Darling, it couldn't have been your fault. It might have happened to anyone, anywhere."

Stella sat up and pushed the tangled golden curls back from her tear-stained face.

"Oh, Biddy . . . it *was* my fault. . . . I shall never forgive myself . . . never . . . all the rest of my life. . . . I shouldn't have put it there."

"But it had always been kept there."

"I know, but it shouldn't have been kept there."

For the night after the Hall garden party Aunt Fanny had evidently been awakened by indigestion and had by mistake taken an overdose of sleeping mixture instead of her usual indigestion mixture. Both bottles stood on the little table by her bed. Stella had come into her room early the next morning and found her dead.

Since then Stella had gone about dry-eyed and stony-lipped, accusing herself with a dull hopelessness that wrung the hearts of those who heard her. Not till today—the day after the funeral—had she broken down.

"The doctor knew it was kept there," said Biddy.

"I know."

"It's his responsibility if anyone's."

"No, no. He didn't love her. . . . I loved her. I should have guarded against it."

"How could you? . . . Listen, Stella. I don't want to seem hard, but your aunt was an old woman. She'd never have been able to get about again. It was the best thing that could have happened."

"Don't," moaned Stella. "You talk as if . . . She wanted to live. I wanted her to live. We were so happy. . . . Biddy——" She rested her elbows on her knees and gazed dreamily in front of her. "We *were* happy. . . . We'd had such a happy talk together the night before she died. I told her that Hugh had asked me to marry him, but that I didn't want to leave her, and—it made her so happy to think that I was going to be there with her—to the end. She'd always dreaded the thought of being left to paid nurses, you know. Over and over again she'd asked me to promise that she never would be. I know she felt so happy that night. She gave me the most beautiful smile when she kissed me goodnight."

Her lips quivered and her voice broke. Biddy flung her arms about her.

"Stella, you've given up your life to her. I don't know anyone else in the world who'd have done it. Everyone says so. You're young and beautiful, and yet you've lived the life of an elderly invalid all these years just for her sake."

"But, Biddy, I loved her. . . . I loved looking after her. . . . Think of all she did for me as a child."

"I know . . . but not many girls feel like that even about their mothers. . . . Darling, you're such a saint, and I can't bear you to torment yourself like this."

And suddenly Biddy broke down too, burrowing her carroty head on Stella's knee and sobbing unrestrainedly. Stella bent over her tenderly, her lips breaking into a tremulous smile.

"Biddy, Biddy. . . . Now, darling, which of us is comforting which? Let's get it clear."

Despite herself Biddy began to giggle, and the two of them clung to each other for a moment, laughing and crying at the same time. Then Mary knocked at the door and said,

"Mr. Hugh Carlswell has called to see you, Miss Stella."

"I'll be down in a moment," said Stella.

She went to the dressing-table and combed back the soft waves of her disordered hair.

"Oh, darling," said Biddy excitedly, "he's come to——"

The glance Stella turned on her was one of grave reproach.

"Biddy, please. . . . As if I could think of anything now but dear Auntie."

She went downstairs to the drawing-room, where Hugh was waiting for her. All the blinds in the house had been kept lowered till after the funeral, and the sunshine that poured through the window seemed unfamiliar and overpowering.

Hugh wore a dark suit and behaved with hushed reverence as if he were in church. He asked her if there were anything he could do for her, and she answered, with a little unsteady smile, that there was nothing just now but that if ever there was she would let him know at once.

"My friends have all been so good to me," she said.

"I hope to be more than a friend," he said gently, and went on quickly, without waiting for her gesture of dissent, "I know you don't want to discuss that now, but I want you to realise that I'm there just across at the Hall, and that, if there's anything in the whole world I or any of us can do, you mustn't hesitate to call on us. My mother told me to give you her love. She hopes to come over and see you later."

He stayed for a few minutes, then took his leave, distantly, respectfully. Stella went slowly back to her bedroom. He had behaved very well. Almost too well. She felt faintly disappointed by the interview. Somehow she had expected him to repeat his proposal, to plead with her, to protest his devotion. She would have been deeply shocked and distressed, of course. She would have reminded him that Aunt Fanny had only been buried yesterday, told him that she was too crushed by grief to think of marriage, let him understand that he must by no means take her acceptance of him for granted. . . . Without that, the interview had seemed somehow tame. She might have been just anyone receiving condolences on her aunt's death—not herself at all.

Then, thinking over the interview, reassurance came to her. It was because she was so triumphantly herself that the interview had been so tame. Merely to be with her had tamed the grosser elements of his nature. . . .

When she re-entered the bedroom Biddy started up eagerly.

"Oh, Stella," she said, "did he——?"

"Hush, dear," said Stella gravely.

For the next few weeks Stella stayed chiefly in the house, appearing only occasionally in the village. Her appearance roused universal compassion. The heavy black crepe-trimmed clothes emphasised her dazzling fairness, and made her seem poignantly fragile and young and bereaved. Even Miss Templeton, seeing her alone in the Markham pew in church, wearing deep mourning, her fair graceful head bent over her prayer-book, felt a sudden lump rise in her throat. And Lady Carlswell, drawing Hugh impulsively into her bedroom one night, said,

"Darling, I'm sorry I was hateful about her. . . . I think she's behaved splendidly. I suppose that I was just jealous."

The rather odd thing was that, though it was years since Aunt Fanny had appeared in public, Stella's slight black-clad figure now conveyed art almost unbearable suggestion of loneliness. Impossible to believe, when one watched it, that actually she had been going about in the village without Aunt Fanny all those years. . . .

Praise of her devotion to her aunt rose like a paean on all sides. She was pointed out as an example to careless daughters.

"I wish you were half as dutiful to me as Stella Markham was to that old aunt of hers."

Miss Farthing, Stella's old governess, had returned to take formal charge of the household and to act as chaperon to Stella. She was a shadowy old lady, with so well developed a gift for effacing herself that people seldom knew whether she were there or not. She sat about in corners, her grey head bent over her needlework, indiscernible from her background.

Except with Stella she had not been a great success as a governess, and she admired Stella, accordingly, looking on her as the justification of her whole career. Stella, on her side, treated her with unfailing kindness and consideration.

"Darling old Penny likes to think that she does the flowers," she said to Hugh with a smile. "She just crams bunches of them into vases—she always did—and she hasn't the faintest suspicion that I do them all over again while she's having her afternoon nap. I wouldn't let her know that for the world."

At the end of six weeks Stella and Hugh became officially engaged. Gradually the heavy black mourning dresses gave place to soft mauve and lilac that suited her equally well. Hugh was radiant with happiness, hardly crediting his good fortune.

"I just can't believe it, darling," he said. "You're so wonderful."

And Stella would make her charming little deprecatory gesture and say, "Oh no, Hugh . . . don't . . . I'm not. . . ."

Lady Carlswell received Stella into the family circle with an affection that satisfied even Hugh. She tried hard to overcome her instinctive dislike of the girl, which she was still conscious of and which she now put down to jealousy.

"After all," she said to her husband, "Hugh's my only son, and I suppose it's natural that I shouldn't consider any woman in the world good enough for him."

"Stella's a dam fine girl," rejoined Sir Miles. "She'll make him a dam fine wife. You've nothing against her, have you?"

"Nothing," said Lady Carlswell, and added, after a slight pause, "Perhaps I'd like her better if I had."

Paul Sanders came home from college for the vacation and stayed with his mother in the little cottage behind the school. He was studying for an examination and seldom appeared except striding over the countryside on the long walks he had always loved. He refused all invitations, making his work an excuse. He came to see Stella, to offer his condolences on her aunt's death and his congratulations on her engagement. He was stiff and aloof and desperately earnest. Stella gave him tea in the drawing-room, which was exactly as it had been in Aunt Fanny's time—draped mirror, gilded bulrushes, and towering wicker fern stand—while Miss Farthing dozed in the yellow brocade tête-à-tête chair. He talked of his college life and work. He was a born student and had found already the *milieu* for which he was best suited, and in which he was happiest. He meant to take a double degree and then, he had been told, a fellowship would almost certainly be offered him. He could envisage no higher future than that of University Professor, but the thought of Stella continued to haunt him, and, in those exalted optimistic moods that sometimes visit one, he had imagined her sharing the life with him, making his happiness complete. . . . Now, seeing her as Hugh Carlswell's fiancée, moving already against a background of Carlswell splendour, he realised how impossible the dream had always been.

"I wish you the best of happiness always," he said as he took his leave of her. "If there's ever anything I can do for you . . . I mean that . . . There's nothing in the whole world I wouldn't do for you . . . nothing." His earnest young face flushed. "I want you always to look on me as a friend."

Stella pressed his hand.

"I value your friendship more than I can say, Paul," she said.

Sometimes she and Hugh met Paul as he was returning from his long tramps over the countryside. Hugh was always particularly pleasant to him, asking after his work, his mother, his plans, refusing to be discouraged by the shortness of his replies.

"I do admire that fellow," he said once as they continued their way after meeting him. "He's raised himself right out of the class he was born in by sheer grit and hard work. You'd take him for a gentleman anywhere."

"He *is* a gentleman," said Stella.

She had always been piqued by Hugh's refusal to consider Paul a possible rival.

"Of course," said Hugh quickly. "I didn't quite mean that. I mean—well, think of his mother."

But Stella didn't want to think of his mother.

"I believe that he's more than half in love with me," she couldn't help saying with a little teasing smile. "Aren't you a tiny bit jealous?"

Hugh looked down at her tenderly. "I don't see how any man who sees you can help being more than half in love with you," he said, "but I wouldn't insult you by being jealous."

Stella couldn't make up her mind whether to be annoyed or gratified by that.

She was, however, happier than she had ever been before. She was surrounded on all sides by an atmosphere of affection and approval. That sense of strain and discord that had so often oppressed her when she lived with Aunt Fanny had gone. She no longer wore that air of wistfulness, that look, as someone put it, of a lost child. Her beauty took on a warmth and sparkle it had never had before. Her engagement to Hugh was made the excuse for a burst of local festivities. Wherever she went she was the centre of the gathering. She moved through a series of enchanting pictures—and if she saw that radiant central figure of the pictures as plainly as the onlooker saw it, who could blame her for that?

There were, here and there, a few false notes in the general harmony. There was Pam. . . . The child got unbearably on Stella's nerves. She couldn't understand the deep affection that the whole Carlswell family seemed to feel for her. They liked to have her always with them, while her very presence humiliated and irritated Stella. To have to kiss the child good-night, as the others did, cost her sometimes an effort almost greater than she could make. The pretty empty face filled her with a revulsion that she tried in vain to master. What made it worse was that the child had a vague elusive likeness to Stella herself. She had the same golden hair, blue eyes, and satin-textured skin. Often, when Hugh held the child on his knee, she had to turn her eyes away so that she should not see them.

She made tentative suggestions to Hugh about sending the child away, but he looked at her blankly.

"Send Pam away?" he said. "*Pam?*"

"I only meant that perhaps they could cure her," she said lamely. "At some of these places they *do* cure cases like that."

"They couldn't cure Pam," he said. "We've had the best specialists in Europe. She has to be kept quiet and happy, and she'll develop as far as she *can* develop. Her nurse, you know, is specially trained. And she does improve."

"But"—she made another effort—"I should have thought that it's too much for your mother."

"Mother?" he said. "Why, Mother loves Pam so much that she's miserable whenever the child's out of her sight. We all feel like that about her. I suppose it's with her being—not quite like other children."

"Of course," she agreed hastily. "I love her, too. That's why I'm so anxious that everything possible should be done."

But she made up her mind that, when she was mistress of Runeham Hall, Pam should be packed off or kept well out of sight.

Then there was her position. Sometimes it seemed to her that Hugh thought more of that than of herself. She was to help his mother in this . . . she was to help his mother in that. . . . It seemed to be taken for granted that when his mother died she was to succeed to all her duties and responsibilities.

When once she uttered a half-hearted protest, Hugh smiled and said,

"I'm afraid you'll have to, darling."

It blurred the picture somehow, made her seem more an imitation of his mother than herself. And yet it was an attractive picture. The position she would occupy held endless possibilities of doing good. Hugh was touched by her shrinking from the worldly importance of her position and her eagerly grasping at the opportunities it offered of helping his poorer tenants.

"Couldn't we have a new barn built for old Peters? He showed me the old one this morning. I don't see how it can be properly repaired. I know that Follett's a good agent, but he's so dilatory."

She was tender-hearted, and, if she heard any story of hardship, could not rest till she had done something to help the victim. She was a frequent visitor at the little cottages in the village. She would read aloud to the invalids and take round baskets of "comforts"—tea, jam, warm garments. She had gone to carefully selected cottages, of course, when she was a little girl, with Aunt Fanny, and later with Miss Farthing, but there was a subtle difference now. She was accepted everywhere as the young squire's bride-to-be. The curtseys were deeper, the "Yes, miss. Thank you kindly, miss" more respectful.

A something of warm humanity that had been lacking before radiated from her.

"How could you have said that she was inhuman?" said Biddy triumphantly to Miss Templeton.

"What I actually said," Miss Templeton reminded her, "was that she was not quite human. I also said that life would probably make a human being of her. I think it's doing so now. Love is a great transmuter."

Sometimes Stella pondered the question as to whether she were really in love with Hugh, and always finally satisfied herself that she was. He was so good-looking, so unfailingly kind and courteous. Always she was conscious of the picture the two of them made together, and the consciousness sent a warm thrill through her, which she was sure was love. She liked to be kissed by him and she liked to feel his arm round her, though his occasional attempts at more intimate love-making horrified her. This was, of course, as it should be, both in her eyes and his. She was "pure" and "modest"—qualities which in those days were looked on as a woman's supreme virtues. Men, on the other hand, even the best of them, were admittedly coarse and animal. In order to have children and thus enter fresh fields of womanhood, a woman set aside her natural purity for certain definite occasions, making it quite clear that she did this unwillingly and against her higher instinct. All nice women, Stella had been given to understand, hated it. It was the price one paid for the privilege of being a mother. It was the cross one carried. . . . Stella was quite prepared to pay this price and carry this cross for the privilege of being a mother. . . . Looking into the future, she saw herself surrounded by a cluster of attractive golden-haired children—small replicas of herself and Hugh. She would be a little more matronly, of course, but just as beautiful. . . . Hugh would worship her. . . .

And so she drifted idly through the hours, in a roseate haze of day dreams, fêted and courted and admired, with the sweet excitement of Hugh's love to dispel any element of monotony the situation might have had . . . till the night of the Carlswell dinner-party.

Chapter Eight

STELLA had not yet met the most important members of the Carlswell family—Sir Robert Carlswell, a cousin of Sir Miles's, who held a post in the Cabinet, and Peter Carlswell, an archaeologist, who had recently returned from an expedition to Bornu in Central Soudan. Sir Miles was delighted when he found that both could accept an invitation for a week-end.

"At last we can have a real family dinner-party in your honour, my dear," he said to Stella.

Carlswells from far and wide, as well as relations of Lady Carlswell, were invited "to meet Hugh's fiancée."

Sir Miles, in his genial old-fashioned way, made much of his future daughter-in-law.

"Now look your best, my dear," he said. "It's you they're coming to see, remember, not us."

And Stella looked radiant that evening, in white satin and tulle, her lovely neck and shoulders bare, her eyes starry, her cheeks flushed. She wore the pearls that had once belonged to Aunt Fanny's mother, and an emerald bracelet given her by Hugh. Her entry into the drawing-room created the expected stir, and in a few moments she was surrounded by an admiring crowd of tall whiskered Carlswells, eager to pay their court. Hugh, standing by her side, his face pale with emotion, felt a deep, almost reverent pride. He was bringing into his beloved family as fair and pure a woman as any other Carlswell had ever brought into it.

"The gel's a ravin' beauty," said a tiaraed dowager to Lady Carlswell. "The boy's got taste."

"Yes, she's lovely," agreed Lady Carlswell with a sigh.

It was during dinner that the first clouds gathered on Stella's horizon. Those Carlswells, assembled to do her honour, gradually began to ignore her. It was as if, having paid their due meed of courtesy to Hugh's lovely young bride-to-be, they could now turn their attention to the realities of life.

They questioned Sir Robert Carlswell, a short thick-set man with moustache and beard cut in imitation of the Prince of Wales's, about the affairs of the day—Kitchener's masterly handling of the situation at Fashoda, Colonel Henry's confession of forgery in the Dreyfus case (two severe blows to France's self-confidence) and Lord Salisbury's surprising choice of young Mr. Curzon, Under Secretary for Foreign Affairs, as Viceroy of India.

Sir Robert appeared to take a somewhat gloomy view of things in general. He hinted darkly that, though the Jameson Raid had fortunately passed off without immediate complications, trouble was brewing in South Africa. He considered that the bankruptcy of Mr. S. T. Hooley marked not only the end of the cycle boom (Fashion had tired suddenly of its new toy, and Battersea Park was no longer the rendezvous of society women in bloomers and men in knickerbockers) but also the beginning of a period of industrial depression. France was commanding the market in motor cars. America was importing light cycles at a price with which our factories could not compete. London itself was in a dangerous state of apathy—emotionally exhausted by the Diamond Jubilee celebrations last year and the death of Mr. Gladstone early this year. "His death," pronounced Sir Robert, "means the death of Liberalism as we know it today."

Peter Carlswell was a shy silent young man, but he was at last induced to talk of his discoveries in Bornu. He described the little towns, surrounded by walls 20 feet thick, with triple gates at each corner, and the huts, built of reeds and clay polished to represent stucco.

"Do the women really stain their faces?" asked someone.

"Yes, they stain their faces indigo, their front teeth black and their canine teeth red. And they tattoo themselves all over."

"How perfectly horrible!" said Stella with a shudder, but no one seemed to be taking any notice of her.

A small pale insignificant-looking Carlswell was, it turned out, an artist of repute and a friend of Whistler's. He had recently met Will Rothenstein, who had come to Oxford from Paris to make his series of Oxford Portraits. After discussing those they went on to talk of the *Yellow Book, Pick-me-up*, and *Pageant*, and the work of the "Beggerstaff Brothers," Phil May, and Aubrey Beardsley.

"I love Leighton's pictures," put in Stella, but again her contribution was ignored. Worse even than this was the fact that the Carlswell women, many of them quite plain and dowdily dressed, displayed a knowledge of politics and art that seemed to Stella little short of an insult. At first she tried to despise this knowledge as unwomanly, to see herself set on a height far above this futile chatter. These ridiculous discussions about politics and art did not belong to a woman's sphere at all. The discussion veered to Woman Suffrage, and there again she was irritated to find that the majority of the guests sympathised with the movement, of which she had always disapproved.

"I was at a meeting the other day," said Robert Carlswell. "A Miss Doreen Blake made an excellent speech."

"Oh yes," said Hugh, "she was staying here in the summer. A charming girl. . . ."

Stella trembled with anger. That hateful friend of Biddy's, whom she had detested ever since she was a little girl! She opened her mouth to say "Surely a woman's sphere is the home," but the discussion had swung back again to Peter Carlswell's expedition to Bornu.

Stella, however, was roused. She could not endure to be ignored any longer. She rushed boldly in. She confused Bornu with Borneo, appeared to think that Lord Salisbury was a Liberal and betrayed a complete ignorance of the working of the British Constitution.

"But surely the whole Cabinet doesn't change just because there's a new Prime Minister?" she said.

There was a constrained silence. The Carlswells did not consider such ignorance either charming or amusing. She saw Hugh flush, and smiled at him sweetly, with an agony of rage and humiliation in her heart. Then someone began to talk of the experiments carried out by Marconi on the Hertzian ray, and a general discussion arose as to whether it could ever become a universal means of communication.

Pam entered soon afterwards and went the round of the table, sitting on the guests' knees in turn and eating nuts and grapes from their plates. Something of the tenderness that her father and mother and Hugh showed her was reflected in the manner of all their guests. Stella despised them for it, hated the child for it and—copied it so faithfully that Hugh sent her a grateful glance across the table.

Pam was at her most irritating tonight. She said that the bite of a bear was responsible for a small scratch on her finger and that a snake had stung her foot on the lawn.

"It did," she persisted. "It did—it did."

"Surely not, darling," said Lady Carlswell, and Sir Miles laughed as if the child had said something clever.

Back in the drawing-room the ladies fell into groups, continuing the discussion of the dining-table. Rage and humiliation still blazed in Stella's heart. She should have been queen of the evening, and—she had been neglected and insulted.

She slipped out of the drawing-room and went along a passage towards the large conservatory that had been built out on the garden side of the house. She couldn't endure their senseless chatter a moment longer. She must be alone for a little while in order to regain her serenity, her poise. . . . Her thoughts went back over the evening. How *could* they have ignored her! It was monstrous, incredible. Her beauty, her gentle wistful charm, should have dominated the whole dinner-table. For reassurance she turned to a full-length mirror that hung on the wall in the passage and stood for a moment, gazing at her reflection . . . letting her lovely mouth break into its slow sweet smile. . . . Her confidence in herself returned with a rush—then she looked down to find Pam standing by her side, studying her own reflection, a monstrous caricature of Stella's smile on the childish lips. That odd likeness between them, the utter fatuousness and imbecility of Pam's smile, sent a wave of blind rage through Stella. It was the rage that always assailed her when she saw the picture of herself blurred or distorted. A mist swam before her eyes. She raised her hand and struck the child as hard as she could across the face, then walked on towards the conservatory, her heart beating wildly. . . .

When she returned to the drawing-room she found Pam sitting on Lady Carlswell's knee. She was still crying and there was a red mark down one side of her face. The guests clustered round, consoling, sympathising.

"What's the matter?" said Stella. "Poor little Pam! I saw her fall down in the passage, but I didn't know she'd hurt herself."

Pam stopped crying and pointed at Stella.

"She hit me," she said indistinctly. "She hit me."

"Pam, darling!" said Lady Carlswell reprovingly. "You mustn't say things like that. You know quite well that Stella didn't hit you."

"She did," said Pam, her blue eyes meeting Stella's. Stella's didn't falter.

"Darling," she said in a tone that was concerned, tender, amused, "I'm so sorry you've hurt yourself, but you *know* I didn't hit you."

One of the ladies had a vinaigrette on a long gold chain and gave it to Pam to play with, and the child was so pleased that she forgot everything else. Lady Carlswell left Pam, happily occupied with her new toy, and came across the room to sit by Stella.

"Stella, my dear," she said, "you mustn't mind Pam. It was outrageous of her to say that, but—she doesn't realise what she's saying. It was just the same to her as that, ridiculous invention about the bear and the snake that she told us of at dinner. She makes up the most absurd stories. I don't know whether she really thinks they're true or not." She put her hand on Stella's and continued, in a voice that was kinder than any Stella had yet heard from her, "I haven't said much to you about Pam, dear. We love her . . . but I know she must be very trying to an outsider."

"You mustn't think of me as an outsider," put in Stella.

"I don't, my dear. And I want to tell you how grateful I am to you for being so kind and patient with her. Don't think I haven't noticed. . . . Pam's a burden that Hugh will have to bear to the end of his days—though he doesn't feel her a burden—and I'm glad that he's found someone as ready to help him as you are. . . . I'm sorry that Pam was at her worst tonight. You'll forgive her, won't you?"

"Of course," said Stella.

She thought Pam's accusation as outrageous as did Lady Carlswell. Already the picture of what had actually happened had faded from her mind, and in its place was one of Pam running down the corridor, tripping up and falling heavily onto the tiled floor of the passage.

"Poor little thing!" she said. "I wish I'd gone to her. . . . I saw her fall, but I didn't realise that she'd hurt herself."

"You couldn't have done anything, my dear," said Lady Carlswell. "You've been very sweet indeed."

Stella felt that the episode had brought her nearer Hugh's mother than she had ever been before.

Pam was fetched to bed by her nurse and shortly afterwards the men came in from the dining-room. Hugh made his way over to Stella and his mother. He looked unusually pale and grave. His mother told him about Pam as they drank their coffee.

"Stella's been so kind about it," she said, laying her hand lightly on Stella's arm. "It was outrageous of the child, of course, but Stella understands. . . . And now, dear, you'll play to us, won't you?"

Stella took her seat at the grand piano, and at once the strain and depression of the last few hours vanished. She played a Chopin waltz and played it extremely well. She had developed her musical talent conscientiously, never shirking the drudgery of long hours of practice. The best music master in Southwood came in to give her lessons each week, and she had always shown herself anxious to learn all he could teach her. The guests listened in silence. These Carlswells had little use for the second-rate in any field, and they recognised Stella's performance as first-rate. As soon as she had finished they surrounded her, congratulating, appraising. And Stella glowed again into radiant happiness. She held her rightful place as queen of the evening. They deferred to her opinion, admired her, courted her. She glanced at Hugh who was standing a little apart. He still looked pale and grave, but to her he had never seemed so attractive. The music had stirred her dormant passion. She longed to leave this hot crowded room and go with him into the shadowy garden, longed to feel his arms about her and his lips against hers. . . .

"It's so hot in here, Hugh," she said. "Let's go out. . . ."

He followed her out of the french windows, down the terrace steps and along the path beneath the high yew hedge. She took his arm and drew close to him, surrendering to the love that filled her whole body with melting sweetness.

"Oh, Hugh," she said, "it's so good to get away from all those empty chatterers . . . to be alone together at last. I got so tired of them at dinner. They talk about such unimportant things. What does it matter who the Prime Minister is or who's a better painter than whom? I feel tonight somehow that all that matters is to be happy and make other people happy. . . ."

They had reached a point where the thick hedge hid them from the house. She expected him to stop and take her in his arms, but he walked on, his face set.

"What is it, Hugh?" she said softly. "You aren't worrying over what your mother told you about Pam, are you? I didn't mind a bit, dear. I quite understand."

He turned and faced her.

"Stella, I've got to tell you," he said hoarsely. "I saw."

She looked at him in silence, and her whole body seemed to turn to ice.

"What do you mean?" she said at last. "You saw what?"

"I came out from dinner before the others, because I wanted to be with you. I was at the end of the corridor. I saw you hit Pam."

Her face was distorted, her beauty turned to a Medusa mask, her white lips drawn back over her teeth.

"You liar!" she said. "I never hit her. I never touched her. How dare you!"

He put his hand on her arm. "Stella," he said unhappily, "I had to tell you, but—I'll never think of it again, I promise you. I'll never tell a soul. It'll be just as if it hadn't happened. Your nerves were upset. It wasn't *you*. I know that it's been a trying time for you and——"

She wrenched her arm away. Her eyes blazed. He was daring to offer her forgiveness. To offer *her* forgiveness.

"You're mad," she said through clenched teeth. "I tell you I never touched the child. How *dare* you insult me?" She tore off her ring and thrust it into his hand. "I never want to see or speak to you again. I——"

Anger choked her. She turned and ran down the path back to the house, leaving him staring after her. She was running away, not so much from him as from the picture he had brought so vividly to life—the picture of herself standing there . . . striking the child. . . .

Lady Carlswell was sympathetic and concerned.

"Yes, my dear, you don't look well. I'll order the carriage at once. I quite understand. I hope this business of Pam's hasn't upset you. . . . You should have told me about your headache before, dear."

The carriage was ready by the time she had put on her cloak. Hugh was there to hand her into it.

"Stella," he pleaded under his breath.

"Goodbye, Hugh," she said. Her blue eyes were blank like the eyes of a doll.

When the carriage had disappeared down the drive his mother laid her hand on his arm.

"There's nothing to look so tragic about, darling," she said in a tone of tender amusement. "It's just an ordinary headache. She'll probably be quite all right again tomorrow."

He turned away from her without speaking.

As Stella drove home her anger turned to panic. I It was as if she were bound and imprisoned in front of that picture. She had to watch the figure in white satin and tulle performing the same action over and over again to eternity like a marionette. It raised its hand and struck the child . . . raised its hand and struck the child . . . raised its hand and struck the child. . . . She tried not to look at it, but she couldn't help looking at it. Hugh, had forced her to. It was there before her eyes in whatever I direction she turned them—a hideous living caricature.

She shrank in sick terror from the thought of meeting him again. He would come to see her tomorrow. . . . A wave of nausea swept over her as she pictured the meeting. Wherever he was, that hateful picture would be. . . . He had seen it. He had made it real to her. It had not been real to her before she knew that he had seen it. To marry him would be to condemn herself to a lifelong contemplation of it. It would drive her mad. . . . She must do something—now, at once. . . .

The carriage drew up before the doors of East Lodge. She descended, bade the old coachman good-night, and entered the house. A tiny glimmer of gas burnt in the hall. The servants always went to bed early, and she had told Miss Farthing not to wait up for her. . . . The house was silent and asleep. She went into the morning-room, where the fire burnt low in the grate, and thick dark curtains were drawn across the window. On the hearth was the saucepan of milk that Miss Farthing had left there. A glass stood on a small silver tray on a low table, together with a plate of biscuits. Mechanically, hardly knowing what she was doing, she began to pour the milk into the glass, but though her expression was grave, calm, remote, her hand shook as if with ague and she gave up the attempt, putting the saucepan back onto the hearth and standing with her elbows on the mantelpiece, her gaze fixed on the dying embers. She remained there motionless for several minutes. So fair and untroubled did she look that she might have stood as a model to one of the popular artists of the day for some such picture as "Girlish Day-dreams," or "After the Ball." But her heart was raging with fear and anger. Suppose Hugh came now. . . . Suppose he roused again the passion that she had glimpsed once already tonight, persuaded her against her will to marry him in spite of what had happened. . . . Suppose she awoke too late to find herself bound for life to a man who had seen *that*, who believed *that*. . . .

Suddenly she seemed to rouse herself from her day-dreams with a slight shiver. She knew now what she must do. . . . Paul, who could never doubt and distrust and misjudge her, who would never believe that cruel lie . . .

She went into the hall and stood for a moment listening. The house was still silent. Slowly and cautiously she opened the big front door again and stepped out into the drive. The moon had risen, shedding its silver light over the garden, throwing long mysterious shadows. . . . She drew her cloak about her and slipped across the lawn, through the kitchen garden, and out by the iron gates into the lane.

Paul himself opened the door of the cottage to her. The colour flooded his face when he saw her standing there in the moonlight—her golden head bare, her dark cloak drawn close about her throat. He stared at her as if he could not believe what he saw.

"May I come in, Paul?"

He still stood, barring her way, paralysed by amazement.

"I'm afraid Mother's out," he stammered.

She slipped past him into the little parlour where he was working. There was an oil lamp in the middle of the round table, which was piled high with dictionaries and notebooks. A notebook lay open in front of his chair, the pen laid down across it as he had risen to answer the door.

She stood looking at him in silence. She had loosened her cloak at the neck, and it fell apart, showing the shimmering satin of her dress and the pearls on her bare white breast. He could see the line of her corsage rising and falling with quick uneven movements. . . . Her beauty took his breath away. The faint perfume that came from her made him feel dizzy. His eyes, in his thin pale student's face, worshipped her bemusedly.

"It was you I came to see, Paul," she said. "Paul . . ."

Her voice broke. . . . She sat down suddenly on his chair at the table and, laying her golden head on his notebook, on the page he had just headed "The Ionian Monists—Anaximander," burst into tears.

"Paul . . . I don't know what to do. I can't go on with it. . . .

Tonight . . . I was so frightened. There's no one to protect me. . . ." She started up and looked around her. "Oh, I oughtn't to have come here, but . . . he's been horrible." She fixed her tear-filled eyes on him. "Oh, Paul, what shall I do . . .?"

He was kneeling by her side, his arms around her, pouring out his love and devotion, offering to give his life for her. . . .

"I knew I never loved him, Paul," she sobbed, "but I'd promised Auntie the night before she died that I'd marry him." (She saw the scene quite plainly. She had just come back from the Hall garden party and told Auntie about Hugh's proposal, and Auntie had begged her to marry him. At last, reluctantly, she had promised. She had been wearing her white silk dress with the embroidered hem, she remembered, and her white leghorn hat.) "Oh, Paul, I've tried to go through with it. Till tonight I thought I could, but tonight——" She dropped her head into her hands again. "Oh, Paul, he was horrible. . . . I can't bear to think of it. . . ."

Paul's face had darkened.

"I'll deal with him."

"No, don't . . . don't, Paul. . . . It's all over. . . . I've given him his ring back. . . . I've told him I can't marry him. . . . Oh, Paul, I shouldn't have come, but I was so frightened and there was no one else. . . ."

She was a persecuted princess and he her knight-errant. He poured out broken phrases of comfort and adoration.

"My darling, I love you so. . . . I've loved you ever since I can remember."

"And I've loved you," she said. "Always. . . . I tried to keep my promise to Auntie, but if she knew how—horrible he was, she wouldn't want me to, would she?"

"No, darling . . . don't think of it again. You're mine now . . . for ever."

"Paul." The blue eyes still swam with tears, but they were calculating and determined. "Paul, I've no one but you to—look after me. We can be married quite soon, can't we?"

There was a silence, in which he came down abruptly from the world of romance to hard reality.

"I've—Stella, I've not got my degree yet."

"Does that matter? You could get some work, couldn't you, without a degree?"

"I suppose so," he said slowly, "but—there's my scholarship. I don't know. . . ."

She broke away from him.

"Oh, you don't love me. . . . I wish I hadn't come. . . . I'm so ashamed. If you loved me you wouldn't think of your scholarship, you'd——"

He took her in his arms again, his thin body trembling.

"I don't care about anything else in the whole world but you. I love you. . . . We'll be married as soon as we can."

She clung to him, laying her golden head on his shoulder.

A wave of happiness swept through her.

She was going to marry Paul—Paul, the only man she had ever really loved.

The nightmare of her engagement to Hugh was over.

Chapter Nine

BELLERTON GRAMMAR SCHOOL was one of those schools that hold
an uneasy place between the secondary and public school. It was
an old foundation but was attended now chiefly by sons of the
small tradesmen in Bellerton or the sons of farmers from the district
around.

Paul Sanders considered himself lucky to have obtained a post
on the staff. It was a very junior post, as befitted a man without
a degree, and meant teaching oddments of Geography, History and
Arithmetic instead of classics on which his soul had been set, but
it was a respectable work with a respectable salary, and Pelham,
the classical master, under patronising pretence of helping him to
"keep up his classics," managed to hand over to him a good share
of his own work.

He sat at his desk now in the common room correcting some
Scholarship Greek Unseens that Pelham had left for him. He knew
that Stella despised him for letting himself be "put on" by Pelham,
and that she could never understand the deep satisfaction the work
gave him.

Even after all these years he dare not let his mind dwell on the
anger and disappointment his decision to give up his scholarship
had caused at the University. He had an exceptionally acute sense
of honour and it distressed him greatly to feel that he had betrayed
those who had set their hopes on him and given him of their best.
But Stella had been adamant, refusing even to consider a compromise.
They must be married at once. He must leave college and get a
post of some sort as best he could. Not that he blamed Stella. That
scoundrel, Carlswell, had given the poor child a shock, and she

had felt that she must at all costs leave Runeham, where everything reminded her of her ill-fated engagement, as soon as possible.

Not once in the six years of his married life had Paul regretted his marriage. He still loved Stella devotedly. If his love had changed from the blind worship of his childhood to a love that knew both how to make allowances for her and how to hide the fact that he was making them, it was none the less real for that. From the beginning he had understood that Stella's spirit was sensitive and fine-wrought. The faintest breath of criticism seared and shrivelled it. He had seen her lovely face go white and anguished at some quite innocent remark that had seemed to her to imply a reproach. She needed the tenderest consideration, and he had learnt to give it her. . . . His love for her had deepened with the coming of the two children—Charles, now aged four, and Oliver, aged two. Looking back, their childhood seemed to him a series of delightful pictures—Stella carrying a baby in her arms with another clinging to her skirts . . . Stella swinging them together on the garden swing . . . two tiny pyjama-clad figures kneeling at Stella's knee . . . Stella seated at the piano with one of them standing on either side, the childish voices upraised in nursery songs. It never occurred to him that he formed no part in these pictures, that he stood outside them, humbly admiring.

He had been afraid at first that Stella would find Bellerton dull, but she had settled down quickly and happily and had made the little house he had taken in High Street near the school, attractively homelike.

They had moved into a larger house when Charles was born. As Stella said, they needed a garden and a nursery. . . . She had chosen a pleasant fair-sized house just outside the town with a rambling old-fashioned garden, laughing down all his objections.

"Darling, I know you couldn't afford it from your salary, but you forget my money. It's going to be *my* extravagance, not yours. It's just the house I want. I'm going to be terribly happy here and make you and Baby happy."

And she had been so light-hearted and eager, busying herself over every detail of the house, making it one of the prettiest, most cheerful houses in the town (she had clever fingers and unerring taste), that he could not find it in his heart to regret the step. But it worried him that she seemed to think her capital inexhaustible. Whenever he said that she could not afford anything, she always fell back gaily upon "my money," buying whatever she fancied or imagined that he fancied, for she was generous and loved to give him presents. Actually her income was not a large one. A good deal of her father's money had been invested in a family business that had since failed, and Aunt Fanny herself had made several unfortunate investments in the hopes of increasing her darling's inheritance. But it was difficult to point this out to Stella without seeming to criticise her for extravagance, and Paul shrank from the scene that would inevitably follow. Even when, as often happened, he found himself saddled with bills for things she had said she would pay for herself and had forgotten, he did not remind her, though on several occasions he had been unable to meet them without considerable trouble and sacrifice.

And, after all, he told himself, she was not really extravagant. She was so attractive and popular that it was only natural she should like to entertain, and she was so lovely that it was only natural that she should like to wear pretty clothes. And even her entertaining was done more for his sake than hers. She refused to join the local "smart set," though its members never ceased trying to induce her to join them. Instead she kept open house for the masters and their wives, the parish church curates and the smattering of professional people in the town. It was generally recognised in Bellerton that young Mrs. Sanders was an "acquisition." Not only was she pretty and attractive and musical, she was also a woman of education and intelligence. For, though Stella had deliberately blotted out from the records of her mind all memory of that fatal Carlswell dinner-party, some unconscious part of her had absorbed the lesson it had to teach. She read the newspapers assiduously and kept herself abreast with what was happening in the world of politics and art. Lonely and unattached young men found in her house an atmosphere of happy home life, with an unostentatious background of culture. There was no stiffness or ceremony. Stella saw to that. She had only one maid and her gardener came one day a week. Visitors were encouraged to help lay the table, wash up, and mow the lawn. Young masters of the Grammar School, young curates of the Parish Church, young men on the lower rungs of all the professions, escaped from stuffy lodgings to play with Charles and Oliver in the garden, loll in the chintz-covered chairs in the charming drawing-room, lark about the kitchen under pretence of "helping," or take part in the musical evenings that were a regular feature of the *ménage*, singing "The Devout Lover," "Sailor, Beware" or, more hilariously, songs from the Scottish Students' Song Book or Songs of a Savoyard. And over all presided Stella—gay, radiant, exquisitely lovely, yet with that touch of austerity, of with-drawnness, that made even the boldest young man treat her with respect.

She had quite a collection of letters from grateful mothers, thanking her for her kindness to their sons, for having thrown open her "happy Christian home" to them and helped them as "only a good woman can help a young man."

The young men themselves, too, thanked her in earnest halting speeches. One or two of them remained bachelors for the rest of their lives, because every other woman they met was so infinitely her inferior.

And here, too, Paul was the onlooker. He watched Stella "mothering" her young men—teasing them, scolding them, mending their clothes, making jellies and beef tea for them when they were ill, taking them to church with her, receiving letters from their mothers—with a tender indulgent smile. How sweet she looked in that plain puritan-like grey dress . . . that simple blue dress . . . that demure little black dress! She seemed to have a lot of new dresses, but when young men have to be cheered and entertained and kept out of harm's way by a good woman, it's an understood thing that the good woman must be attractive and well dressed. So he gave her that tender indulgent smile and went to the study to correct the piles of exercise books that always awaited him, and to browse in a furtive guilty way among the classics that he felt he had somehow betrayed.

Mr. Dale, the head master, approved of Stella and was a frequent visitor at Beechcroft. After being treated as a demi-god at school, he enjoyed being laughed at and ordered about by Stella. Though he was quite unaware of it, he was more than a little in love with her, and frequently envied Paul his charming home and wife and children. He was in type not unlike Paul—studious, shy, conscientious—and Stella knew just how to manage him, rallying him when he was depressed, encouraging him to confide his troubles and difficulties in her. Soon she came to know more about the school than Paul himself knew. "Better not tell your husband," he would say sometimes when he had given her some more than usually confidential piece of information. He would discuss the young masters and the elder boys with her, she would plead for culprits, urge him to lenience, soothe away his irritation. She became, in fact, a sort of unofficial "head master's wife." And her reputation stood so high in the little town that no one ventured to breathe even a hint against it. . . .

The news that Mr. Dale had married during the summer holidays had come as rather a shock to her. It wasn't so much the thought of Mr. Dale himself, though he was a good-looking man and she had found his interest flattering; it was rather the thought of her own position that secretly troubled her. It so happened that in all these years till now her position at the School had been unchallenged. Few of the masters were married, and the wives of those few were drab insignificant women who added themselves willingly to the circle of her admirers. A head master's wife would be something quite different. Paul, too, had been troubled by the news, though he could not have told exactly why. He would not have admitted, even in his most secret thoughts, that Stella seemed to cultivate women who were second-rate and characterless, avoiding and depreciating any who could challenge comparison with her. There was no doubt that she had, during the years she had been in Bellerton, built up for herself a position that would be difficult to sustain if the head master were married. Unless, of course, his wife should prove to be one of those colourless women who seemed to be content to follow Stella's lead and bask in the sunshine of her favour. Knowing Dale, he didn't think this likely. . . .

He dreaded any rebuff or slight for Stella, so acutely sensitive was she, so easily hurt. He realised suddenly how large Stella's sensitiveness loomed on his horizon, in what constant fear he lived of hurting her, of seeing her hurt by others. At first, he remembered, it had been sweet to reassure and comfort her. He blamed himself for the fact that he was no longer thrilled and touched by her turning to him for consolation, that those scenes no longer seemed to him a renewal and glorifying of their love.

Sometimes now, when he was afraid that she had been hurt, he would make an excuse to be out of the house, so as to avoid the task of reassuring, sympathising, consoling. . . . He was bitterly ashamed of this. He had known from the beginning that he was of coarser grain than she was, that she needed his protection against a world that was too rough and crude for her, and whenever, through cowardice, he shirked the issue, he felt that he had deliberately betrayed her trust.

He had been relieved, on meeting Mrs. Dale at the beginning of the term, to find her a sensible, pleasant, good-natured girl—but no rival to Stella in looks or charm. She was friendly and unassuming, with obviously no exaggerated idea of her importance as a head master's wife. There was an air of serenity – about her that made Paul, again to his horror, feel a little envious . . . so that he had to remind himself how serene Stella herself was and try to forget how anxiously he watched her serenity, prepared always for the cracks that could appear so suddenly and unexpectedly in its surface.

The two had so far got on together excellently. Lorna Dale admired Stella and made no attempt to assert her own position.

"Your wife's the loveliest thing I've ever seen," she had said to Paul. "Everyone sang her praises to me, and now I've met her I'm not surprised."

To her husband she had said,

"She's adorable and I'm not surprised you were in love with her, but——"

"Yes?" he had said, smiling down at her. "But what?"

She wrinkled her brows.

"I don't quite know. She's like someone you dream about or see in a play. Too good to be true." Her round face dimpled with laughter. "Now you'll say I'm jealous. I'm not really. I like her, but she's the only person I've ever met whom I couldn't imagine doing anything foolish or undignified. . . . It's—just a little inhuman."

"She honestly *is* like that," her husband assured her. "She's a very rare character. I'm glad she's here to help you get into the swing of things. She's been the making of some of the young louts we've had on the staff."

"I don't think I'll attempt to rival her there," she said.

He twinkled at her.

"I don't think I want you to, but"—he grew serious—"she has the most amazing tact and understanding. I've even put her on to recalcitrant parents, and she's always made them see reason."

His wife looked up at him with a smile that was affectionate, whimsical and just a little rueful.

"It's a good thing I'm not inclined to be jealous," she said.

He had almost come to the end of the Unseens now. He made the corrections in the small neat cultured hand, writing "Good" against Spencer's translation of $\phi\omega\rho\hat{\omega}\nu\,\lambda\iota\mu\acute{\eta}\nu$ as "Smuggler's Creek," then his pen rested in mid-air and his eyes grew dreamy. How he would have loved to teach these young scholars himself, instead of drumming Geography and Arithmetic into grubby and reluctant fourth forms! Still, these occasional corrections for Pelham were a consolation to him. He was a better classical scholar than Pelham, and Pelham had got into the way of submitting disputed points to him and asking him to translate obscure passages. Pelham was touchy and jealous of his position, and Paul had to go very carefully, making a pretence sometimes of being the one who asked help instead of the one who gave it. To abase his pride thus was, he considered, not an unduly high price to pay for this small share in the work he loved, this inglorious shadow of what he had once meant to be his career. It was an odd coincidence, he thought, that he should have to go so carefully both at home and at school—with

Stella and with Pelham—then was ashamed of the disloyalty of the thought. But it had turned his mind to Stella, and he glanced hastily at his watch. He mustn't be late home. Stella was having a tea-party, and he had promised her that he would be in time for it.

He finished the last of the corrections, put the pile in Pelham's pigeon-hole, together with his fair copy of the translation, and went to the cloakroom for his hat and coat.

He hurried through the main street of the town—a tall, stooping figure, his good-looking face a little more lined and worn than his years warranted. He mustn't be late. Stella would be "hurt" if he were late. He had a vague idea that it was a very special tea-party—he didn't know why. The usual people were coming, but it was a special tea-party. Stella had bought a new dress for it and had taken a lot of trouble over the preparations.

He was out of breath when he reached the green wooden gate that led into the shady garden. The house was squarely Georgian, of mellow red brick, set well back from the road. It was larger and more imposing-looking than that of any of the other masters, even the Dales, and sometimes he felt a little uncomfortable about it, but it was, after all, Stella's business. If she liked to spend her money on a house that was certainly a better setting for her beauty than any he could have provided, it would have been small-minded and ungenerous of him to object. She had made it charming inside, too, picking up at sales pieces of Sheraton and Chippendale, when most people were still content with horse hair, bamboo and heavily ornamented monuments of mahogany, making chair-covers and curtains of flowered cretonne, instead of the ubiquitous damask and plush.

She came into the hall to meet him, and he drew a secret sigh of relief as he saw that she was smiling a welcome. She would have smiled a welcome in any case, but experience had made him an expert at assessing her smiles, and he knew the almost imperceptible tension in them that concealed displeasure.

"You naughty boy!" she said affectionately, holding up her face to be kissed. "You're late."

"I'm sorry, darling," he said, kissing her, then holding her at arm's length. "My word! Aren't you a swell!"

She had on a new dress of wine-coloured satin, with a flounced train and long tight sleeves that ended in falls of lace matching the lace yoke. Her golden hair was carefully dressed.

"I'll forgive you," she said. "I do look rather nice, don't I? You're not really late. No one's arrived yet. Come and look at the room."

She led him into the drawing-room, which was arranged for the tea-party, with a lace-edged cloth on the low table by the fire, gleaming silver and china, elaborately iced cakes on dainty hand-made d'oyleys. There were flowers everywhere—white lilac, tulips, banks of lilies. He wondered how much she had spent on them.

"It's all very—swagger, isn't it?" he said.

She laughed.

"Why not?" she said. "There's a letter for you from your mother. Come and sit down and read it. . . . Oh, Spencer's coming to help Janet hand the tea round. I asked him yesterday. He went quite pale with joy."

Spencer was the head boy—a tall good-looking youth who had adored Stella ever since she came to Bellerton and was one of her favourites. She had never included the boys in her tea-parties before, and he began dimly to understand the importance of this one. It was to be a triumphant assertion of her position. It was to show that she did not intend to yield it to the new Mrs. Dale. Here, in this charming flower-decked room—not in the Dales' austere little room, its plain walls hung with Arundel Prints—the heart of the school's social life was to remain. Here was her court of satellites, with Spencer her devoted page. He understood this vaguely, felt for Stella something that was partly admiration, partly fear, and wholly tenderness—then sat down to read his mother's letter. She wrote to say that she would not be able to come to stay with them this summer as usual. He was sorry—and yet at the same time guiltily relieved. He loved his mother, but it was hard not to feel a little ashamed of her in this exquisite house of Stella's. She dressed garishly, she frequently dropped her aitches, she committed innumerable breaches of good manners, as Stella and her kind understood them, and she spoilt the children—buying them cheap sticky sweets (which Stella surreptitiously threw into the fire), pleading for them to be let off punishments when they had been naughty. Stella was uniformly kind and affectionate to her, and yet—without, he was convinced, meaning to—she managed somehow to draw attention to her faults of manners and breeding.

Only last week she had corrected Charles for some lapse of manners at table and added, "I know that Grannie does it, but she doesn't know any better." She had seen Paul flush and had been sweetly contrite afterwards. "Darling, I'm so sorry I said that. You know that we all love Grannie. I only meant that they mustn't copy her in everything. It didn't hurt you, dearest, did it?"

So that he couldn't conquer a faint relief when he heard that the visit was not to take place this year. His mother gave no reason for her decision, but ended the letter:

"You'll come as usual and spend a week with me in the autumn, won't you, dear?"

He always enjoyed the week he spent alone with her each year. She had left Runeham and lived now in a small bungalow in Hythe. There they sank back into their old relationship of easy affection, making the old childish jokes, as they never did when Stella was present. He felt ill-at-ease when she stayed with them at Bellerton. She, too, was different then somehow—timid, on her guard, anxious not to offend.

It had occurred to him more than once that she seemed to avoid mentioning Stella and to become silent and constrained when he mentioned her. Oh well, he thought indulgently, I don't suppose that any mother quite hits it off with her daughter-in-law, and she's certainly nothing to complain of in Stella's behaviour to her.

He handed the letter to Stella, and as she read it her face fell.

"I'm so sorry she can't come," she said. "Dear Grannie! the children will be heartbroken. Do you think if I write . . .?"

He shook his head, touched by her attitude.

"I don't think so. . . . It's rather a long journey for her. She's not as young as she was. . . . Who's your letter from?"

"From Biddy. She can come for August."

"Oh good!" he replied.

Secretly he found Biddy Lytton, with her volatile enthusiasm for Stella, a little wearing. He loved Stella, but it was irritating to have her virtues perpetually pointed out to him by a third person. Miss Farthing, who also paid them regular visits, irritated him in the same way.

Stella looked up from her letter with dancing eyes.

"I believe you're jealous of Biddy," she said.

"Perhaps I am,' he said with an answering smile. "Well, I suppose I must go and wash."

When he came down the party was in full swing, though the Dales had not yet arrived. Stella had never looked so lovely, never queened it so triumphantly. The whole room formed her court. There were no rival groups. Everyone seemed to be waiting eagerly for a chance to speak to her. Spencer hung about her chair in bemused adoration, flushing deeply when once she laid her hand on his arm.

Paul entered and, taking his place in an inconspicuous corner of the room next the junior science master, began to discuss with him some question of school organisation. Stella smiled at him affectionately, feeling a sudden rush of love for him. Dear old Paul—so stupid and dull and ordinary! It was lovely to feel that she had rescued him from the dreadful surroundings he had grown up in, dragged him out of his frowzy student's rut, given him this happy home, this circle of interesting friends. He couldn't, of course, realise all the hard work and sacrifice it had meant on her part, but she didn't mind that. She hadn't done it because she wanted gratitude. She'd done it for his sake—for the sake of his position and his career. Probably he didn't even realise how much he owed to her. Men never did. It was enough that she had made him happy. A heady sense of achievement possessed her. This afternoon marked, as she had meant it to mark, her final victory. So a queen might have felt, looking round on a room full of loyal and devoted subjects. It had been foolish of her even to consider the possibility of a rival. The allegiance of these people was hers . . . and hers only.

Then the Dales entered. Stella greeted them affectionately, even kissing Mrs. Dale in her delight at finding her dressed in a drab-looking grey serge dress and a green jacket with a plain black straw hat. No, there was no rival here. . . .

Janet brought in the tea, and there arose the buzz of laughter and conversation that marks the successful party. The two little boys returned from their walk with Nurse and came into the drawing-room. The ladies received them with cries of rapture. Paul, as often, found it a little difficult to realise that these beautifully dressed, beautifully mannered little creatures were his flesh and blood. . . . Then Nurse bore them off and a chorus of praise arose on all sides.

"They *are* rather sweet," said Stella. "At least Daddy and I think they are," and flashed an affectionate smile at Paul across the room. He smiled back, faintly embarrassed. It always took him by surprise when she admitted him, as it were, to the centre of the picture. He was quite content with his usual rôle of appreciative onlooker. . . .

It was some time after this and only very gradually that Paul began to notice a tension in the atmosphere. At first he couldn't understand it. Then he realised that too many people were listening to Mrs. Dale. . . . She sat at the opposite end of the room from Stella—quite insignificant-looking in a hat that didn't suit her and a jacket that didn't match her dress—but her round rosy face was alight with humour, and her soft gentle laughter was like a refreshing spring in the somewhat sultry atmosphere of Stella-worship. She was describing a holiday that she had spent in Ireland the year before. At first she had been talking—in her low musical voice—to the people next her, but more and more of the guests stopped their conversation to listen, till Stella was left almost isolated behind her tea-table. Mrs. Dale continued to describe her Irish holiday, wholly unaware of the enormity of the offence she was committing. A burst of laughter rose as she reached the end of an anecdote. Through it came Stella's voice, as hard and cold as ice.

"I'm afraid I can't see anything funny in ignorance and untruthfulness."

There was a moment's constrained silence, then Mrs. Dale said, without embarrassment or rancour,

"I know, Mrs. Sanders. I understand how you feel. They've been treated most unfairly, and it *is* unkind to make fun of them, when, I suppose, we're responsible for the appalling conditions most of them live in. I'm afraid that I'm inclined to let my tongue run away with me."

It was an apology that completely vindicated Stella. Everything should have been all right. Everything would have been all right . . . but just then the appalling, incredible thing happened.

Spencer was trying to pass behind Stella with the cake-stand, and there was insufficient room, so he held it high above her head. In doing so he caught one of the wicker legs in the carefully piled erection of her hair. Aghast at what he had done, he pulled it clumsily away. It dragged out a long strand of hair that fell over her face. At the same time a cream bun fell from one of the plates, deposited its cream on the lace at her breast and slid down to the silk of her knee. One of the junior masters tittered. In that titter Stella saw herself—the long strand of hair falling over her face, the blob of cream sliding ludicrously down her bodice. She turned on Spencer, her face brick-red.

"You clumsy idiot!" she said in a voice that cut like a file through the sudden silence of the room.

Spencer gave her a stricken look and fled, running out of the front door and past the window as if pursued, his face a mask of horror. Inside the room, everyone hastened to repair the damage, picking up the cakes that were rolling about the floor. Stella took back the strand of hair and secured it again among the gleaming coils. Mrs. Dale picked up a tea napkin and carefully wiped the cream from her dress. Stella, who would gladly have killed her, thanked her prettily. Her agitation had vanished as suddenly as it had appeared, though, now that the flush had faded, her cheeks were paler than usual.

"It's quite all right," she laughed. "No harm's done. The dress will clean perfectly. Poor Spencer! I believe he actually took my teasing seriously."

There was a constrained silence, then well-meaning guests threw themselves into the breach, making frantic conversation about whatever they happened to remember from their morning's reading of the newspaper—Lord Kitchener's disagreement with Lord Curzon in Egypt, the visit of the German Emperor to Tangiers, the progress of the Congo Reform Association—but the party was definitely a failure and the guests departed earlier than usual, with a sense of relief, almost of escape.

Mr. Dale was rather silent as he walked home with his wife. At last he said unhappily,

"You mustn't judge her by what happened this afternoon."

"But I liked her for the first time," protested his wife. "She seemed suddenly to turn into a human being. If she'd boxed Spencer's ears, as she wanted to, I'd have liked her still more."

"You wouldn't have boxed his ears."

"No," said his wife reflectively, "because I don't care how I look. But if I were as lovely as that and cared so much about being lovely and felt as she did about being made to look a sight, I'd have boxed them."

Paul, after seeing off the last guest at the front door, went back to the drawing-room slowly and with a sinking heart. Every nerve in his body shrank from the inevitable scene. Stella had been turned for one fleeting second into a figure of fun, and someone, presumably himself, would have to pay for it. He didn't put it like that, of course. He told himself that she must have been deeply hurt and distressed by the incident. But in effect it came to the same thing.

When he entered the drawing-room she was standing before the mirror, rearranging the lace of her dress. He stood watching her warily. She turned to him with a smile.

"Well," she said, "it went off quite well, didn't it?"

He was relieved but still on his guard. He knew that it wasn't really going to be dismissed as easily as that.

"Is your dress spoilt?" he said, feeling that sooner or later the thing had to be mentioned.

"My dress?" she said carelessly. "Oh no, it'll clean quite well. I shouldn't probably have been able to wear it more than twice without cleaning, anyway. If I'd escaped Spencer, the babies would have put jammy fingers onto it." She laughed. "Poor old Spencer! I believe he thought I was in earnest. It'll give me something to tease him about, anyway."

For the rest of the evening she was artlessly gay and light-spirited, chattering about school affairs, telling him bits of local gossip, teasing him affectionately, calling him her "old bookworm" when, in order to relieve the oppression that weighed upon his spirit, he took refuge in his worn volume of Homer. He waited—wary, apprehensive. . . . The blow fell just as she was going to bed. She gathered up her needlework, then sat down again and put her hand to her head.

"I've got such a headache, dear," she said.

He laid his book aside.

"I'm sorry. . . ."

"I nearly always have one nowadays." Her blue eyes rested on him—grave, tender, full of compunction. "I haven't wanted to worry you because I knew how you liked your work here, but I haven't felt well for some time. Perhaps I'd better consult Dr. Blakelock. I don't think that Bellerton really suits me. . . ."

Chapter Ten

BIDDY sat on the window-sill of Doreen's Chelsea flat, watching the seagulls as they swept the grey river below with flashes of white wings.

"They're lovely, aren't they?" she said.

"They're all right in the distance," admitted Doreen. "I don't like them at close quarters. Their expression reminds me of the Albert Memorial."

"But they're so picturesque," said Biddy.

"Oh yes," agreed Doreen with a faint smile, "they're picturesque."

The two cousins made a striking contrast—Doreen, tall, beautiful, with her air of distinction and sophistication, Biddy as dumpy and plain and appallingly dressed as ever. She had had an orgy of dressmaking in preparation for this visit, had chosen the gayest materials procurable in its honour and had put the garments together in such a state of excitement that pieces meant for one dress actually appeared in another. Her chaotic packing had deprived her hats of any shape they may originally have had, and one or two strands of her stiff carroty hair escaped her "bun" to hang down her back, however often she pinned them back.

Doreen had come to the Chelsea flat after her mother's death and had written two novels in the last three years, using a pen name so as not to appear to be exploiting her father's reputation. The first had been praised by discerning critics but had been ignored by the public; the second, published last year, had seemed to satisfy both critics and public and had secured for her a sound reputation as a novelist.

Biddy had been wildly excited by her cousin's success and had sent a copy of the first book to Stella, who in her reply had praised the book, but stressed various particulars in which she considered that the heroine had failed in "womanliness." "But then, darling," she had ended, "you know how terribly old-fashioned I am. Doreen, of course, is much more up-to-date."

Biddy had come to stay with Doreen for the Coronation but, frantically loyal as Biddy was, the high-light of the whole fortnight in her eyes was the visit they were going to pay Stella today.

"It'll be lovely to see her again," she said. "I've not seen her for three years, you know. The boys are eleven and nine now. She's a wonderful mother." She sighed. "Poor Stella!"

"Why 'poor Stella'?" said Doreen.

"She's had such a dreadful time," answered Biddy.

"Why? She's got a good husband and——"

"A good husband?" interrupted Biddy indignantly. "Paul? Why, Doreen, he's lost job after job. He's a junior clerk in a Peckham warehouse now, you know. Think of Stella—*Stella*—living in a poky little house in Peckham, on less than lots of working men earn. Yet she never complains."

Doreen rose and stood looking down over the river.

"Is it Paul's fault that he's lost his jobs?" she said.

"Of course," said Biddy. "Whose else should it be?"

"I thought that they left Bellerton because of Stella's health."

"Well, Stella said so, but—you know what Stella is. She's so *loyal*. She's always tried to cover up Paul's failings. I guessed at the time that Paul had lost the job through incompetence and, though she's never said so in so many words, she's given me quite plainly to understand that that's what did happen. He's so shiftless and inefficient. Why, after Bellerton he had three teaching jobs and lost them all. After that, of course, he had to take what he could get. If it weren't for Stella, I can't think what would have happened to him. She's done all that a wife could possibly do for her husband, but he's dragged her lower and lower ever since they were married."

Doreen looked at her, faintly amused.

"You'd never see any faults in your beloved Stella, would you?" she said.

"There aren't any faults to see in Stella," said Biddy stoutly. "You don't know her as I do, Doreen. You don't know how unselfish and generous she is. She's spent practically all the money her aunt left her on Paul and the children. When I compare the life she's leading now with the sort of life she'd be leading if she'd married Hugh Carlswell——"

"Why didn't she marry Hugh? I've never quite understood that. They were engaged, weren't they?"

A shadow passed over Biddy's face.

"Haven't I told you? He was terribly in love with her and—I suppose he lost his head. Stella's so sensitive and fastidious, you know, and he frightened her."

"Perhaps," said Doreen slowly. "I mean, I can understand that happening, but—surely if they loved each other that shouldn't have been more than a temporary estrangement. Hugh's not a cad."

"I know," said Biddy, "and it would have been all right if it hadn't been for Paul. It was his opportunity, you see, and he used it to turn her against Hugh and to persuade her almost against her will to marry him. Oh, I know that Paul's well-meaning enough, but I can't help thinking of him as Stella's evil genius. Right from the beginning he's been that. I know it sounds wicked, Doreen, but sometimes I think that the best thing that could happen would be for Paul to die, then Stella could marry Hugh."

"Do you think Hugh would want to marry her?"

"Oh, Doreen! What man wouldn't? Even after all she's been through, she's still the loveliest thing you can imagine. And she's sweeter than ever. You know, adversity's supposed to make a character either worse or nobler. Well, it's made Stella even more wonderful than she was before."

"I'm rather anxious to meet this ennobled Stella," said Doreen.

"Well, you're going to," smiled Biddy, "and it's time we set off now. She's expecting us to lunch." She smiled at Doreen—her frank ingenuous smile. "It's no use trying to annoy me. You've never been fair to Stella, but you'll see today. You'll understand today. . . ."

"I hope I shall," said Doreen. "I want to understand."

It was a small drab-looking house in a small drab-looking street in Peckham. Stella herself came to the door, wearing a blue drill overall. Doreen had seen her last in the Bellerton days, exquisite in a dress of cream lace. She looked just as lovely, just as exquisite, in the cheap overall. The blue eyes were smiling, the sweet mouth serene, the skin still as smooth-textured and flawless as a baby's.

She kissed Biddy affectionately and held out a slim cool hand to Doreen.

"How good of you to come slumming like this!" she said gaily. "Come in. There's no ceremony in this house. It's too small for ceremony. Hang your things on the hat-stand and come straight into the kitchen. Dinner's nearly ready. It's dinner here, remember, not lunch."

They followed her into the kitchen. It was small but spotlessly clean. Blue and white check curtains hung at the windows, and the top of the dresser was covered with blue and white check American cloth. Everything was in its place and everything shone. The doors of the china cupboard shone, the china shone, the glass shone, the cooking utensils shone. The floor was covered with linoleum, and there was a rag rug in front of the open fire, on which a large saucepan was cooking. The table was spread with a white cloth and laid for the meal.

"Sit down at the table," said Stella, busying herself at the fireplace over the saucepan, "and talk to me. Tell me the news while I dish up. We have all our meals in the kitchen. We can have things beautifully hot, straight from the saucepan's mouth."

Biddy sat watching her, every now and then throwing a triumphant glance at Doreen. Doreen, on whom this bright artless manner of Stella's jarred intolerably, avoided Biddy's eyes.

Though Stella had asked them to talk to her, it was she who did the talking, describing the routine of the little house and by implication, as it seemed to Doreen, vaunting her own excellence as a housekeeper.

"I'm a poor man's wife now," she said with an air of gallant lightheartedness. "I have to count every penny. Literally every penny. An unexpected expense—such as a doctor's bill—keeps me awake all night. Oh, I don't mean that I mind. In a way it's fun. We've got each other and we manage."

"You mean *you* manage," said Biddy.

"Oh well," said Stella with a deprecating little laugh, "that's the woman's job, isn't it? Men aren't good managers. At least," with a sigh, "poor old Paul isn't."

The two boys came in from school as she was dishing up the meal. Charles, the elder one, resembled Stella, but with nothing of effeminacy about him. He was a handsome, well-built boy and looked over-serious for his age. Doreen was struck by the way his eyes met hers, levelly, almost sternly, without a trace of self-consciousness, as he greeted her. He smiled seldom and had an abrupt but wholly courteous way of speaking.

Oliver, the younger, was more like Paul, slight and delicate-looking, with dark heavily lashed eyes and a pale narrow face. He greeted the visitors shyly and flushed with embarrassment when Biddy threw her arms round him and kissed him.

Doreen watched them as they helped their mother with the final preparations of the meal. Their manners were excellent, and, grudgingly, Doreen had to admit to herself that the little house was efficiently and economically run.

Paul came in soon after they had begun the meal. He looked so much older that at first Doreen did not recognise him. His face was lined, his hair streaked with grey, his shoulders bent. The shabbiness and shapelessness of his suit emphasised his general air of failure. He looked desperately tired. He greeted the visitors, stooped to kiss the glowing face that Stella lifted to him, then went upstairs to wash.

"Poor old Paul," sighed Stella as the door closed on him. "He was born under an unlucky star. But he's kept this job for nearly a year, so we've quite a lot to be thankful for."

A pity to talk like that in front of the boys, thought Doreen, but they were apparently accustomed to it, though she fancied that the younger one looked slightly embarrassed. Biddy continued to beam adoration at all three of them. Paul returned and took his place at the head of the table. Stella ladled him out some stew from the saucepan and set the plate in front of him.

"Excuse my hands," she said, smiling at Doreen and Biddy. "I know they're past hope. You can't expect a working woman to have nice hands, you know."

"You used to have such lovely hands," said Biddy.

"I know," said Stella with a wistful smile. "That was before I had to scrub floors and black grates."

Paul spoke for the first time. "Need you scrub floors and black grates?" he said. "Couldn't the charwoman do it?"

"She has so much to do," said Stella, "and if I work with her as hard as I can it means that she's finished sooner and there's less to pay. You see, *I've* got the budget to consider."

"Don't you ever play the piano now, Stella?" asked Biddy.

Stella laughed.

"The piano? With these hands?" She spread them out again. They were roughened, certainly, but not, so far as Doreen could see, so as to prevent her playing the piano if she wanted to. "How I wish I could! But we haven't a piano now, in any case. We had to sell it to pay for the last move but one, and we haven't been able to afford another. It doesn't worry me in the least. It's just one of the many things I've learnt to do without."

It was an enjoyable well-cooked meal, but, despite Stella's smiling cheerfulness and Biddy's adoring eagerness, there was a constraint in the atmosphere. The two boys were very silent.

"It's *lovely* stew!" said Biddy, enthusiastically.

"Oh, stew!" smiled Stella. "One becomes an expert in stews when one has to count the halfpennies. I remember Auntie was always very suspicious of stews. She used to say that you never knew what was in them. . . . Poor Auntie!" She laughed—the gay little laugh that jarred so on Doreen's nerves. "How horrified she'd be if she could see me now! Such a silly attitude, isn't it? After all, housework's one of the few really useful jobs in the world. When I get tired I tell myself that."

"Do you get *very* tired, darling?" said Biddy compassionately.

"Sometimes," admitted Stella as if reluctantly. "Only sometimes.

Especially when I have to go out shopping after a heavy morning's work. You ladies of leisure"—she rallied her visitors brightly—"don't know what it is to toil up from the town with a basket full of groceries."

"There's the bus," put in Paul quietly.

"Oh, the bus," said his wife, smiling at him affectionately. "They don't give you rides on a bus for nothing, you know, darling. And twopence saved on a bus fare means twopence towards the weekly bills. Poor old Paul! He hasn't any money sense at all. Lucky for you—isn't it, darling?—that you married a wife who *can* count the pennies."

Paul made as if to speak, then gave it up with a faint shrug of his bent shoulders. He must have had to play his part in the little scene so often, thought Doreen. He must be sick and tired of it.

"You know, Paul minds being poor far more than I do," smiled Stella, "which is absurd when you consider that he's used to it and I'm not. Just shows the general contrariness of the male sex, doesn't it? After all, when I was a little girl I used to have my meals in state, with a parlourmaid to wait on me, while Paul used to have his at the kitchen table just like this. Only I'm sure he had a nicer time than I did, because Auntie was always worrying me about my table manners, and I'm quite sure Paul's mother never worried him about his."

Doreen glanced at Paul, but his face was expressionless. Stella continued on that note of tender compassion that her voice could strike so effectively.

"And with that dreadful father of his I'm sure that his meals in the kitchen weren't half as pleasant as this. Anyway, I try to console myself by thinking so, when I feel worried at not being able to have things nicer for my poor old man."

They were uncomfortably crowded at the little kitchen table, and it occurred to Doreen that, with two guests expected, Stella might surely have carried the meal into the sitting-room that they had seen opening off the hall and containing a fair-sized dining-table, might also have dispensed with the drill overall, which she still wore. But one had to admit that the Picture of a Lady who has

Married Beneath Her Gaily and Gallantly enduring Poverty would have been much less effective.

They had finished the first course, and the boys got up to change the plates. Doreen watched them with interest. Charles was evidently Stella's page-in-chief. Once, when she dropped her table napkin and Oliver was about to pick it up, Charles pushed him away in order to pick it up himself. When she wanted to show Biddy something in the newspaper and Paul half-rose in his seat to get it, she said pointedly, "Fetch it for me, Charles, will you?" Paul sat down again and Charles went out, with a suggestion of triumph in his walk.

"I don't know what I'd do without this boy of mine," she said, laying her hand tenderly on his arm when he returned with it. "He's such a help. When he was a little boy he used to say that he was going to give me lots and lots of money and a beautiful house and a butler when he grew up."

"I still am," said Charles, his young face set and earnest.

"Well, it's a good thing that someone in the family's going to make a little money, because"—she threw the familiar affectionate smile at Paul across the table—"I don't think that Daddy ever will."

Doreen noticed that Paul avoided speaking to Charles, and that, when he did speak, Charles answered him shortly, with a faint touch of contempt in his manner. Oliver seemed to feel the tension in the atmosphere. His face looked strained and anxious, and he threw several unhappy glances at his father during the course of the meal, even trying once or twice to draw him into the conversation. There was evidently a timid half-furtive bond of friendship between them, though it was plain that Oliver, too, was devoted to Stella. He's being torn between them, thought Doreen. That's why he looks so unhappy.

Once when Paul said quietly, "I shall be back by six tonight, Nollo, if you'd like a walk," Stella broke in, with unusual sharpness, "I don't want Oliver to go for a walk, Paul. His home work takes him all evening, and I want him to get to bed early. He gets quite enough walking going to and from school." She turned smiling to the others. "Do you know, this darling old idiot of a husband of mine actually began to teach Oliver Greek, and the ridiculous child was so anxious to learn that I had to go and see his head master before I could get it stopped."

"It wouldn't have done him any harm," said Paul. "He was keen enough."

He spoke wearily, as if the subject no longer interested him.

"Oh, keen!" smiled Stella. "He was too keen. Mr. Beauchamp agreed that it would be too much for him."

"Well . . . it's time I got back to work," said Paul, rising.

Soon afterwards the boys returned to school, and Stella and Biddy washed up, helped half-heartedly by Doreen. (She could so easily have left it till we'd gone, she thought.) Laughingly, Stella showed them all the details of her domestic arrangements.

"Oh, I know that you only daughters of devoted parents can have all the gadgets you like, and of course it's understood,"—a faint sneer invaded the sweet voice,—"that authoresses are above all such mundane things, but this is how the humble poor live."

Once when Biddy mentioned Hugh, Stella turned her face away, biting her lip.

"Don't, Biddy," she said in a low unsteady voice. "I don't want to—think about that."

When they took their leave Biddy flung her arms round Stella's neck.

"Darling," she said, "you're so brave and—oh, it must be so dreadful for you."

Stella laughed.

"Biddy, you ridiculous child! I'm perfectly happy. We're poor, but we love each other and we've got the children. I know it's hard work, and I *do* get tired and disheartened sometimes, but when I do I just remind myself that I'm making Paul and the boys happy, and that's all that matters to me."

"What did you think of her?" said Biddy as they walked away.

"She used to be more subtle," said Doreen slowly. "It was all—just a little crude."

"What *do* you mean?" said Biddy. "But she *is* wonderful, isn't she?"

"Oh yes," agreed Doreen. "She's wonderful. . . ."

Chapter Eleven

MISS TEMPLETON'S drawing-room—uncompromisingly old-fashioned—was on the first floor. There were Nottingham lace curtains at the windows, crocheted mats on the tables and knitted antimacassars on the chairs. A giant palm stood in one corner of the room, reaching almost to the ceiling. (This palm, in various malignant guises, invaded the dreams of the under-housemaid who had to carry up the steps to dust the upper branches once a week.) In the china cabinet between the two long windows reposed the heterogeneous medley that usually filled such receptacles—a Crown Derby tea service from which no one had ever drunk tea, a collection of Goss china, some Japanese fans, a group of ebony elephants, several carved ivory figures, pieces of jade, coral, amber and rose quartz, a medal won by Miss Templeton's father in the Boer war, and another one worn by her grandfather in the Crimean, as well as innumerable "souvenirs" brought by her friends and relatives from their travels abroad. The "silver table" was covered with shining knicknacks, the draped mantelpiece with framed photographs of Miss Templeton's "old girls" in presentation dress, riding habits, wedding dress, with fiancés, husbands and ever-growing families.

The room, though large, was overcrowded, as so many of Miss Templeton's pupils gave her presents of their own handiwork, and Miss Templeton liked to have them about her. There were embroidered cushions, embroidered fire screens, embroidered footstools; there was a hand-woven waste-paper basket and a hand-painted drain-pipe—originally intended as an umbrella-stand but used by Miss Templeton to keep her fire irons in. On the rosewood cottage piano stood a school group taken last year, and enclosed in a gigantic frame of poker-work made by the head girl. The walls were covered by water-colours of varying merit presented by affectionate pupils, and even the white-painted panels of the door bore a design of red roses (fortunately by now somewhat faded) executed—under the supervision of the art master—by the first pupil who had entered the school.

Miss Templeton sat in her favourite chair—low, armless, comfortably curved—her neat grey head bent over her tapestry work. She wore a dress of grey silk with "tucker" and cuffs of finest cambric. A gold pencil-case, at the end of a long chain, hung round her neck, and her watch was pinned to her grey silk bodice by a gold brooch.

At the end of Biddy's visit to London, Doreen had come back with her to Runeham to stay at the Vicarage for a few weeks. The two had been invited to Runeham Hill School to have tea with Miss Templeton, and after tea Biddy had gone out into the garden to talk to some of the pupils.

Biddy, eternally young in spirit, always had one or two special friends among Miss Templeton's pupils.

Doreen stood at the window, looking down at the garden, where the elder pupils in dark ankle-length skirts, white shirt blouses with stiff linen collars and ties, their hair, in long plaits or shortened "door knockers," adorned by enormous bows of broad black ribbon, strolled arm in arm along the shady paths.

"What was it like really?" said Miss Templeton suddenly. "We've had the usual song of praise from Biddy, but—what was it like really?"

Doreen turned from the window. She wore the grotesque too-heavy hat and long "hobble-skirted" dress then in fashion, but, unlike most of that fashion's adherents, was tall enough not to look ridiculous.

"It was dreadful," she said. "It was worse than anything I'd imagined."

"She's a model of competent housewifery now, according to

Biddy. She spends less on clothes, in the whole year, than she used to spend on a single dress when she lived in Bellerton."

"Of course," said Doreen. "It's a different scene. It requires a different setting. Then she was the attractive young woman exerting an influence for good by sheer charm. It required, of course, an expensive setting. The present scene definitely requires an inexpensive one. She's quite an artist in her own way."

"She squandered all her aunt's money," said Miss Templeton. "I expect she regrets it now."

"I don't think she does," said Doreen. "I think that actually she prefers a small canvas, and poverty gives you a small canvas. Money means a large canvas, and it's always more difficult to be the central figure on a large canvas."

Miss Templeton nodded, and carefully drew out a needleful of rose-coloured wool.

"What's she like to Paul?" she asked.

"Perfectly sweet and indescribably devilish," answered Doreen. "Oh, you mustn't take me too seriously. I dislike her so much that I suppose I'm not quite fair to her."

"Does she still love Paul?"

"I don't know. He's necessary to her, of course. He provides her with her cues. She acts her scene round him. . . . Probably she's as fond of him as she could be of anyone. He mustn't speak out of his part, and he mustn't have any independent existence for the boys. They're only to see him in the role she gives him. She's very particular about that." She was silent for a few moments, then went on, "I don't think that people are people to her any longer. They're just mirrors. If she can see the right picture of herself in them, she likes them. If she can't, she dislikes them. I'm not sure whether Paul still reflects the picture she wants to see. It's possible that she won't realise it at first even when he stops. She's less perceptive than she used to be. She's gradually coarsening. . . ."

"Does Paul still love her?"

"There again—I don't know. She's still very lovely and she can be very sweet. Probably he's as much in love with her as she wants him to be. He was—tired the day we saw him, and she was keeping him very strictly to his part. I expect there are times when she is very sweet to him. It must be difficult for any man not to be in love with her if she wants him to be. But—he hasn't to have any claims on the boys. They have to belong to her entirely."

"A lot of mothers are possessive," said Miss Templeton, speaking from a vast and sinister store of knowledge. "I could tell you some things about *that*."

Doreen moved from the window and sat down on a small three-cornered chair, cupping her chin on her hand and gazing into space.

"I don't think she's—possessive exactly. It's that—she must see herself the centre of her immediate circle. I don't think she'd much mind who formed her immediate circle, but at present it's Paul and the boys."

Miss Templeton sighed.

"Poor Paul! I used to help him with his Latin when he was a little boy. He was the cleverest child I've ever taught. He ought to have had a distinguished career."

"He would have had if it hadn't been for Stella."

Miss Templeton finished off the rose-coloured thread and selected a green one before she said,

"Stella was quite a clever child, too, but, of course, she was never properly taught."

"She's clever enough now," said Doreen. "Biddy was right about that. She's an extremely competent housewife. And she must have picked it all up by herself in the last few years."

"I wonder what started the trouble," said Miss Templeton reflectively. "My own belief is that it began with the old aunt. She set up a sort of graven image that was partly herself and partly Stella and worshipped it and taught Stella to worship it. She fed her own vanity on the child and the child's at the same time."

"Perhaps," agreed Doreen. "It's amazing, though, how she's always been able to inspire devotion. She was adored at Bellerton. Her boys adore her now, and I think Paul still loves her as much as she'll let him."

"Oh well," said Miss Templeton, turning the canvas over to finish off a thread, "Hugh Carlswell was spared something."

Doreen looked quickly away, and Miss Templeton shot her a keen glance. She had guessed some time ago why Doreen, with her successful career and brilliant circle of friends in London, still found time for this annual visit to Runeham.

"Have you seen the Carlswells yet?"

Doreen shook her head.

"Not yet. We're going there tonight."

"You heard about Pam's death?"

"Yes . . . Biddy told me."

"I think they felt it more than they'd have felt it if the child had been normal. Their lives were so completely wrapped up in her. They hardly know what to do with themselves now that she's, gone. Lady Carlswell was absolutely broken by it. And Hugh—well, you know how devoted Hugh was to her."

"I know," said Doreen in a low voice.

Then Biddy burst in from the garden, happy and exuberant.

She had shown the pupils her picture post-cards of London and described every detail of the Coronation procession.

"It was simply wonderful. The King looked so dignified and kingly, and the Queen looked so handsome and motherly and Queen Alexandra looked so brave and beautiful, and the little princes made one's heart ache somehow. Prince Edward looked wonderful, so grave and princely. The Crown Prince of Germany was there, but he looked terribly plain beside our Royal family. I felt so proud of them, I cried and cried. . . ."

She ended by inviting all the prefects to tea at the Vicarage on Sunday (Mrs. Lytton loved feeding schoolgirls and Mr. Lytton loved teasing them), then, hearing the clock strike six, ran upstairs to her hostess.

"We ought to be going, oughtn't we, Doreen?" she said breathlessly. "We're dining at the Hall tonight, you know."

There was an air of depression over the Carlswell dinner-table, which each member of the family sought unavailingly to dispel.

Pam's death had left a blank that nothing could fill, for so long had the life of the house revolved round that lovely little body and empty mind.

"We ought to be glad really," Lady Carlswell had said to Doreen before dinner. "I used to lie awake at night worrying about what would happen to her when we died. . . . Hugh loved her, but his wife mightn't have been kind to her." She sighed.

"I wish that Hugh would go about more and meet more people. Of course, there's a lot to do here now that my husband's so lame, but Hugh's not much over thirty, and he seems to be turning into a settled old bachelor. It worries me sometimes. I feel that, Pam being what she was, we encouraged the boy to confine his life too much to the home. Pam couldn't go out, of course, and she fretted when Hugh wasn't there, and Hugh couldn't bear to hurt her. We shouldn't have let him sacrifice himself to her as he did. He could never ask his friends to the house because of Pam. She took odd dislikes . . . and I suppose that normal young men do shrink from anything—abnormal. He invited one or two of his friends to stay here when he was at college, but I could see that it wasn't a success. Perhaps we should have kept Pam more in the background, but she loved to be with us, and—well, you know how we all loved to have her."

"Hugh's young," said Doreen slowly. "He'll soon pick up the threads of ordinary life again."

"He's old for his age," said Lady Carlswell. "I feel now that in doing my duty to Pam I failed in my duty to Hugh. . . . I sometimes wish——" She broke off and sighed. "I never understood what happened about Stella Markham, but it would have been better for Hugh to have married. Biddy says that she's made Paul Sanders a wonderful wife."

Doreen watched Hugh at dinner. His air of gravity and responsibility had deepened, and he seldom laughed. Something of pathos seemed to invest the whole family, though they had everything that is supposed to count as happiness. Doreen wondered how often in his dreams Hugh had seen Stella sitting there in his mother's place. . . . His manner to his father and mother was curiously tender.

They seemed lost, bewildered, as if the mainspring of their lives had suddenly broken. After all, thought Doreen, they had never known the gradual alienation that the growth of a child's individuality so often brings. Pam's mind had remained the mind of a child, and they had been her whole world till her death.

After dinner Sir Miles went to doze in the library, while Lady Carlswell discussed village affairs with Biddy.

Hugh and Doreen strolled out into the garden. It was that hour of twilight when the trees and grass seem to take on a light of their own and shine through the dusk.

Doreen wore a fur wrap over her evening dress of amber satin and her smooth dark hair was neatly coiled at the back of her head. She looked very graceful and beautiful as she walked slowly by Hugh's side across the lawn. He was tall, but her shapely head came above his shoulder. It occurred to him how little her face ever revealed her thoughts. There was always that remoteness, that faint air of disdain about her. She reminded him of his mother. He wondered if that had first made him love her.

"I'm so sorry about Pam, Hugh," she was saying. "Your mother feels it terribly, doesn't she?"

"Yes," said Hugh, "they both do. I suppose that it's really the best thing that could have happened to the child, but they miss her so. My mother had her with her all day, and my father used to play with her every evening. It's left things—empty for them."

She nodded.

"I know. . . ."

She was going towards the rose garden, but he laid his hand on her arm to stop her. Stella was sitting there in her white dress, her golden beauty shining through the dusk. . . .

"Not there," he said in a low voice.

Doreen looked at him in faint surprise and went with him down the path beneath the yew hedge to a seat that overlooked a sunk garden and in day-time gave a view of the distant park.

They sat down and Doreen leant back, gazing dreamily into the distance.

There was no constraint in the silence. Hugh realised that she was one of the few women he knew to whom one felt one need not talk.

"Doreen," he said at last, "I didn't say this to you before, because of Pam—I felt that it wasn't fair to any woman to ask her to take on that responsibility—but—will you marry me?"

She did not move or take her eyes from the shadowy distance. She had come to look upon her love for Hugh as something that she must carry hidden in her heart for the rest of her life. She felt at first too much shaken by his proposal to speak. Then she said slowly,

"I must get this clear, Hugh. I'm not the kind of person who drags up relationships by the roots to examine them, but—is it that you feel you ought to carry on the family and that you think I'd—it's difficult not to put it crudely—be a suitable mistress for Runeham Hall?"

He was silent for some moments before he spoke.

"I, too, want to be quite honest," he said at last. "There is something of that in it, of course, but—I do love you."

"Not as you loved Stella," she put in quickly, almost breathlessly.

He thought of the ecstatic love that had filled his childhood and youth with radiance.

"I was young," he said. "It was different. . . ."

"I know," she said in a low voice. "Hugh, I'll never refer to this again, but—will you tell me what happened about Stella?"

He was silent again, his brows drawn together into a frown. The memory of Stella striking Pam was so fantastic and unreal that he had long ceased to believe it. He had come to the conclusion that he could not possibly have seen what he thought he had seen. The whole history of Stella belied it. The child Stella, so tender and pitiful, gazing at the dead bird, her blue eyes dark with tears; the girl Stella wasting the golden hours of her youth in attendance on her fractious, bedridden old aunt; and now the woman Stella (he had heard every stage of the story from Biddy) bravely shouldering her burden of poverty, smoothing the path of the spiritless failure who was her husband, giving him comfort and love and loyalty, bringing up her children with unfailing tenderness and care. No, whatever he had seen he could not have seen—that. Thinking it over, a dozen explanations had offered themselves to him. She had been putting up her hand to straighten her hair before the mirror, then, seeing the child slip, had put it down quickly to try to save her. She had been playing with the child. . . . One's eyes could trick one in innumerable ways. And just because one of Pam's absurd stories fitted in with what he thought he had seen, he had believed it rather than his lifelong knowledge of Stella. He had failed her, driven her into an unhappy marriage. The thought had tortured him for years. He made a little helpless gesture.

"I don't know, Doreen. I don't—understand. Only it was my fault."

"I see," she said slowly.

"Oh, it wasn't what people thought," he said bitterly (for he had heard the current stories of his having outraged Stella's modesty by an attempt at violent love-making). "It was that—I accused her of something she hadn't done and she was so hurt that she turned to Paul Sanders, and it was the chance he had been waiting for. He's dragged her further and further down. . . . Well, you know all about that. You've seen them, haven't you?"

"Yes," she said.

She was going to say more but stopped suddenly. With a flash of intuition she knew that the one way by which she could lose Hugh's love was by trying to tear aside the veil of illusion through which he saw Stella.

"Doreen, you haven't answered me yet. . . . Will you marry me?"

It occurred to her that he had not asked her if she loved him.

She murmured "Yes." He put his arms about her, and she raised her face to his.

Between them she seemed to see Stella's face—the sweet lips parted in their faint wistful smile.

Chapter Twelve

STELLA stood by her bedroom window reading the newspaper cutting from the *Southwood Mercury* that Biddy had sent her. She read it over and over again till she felt she must know it by heart. The bride had been married from Runeham Vicarage. . . . She had worn a dress of ivory satin and a Brussels lace wedding veil that had belonged to her mother. . . . The newly-married couple had left for a honeymoon in France and Italy.

So he had married Doreen Blake. . . . And Pam had died. Stella had always liked to think of Pam's being there to complicate the life of any woman who married Hugh. She had heard from Biddy of Doreen's engagement, of course, but somehow it had not seemed real to her till now. She could not bring herself to believe that Hugh could really marry anyone else. He had loved her so desperately. . . . If it hadn't been for Paul they would have been married. . . .

Hatred of Paul leapt and blazed up suddenly in her heart. . . . This weakling, this failure, who had ruined her life. . . . She caught sight of her face in the glass—twisted into lines of anger and bitterness—and quickly schooled it back into its normal lines of sweetness and serenity. At least, she told herself, she had the children. They gave her life meaning and purpose. She could dedicate it to them. . . . Looking back, she thought how little she had ever lived to herself. With talents, beauty, charm, that should surely have justified her in doing so, she had consistently sacrificed herself to others—first her aunt, then her husband. Poor Paul! (She smothered the flame of hatred, burying the sparks deep into her heart as if they had never been.) Where would he have been without her? If he had selfishly accepted all she had done for him without realising the sacrifices it involved ... well, that, too, was just part of the burden she had to carry. And both he and the children adored her. ... She was their light, their guiding star. ... Without her, without her love, her gallant courage and cheerfulness, she could not bear to think what would happen to them. It added to her burden that there was so little real affection between Paul and his sons. She was sorry about that. She had done all she could to hide his failings from them, to win their respect and affection for him, but the task had been too much even for her.

She folded up the cutting and slipped it into a drawer with a little sigh. She was grieved that Hugh should be marrying a woman who would bring him so little happiness. Doreen Blake was hard, cold and selfish. She sighed again, smiled sadly to herself, and went slowly downstairs to the little sitting-room.

She opened the door and stood for a few moments in the doorway, motionless.

Paul sat in the shabby armchair before the fire, smoking a pipe, and on the arm of it perched Oliver, his arm round Paul's shoulder.

"We shall be in good company," Paul was saying. "Wordsworth and Southey and Coleridge and Shelley and Keats went there."

Oliver turned and saw her, and, with a sudden flush, withdrew his arm.

Paul looked at her calmly, his pipe still in his mouth.

"Nollo and I have been making holiday plans," he said.

"Holiday plans?" she repeated.

She had gone very pale.

"Yes. If I can fix my holidays at the same time as his—and I'm pretty sure I can—we're arranging to have a fortnight's walking tour in the Lakes." He looked up at the boy. "It's going to be grand, isn't it, Nollo?"

The boy's eyes met his with a sort of dogged loyalty.

"Yes, I'd love it," he said.

Stella entered the room. Her face was still pale but she was smiling tenderly.

"It's a splendid plan," she said.

Oliver breathed a quick sigh of relief.

"Where did you say the maps were, Father?" he said.

"In the tin trunk in the box-room," said Paul.

"May I get them now?"

"Rather!"

"I didn't know you'd got maps and things all ready," said Stella, when the boy had gone from the room.

"I've had them for years," said Paul slowly. "I'd arranged to do the trip with a man I knew at college after we'd finished our Finals."

"I remember. . . . Paul, I'd so *love* you to have this holiday. The only thing that worries me a little is Nollo's health. He isn't strong. I don't honestly think that he could stand the strain of a walking tour."

"I asked the doctor about it," said Paul. "I met him by chance yesterday. He said it would do him good."

"I'm so glad."

There was a short silence. Then she said,

"The only other thing that occurs to me is that Mr. Beauchamp said that he ought to have extra coaching in Maths, next holidays. I don't know . . ."

"I'll go and see him about that," said Paul.

"Oh no, it doesn't matter," she said hastily.

"You've no objection to the plan, then, I gather, except Nollo's health," he said, "and I'll undertake to see that he doesn't overdo it."

His eyes met hers in a long unflinching look, and she read a new determination in them. Her intuition was keen enough. She knew that this was one of the rare occasions when he meant to have his own way.

"Of course I haven't," she said lightly. "All I want is for you to be happy. You surely ought to know that by now. I'm just a fussy old mother hen, and I don't believe that anyone can really look after any of you but me."

Oliver came back with the maps. The strained anxious expression that his pale face usually wore had vanished. He looked eager and happy.

"Well, I'll leave you to plan routes and timetables and all the rest of it," she said.

She smiled at Paul, dropped a kiss onto Oliver's dark head, and left the room.

Her heart was beating loudly and unevenly as she went upstairs. The thought of the proposed holiday seemed to hang over her like some black shadow, menacing her whole future. Her mind shrank in panic from the picture of Paul and Oliver tramping together over the hills, sitting together in inn parlours, talking over the events of the day, laughing over its humours.

They would have an endless fund of shared experiences in which she had no part, of little private jokes to which she had no key. It would form a bond between them for ever afterwards, and she would be outside it . . . outside. . . .

She closed her bedroom door and stood for a moment gazing into space, her lips tightly compressed.

At first she couldn't think what to do.

Then she remembered the letter. . . .

She had found the letter several years ago. It was proof of a short unhappy love affair that Paul had had with a typist at an office in Battersea where he had once worked. She had at the time been faintly disgusted, faintly amused, but not slow to realise that sooner or later the possession of it might be useful to her. She had put it aside in her armoury, as it were, against the time when it might prove a useful weapon. It was, she knew, his only lapse from fidelity, and the girl had been a pathetic waif of a creature, whose conscience had been almost as uneasy as Paul's over the affair. Though passionately in love with each other, they had parted, and she had gone North to work in an uncle's shop—an uncle who was a pillar of that narrow evangelical society in which she had been brought up and from whose influence even her love for Paul had not been able to free her. Paul, on his side, had been deeply remorseful, for, despite occasional uncertainties and bewilderment, Stella still meant to him all that she had meant to him throughout his boyhood and youth. She was still the ideal of womanhood, the perfection of purity and high purpose.

Since Oliver's birth she had gently but very firmly refused to live with him.

"I'm sorry, Paul, but to me that's—a sort of sacrament, an act of creation. I couldn't bear to debase it to an act of physical gratification."

She was, as he had long known, cold sexually and was perhaps relieved to have a reason for discontinuing a process that had always slightly disgusted her; but that it did disgust her proved her, in his eyes as well as hers, to be a woman of exceptional fastidiousness. Though he had loved Milly, the thought of Stella always seemed to haunt him when he was with her, and he made only a half-hearted attempt to prevent her putting an end to the affair. It was a letter from Milly that Stella had found, slipped into the pages of a copy of Gibbon's *Decline and Fall of the Roman Empire* in his bookcase, when she was spring-cleaning. Probably he had had it in his hand when she came into the room and had thrust it into the book he was reading, and then thought that he had destroyed it as he had destroyed her other letters. It was a disjointed desperate little letter:

> I shall never love anyone else. It's like heaven just to be with you. I know it's wicked and sometimes I'm so miserable I could die and sometimes I'm so happy I can't bear it. . . .

The letter was in two pieces, as if he had just torn it across, meaning to burn it, when he had been interrupted. Stella had thrown away the top piece that contained the date. She took it out now and stood reading it, a faint smile on her lips.

Then, as if coming to a sudden decision, she went to the top of the stairs and listened. She could hear voices from the sitting-room downstairs. Charles had evidently come in and, interested in the proposed holiday, had joined in the discussion.

"Why don't you take the train to Penrith and start from there?" he was saying. "And, I say, you ought to have a shot at Skiddaw."

Their voices sank lower and she couldn't hear what they were saying. . . . Paul's rare laugh rang out.

"Paul!" she called over the banisters.

"Coming!" said Paul.

He ran upstairs with a boyish spring, unusual in him, two steps at a time.

"Yes, dear," he said, entering the bedroom.

"Shut the door, Paul," she said.

He looked at her in surprise. She was pale, her lips were set in a tight line of suffering. She was in fact now experiencing all the emotions that a loving wife should feel, on suddenly discovering her husband's infidelity. She handed him the letter.

"I've just found this, Paul," she said.

He looked at it and his thin face flamed crimson.

"I didn't know," he stammered. "I——"

"Don't attempt to deny it, Paul," she said in a low voice. "After all, a letter like that speaks for itself, doesn't it?"

"I—I know," he said. "But, Stella—it was years ago. It was——"

"Paul, you don't expect me to believe that, do you? I've just found it slipped into this book."

"I suppose no one's opened the book since then," he said doggedly. "I'm—sorry about it, Stella. As you say, it speaks for itself. But it was over and done with years ago. Do you believe me?"

She looked at him sadly.

"I'd like to, Paul . . . but, if you were capable of deceiving me over this, you're capable of deceiving me over other things. There's no date, of course," she added bitterly. "That makes things easier for you, doesn't it?"

"Stella, you *must* believe me. It was—three years ago. Won't you listen? I want to tell you——"

She raised her hand.

"I don't want to hear about it," she said, "and, after all, it's quite immaterial whether it was three years ago or whether it's still going on. In essence, it's the same. In either case you've—betrayed me." Her lips curved into a tremulous unhappy smile. "You've not been a very good husband to me, have you? I think I've put up with more than most wives would have put up with. I've never reproached you because I've had to work my fingers to the bone for you and bring up my children on a workman's wages, have I? But somehow I've always taken for granted that you were faithful."

He looked at her in silence for a few moments, then said again in a dull toneless voice,

"I'm sorry, Stella. . . . I suppose I've no right to expect you to believe me, but it's the only time it happened, and—it only lasted for three months. I haven't even heard from her since."

Stella's grave blue eyes were fixed on his.

"I'll try to believe you," she said. "I—I can't pretend that it hasn't hurt me terribly. I suppose that some women take this sort of thing as a matter of course. I—can't do that. It's hurt me so much that—I don't think I can ever feel the same to you again. But I'll try to. There's—no question of forgiveness, because you know that whatever you did I'd forgive you . . . but it's going to be very difficult to—forget." Her eyes brimmed suddenly with tears and her lips quivered. She turned to the door. "Don't follow me, Paul," she said unsteadily. "I must—get things straight by myself. I'll come back in a moment."

Paul stood by the window, looking down at the street, his hands in his pockets, his mouth tightly set, his thin cheeks deeply furrowed.

His mind went back over the years of his marriage. He remembered how desperately he had tried to find the real woman behind the wall of her cold sweetness and reserve, how finally in despair he had come to the conclusion that it was his own unworthiness that had made him fail in the search. He was not the man who could reach and hold her. Her spirit was too fine and delicate for his clumsy fingers. Then had come a time when his mind had wandered in a darkness of bewilderment, among things he dared not let himself see. That sense of bewilderment remained. He should have been feeling, he knew, contrite, ashamed, grateful to her for her forgiveness, but all he was conscious of was that feeling of lost bewilderment. . . . He seemed to be wandering among monstrous veiled shapes at which he dared not look.

He could hear her voice downstairs—the sweet low voice that had once thrilled every nerve in his body. Even now it summoned to his imagination a vivid picture of the Stella he had once believed in, the Stella whom, despite everything, he strove desperately to believe in still.

Then she came into the bedroom again. Her face was smiling and radiant.

"Paul, dear," she said, holding out both her hands, "I'm sorry if I—seemed unforgiving. I wasn't really. It was a shock to me, but now—let's put it right behind us, as if it had never been. I'm so glad I know. After all, the one fatal thing is—dishonesty, isn't it? I've always felt that. I can't pretend. I've—*got* to be honest, to have things in the open. I've told the boys everything, dear, and they forgive you just as I do, and are never going to think of it again. We shall all be much happier together now that the thing's out in the open, that we've all been honest with each other. And now, dearest, as far as I'm concerned, it's all over and done with for ever."

She put up her hands, drew his head down and kissed him tenderly on the lips.

He went downstairs, slowly, dazedly.

The two boys were in the sitting-room where he had left them. On the table were still the notes and plans for the walking holiday. As he entered Charles got up, his face white and tense, and walked out of the room without looking at him. Paul turned to Oliver. Oliver's eyes were red, his cheeks flushed and tear-stained. He seemed to meet Paul's gaze with an effort . . . then sprang suddenly to his feet, swept together notes and plans from the table, flung them on the fire, and rushed from the room.

Chapter Thirteen

PAUL lay in bed, watching the patch of sky that he could just see over the roof of the house opposite. He had been in bed now for three months. The attacks of indigestion from which he had suffered for several years had turned out not to be indigestion after all, but heart trouble. The doctors had enjoined complete rest and were still enjoining it after three months. Stella had nursed him devotedly. She was an excellent nurse, deft and skilful, taking endless pains to make him comfortable, always cheerful and uncomplaining. He felt bitterly ashamed of the dark moments when his mind had wandered, sometimes still wandered, among those monstrous veiled shapes. . . .

He could hear the soft murmur of voices from below. Biddy Lytton was in London for the day, and she and Stella were having tea together in the little sitting-room downstairs. Biddy's company bored and wearied him, but he was glad for Stella's sake that she had come. So little pleasure fell to Stella's lot nowadays. . . . She seldom left him for longer than it took to do the housework and necessary household shopping.

He turned his head wearily on the pillow. It was a sultry airless day in late August. London groaned and sweltered in a heat wave. Upon the little Peckham house the sun beat down mercilessly, shedding a dry harsh heat like the heat of a furnace. It seemed to press down on Paul like a tangible weight. The open window framed a grey quivering haze. Somewhere there were fresh uplands, mountain streams, cool stretches of purple heather. He tried to think of them. . . .

Downstairs Stella lay back in her chair and let Biddy pour out the tea.

"You look tired to death, darling," said Biddy solicitously.

"I am tired," admitted Stella, with her faint smile. "It's so hot, and Paul needs a good deal of waiting on, you know. I suppose all invalids get like that. They don't realise how much trouble they give."

"I'm afraid Paul's dreadfully selfish," said Biddy severely.

"Oh no, he's not really selfish," protested Stella.

"You wouldn't say so, of course," said Biddy, "but I'm not blind, Stella."

"Well," conceded Stella, "let's say not more selfish than men usually are. They always expect to be waited on, even when they're well. I know that I think of Hell as an endless going up and down stairs with trays for invalids."

"I can't bear it, Stella," said Biddy with a catch in her voice. "To watch you—*you*—turned into a drudge——"

"Why me more than anyone else?"

"You're so lovely. . . ."

"Oh, as to *that*," Stella threw a glance at her reflection in the mirror on the wall, "I don't see that *that* makes any difference. . . . And as to being a drudge, I don't think of it like that, Biddy. I hate the word. It isn't drudgery. It's service. That's all I've ever asked of life—to be able to be of service, to be able to *help* people. I'm proud of having been able to make things easy for Paul. From the beginning I've never wanted more than that."

"Anybody but you would have grown bitter and discontented," said Biddy.

"Well, I'm not anyone but me," said Stella with a smile, "and I haven't grown bitter and discontented. Sometimes it *does* get me down a little, but not for long. Only when I'm over-tired. . . . Generally I love being able to do it. After all, to feel that one's of use in the world is the greatest happiness in life."

"Oh, Stella, you're so wonderful!" put in Biddy.

Stella laughed.

"Me, wonderful! Don't be ridiculous. I'm a very lucky woman.

I've got my darling old Paul, and I've got the two finest boys in the world."

"You've certainly got the two finest boys in the world," said Biddy. "I do hope I shall see them before I go."

"I'm afraid you won't if you insist on catching that wretched train, because they're both staying late at school for cricket."

"I must catch it, Stella darling, because of Daddy and Mummy. I don't like leaving them for too long these days. You must give my love to the boys. Are they getting on all right?"

"Yes. . . . They're such good boys, Biddy. They spoil me, you know. They're not happy, either of them, unless they're waiting on me."

"I hope they help you with looking after Paul," said Biddy.

Stella's face clouded.

"That's—one of the things I'm rather unhappy about. They've never—got on very well with Paul, you know. I've done all I can to make them understand him better and to make him understand them, but—well, there you are. They'd do anything on earth for me, but—they're not at their ease with Paul. They seem to avoid him, resent him."

"I don't wonder," said Biddy bitterly. "When I think of what he's done to you, I resent him myself."

Stella was silent for a long time, then said slowly, "I don't pretend that Paul's been a good husband, Biddy. He could never keep a job and—he's not been faithful to me. I told you about that, didn't I?" Biddy nodded, her mouth a tight line. "But it hasn't made any difference to my feeling for him. In a way it's made him even more to me, because I feel that he needs me so. Without me—well, I can't bear to think what would have happened to him. . . . Now, darling, that's quite enough about me. Tell me about Runeham. Are your mother and father all right?"

"Yes. . . . Daddy's getting so blind that he can hardly see at all, but he knows all the prayer-book and most of the Bible by heart, so he can still manage the services all right."

Stella smiled.

"And—Hugh?" she said. "I do hope that he and Doreen are happy?"

"I think they are," said Biddy. "They're both so reserved that it's not easy to tell, but they seem quite happy. Doreen's going to have a baby in the spring, you know."

Something seemed to freeze in Stella's heart as she said,

"I'm so glad."

"She wants to learn to drive a car," Biddy rattled on, "but Hugh won't let her—yet. They've got a lovely Rolls-Royce, but Doreen wants to have a little one of her own just to run about in. I suppose she'll have it after the baby's come."

"She's a lucky woman," said Stella.

"I'm specially glad about the baby for Hugh's sake. It was dreadful for him, losing both his parents so suddenly. Everyone thought that Lady Carlswell's bronchitis was just an ordinary spring ailment, then it turned suddenly to pneumonia and she died in two days. Poor Sir Miles looked so dreadful at the funeral that I wasn't surprised to hear he'd had a stroke that same night. He never recovered consciousness, you know. I think they'd never really got over Pam's death."

"So now Doreen is Lady Carlswell . . ." said Stella.

"Yes. It makes her frightfully busy, of course."

There was something very set and bright in Stella's smile as she said,

"Somehow, I can't imagine a typical Chelsea-ite like Doreen fitting into Runeham Hall."

"Oh . . . I don't think she's really a Chelsea-ite, Stella."

"You mean she's given up her writing?"

"N-no. She's not done that. She had a book published this spring. It was quite successful, too. . . . She somehow manages to do all the things she has to do as Hugh's wife, and keep up her writing."

"I should have thought it rather unwise to attempt to keep up her writing."

"Well, of course, people have a way of imagining that just because Doreen knows them she must have put them in her books. Lady Pelliter took offence because she said that Doreen's description of the charwoman was taken from her. She was furious about it and, of course, Doreen hadn't even *thought* of her."

Stella smiled.

"She'll end by getting herself into trouble," she said. "Hugh loathes anything in the way of publicity."

"I know," agreed Biddy, "but he was awfully proud of her book."

"It's marvellous to think of anyone with time to spend on writing," went on Stella with a little wistful sigh. "By the time I've settled Paul for the night I'm so tired that I can hardly move."

"Darling!" murmured Biddy fervently.

"And, of course, I have to keep things so quiet for him," went on Stella. "The boys are very good—they go about like mice—but I'm always having to send away noisy children and organ-grinders and so on from the street. The doctor says that any shock—even a slight one—might bring on an attack and that any attack might prove fatal. I can't take any risks."

"Couldn't you move to a quieter place?"

"How I wish we could!" sighed Stella, "but we can't afford it. You've no idea, Biddy, what a tiny pension Paul's firm allows him. Just as little as they dare. . . ."

"Stella," burst out Biddy impulsively, "I wish you'd let me help. I——"

Stella put up her hand.

"Please, Biddy," she said. "Don't spoil our friendship."

"It wouldn't, Stella——"

"It would, dear. I must fight my own battles and stand on my own feet. For you to give me money would kill our friendship, and I value it much more highly than anything your money could do for me. And I've got, I hope, the right sense of values. Money means very little to me. It's quite one of the inessentials in my eyes, I'm glad to say. One must, of course, have enough to live on, but"—she shrugged—"I've never wanted more than that. I think that it's soul-destroying to have more money than one actually needs. In a way it's soul-destroying even to have as much as one needs . . . I love"—she smiled—"to have to screw and scrape and plan and scheme for my dear ones. If I feel I'm making sixpence

148

do the work of a shilling in my little home—well, Biddy, I feel that I've done something far more worth doing than if I'd just gone out and spent a shilling without having to think about it twice. You know, poverty not only keeps one's wits sharp, it keeps one's soul alive. ... I'd have had everything I wanted as Hugh's wife, but I wouldn't have been able to give him what I've been able to give Paul."

"If only Paul appreciated it!" said Biddy.

"One doesn't look for appreciation," said Stella. "Appreciation is a sort of payment, and there's no merit in giving if one does it for payment. ... Well, that's my philosophy of life. It's very home-made, I know, but there it is for what it's worth."

Biddy's eyes were moist.

"You're just the greatest saint I've ever known, Stella," she said. "I used to think that Daddy was." She smiled reminiscently. "Daddy's only done one worldly thing in his life, and that didn't come off. He chose a rich aunt for my godmother and she promptly decamped to the South of France and hasn't been heard of since. Oh, dear!" She looked at her watch. 'I don't want to go, but I shall miss my train if I don't."

"I'm sorry you've not seen the boys," said Stella.

"So am I. Give them my love, won't you? ... And, Stella darling, you won't refuse a little present for them, will you?"

Stella's face softened.

"No," she said, "I won't refuse it for them." She took the notes that Biddy held out. "Thank you, darling. I'll divide it and add it to their savings. You're far too good to them."

When Biddy had gone, Stella put on her overall, washed up the tea things and tidied the sitting-room. She didn't see the little room, immaculately tidy, immaculately clean. She didn't even, as she generally did, see herself moving about in it—a lovely graceful goddess of the home. She saw Doreen, sitting at the foot of the big mahogany dining-table at Runeham Hall, the Carlswell pearls round her white neck, smiling at Hugh, who sat opposite her—Doreen, who was going to bear his child. The picture changed to other pictures. Doreen stepping into her Rolls-Royce, the chauffeur holding the door open, a footman spreading a rug over her knees. ... Doreen riding through the park on horseback by Hugh's side. ... Doreen moving about the old house, beautifully gowned, surrounded by luxury, waited on by obsequious servants. ... She tried to summon the pictures of herself that generally filled her mind's eye so satisfactorily—gentle, unselfish, nursing her sick husband devotedly, making poverty a blessing for both him and the children by her cheerfulness and courage ... but for the first time the picture failed her. It turned into the picture of a dreary drudge beside those radiant visions of Doreen.

She went slowly upstairs to the bedroom, where Paul lay, his body painfully thin beneath the cheap cotton coverlet. He moved his grey sunken face towards her, and again hatred for him blazed up in her, making her tremble, draining all the breath from her body. She mastered herself with an effort. ...

"Well, darling," she said affectionately. "Sorry I've been away so long. Had a good afternoon?"

He had had a very bad afternoon. One of the worst attacks of pain he had had since the beginning of his illness had seized him, so intense that the sweat had poured down his face. But it had passed now, and he was glad to think that he had not disturbed her. His one aim was to give her as little trouble as possible. ...

"Not too bad," he said reassuringly.

She straightened the coverlet, and stroked the hair back from his damp forehead with a lingering caressing touch, while hatred for him still leapt and blazed in her heart. Then she went to the window and drew the curtain so that the light should not fall on his face. The room felt oppressively hot and airless. Doreen in cool gossamer dresses under shady trees pouring out tea ... Doreen ... Doreen ... Doreen. ... Doreen's picture taking the place of the picture that had been her stay and comfort all those years.

She sat down in the basket chair by the window.

"I didn't bring you up any tea, dear, because you said you didn't want any, but I can easily make you a cup."

"No thank you," he said.

He looked at her, thinking how exquisitely fresh she looked, despite the heat, in the crisp white linen overall that she always wore in the sick-room. The room, too, was as fresh and spotless as her care could make it. There were newly laundered covers on dressing-table and chest of drawers. A bowl of roses stood on the table by his bed. She dragged herself to her feet with an effort and, taking a bottle of eau-de-cologne, moistened his forehead and wrists with it.

"It's hot, isn't it, darling?" she said. "This will cool you a little."

"You're very good to me, Stella," he said slowly. "I'm not much use at putting things into words, but—you know I'm grateful to you for all you do for me."

"It's nothing," she said cheerfully. "After all, I got broken in to this sort of thing with Auntie."

He was silent. . . . It hurt him to be compared to an old woman, who, she had always given him to understand, was fractious and selfish and exacting. Catching the sidelong glance she threw him, he knew suddenly that she had meant to hurt him. The old bewilderment swept over him.

"Did you enjoy Biddy's visit?" he asked, after a pause.

"Yes. . . . It was lovely to hear news of Runeham again. It made me feel homesick."

He was silent for so long that she thought he had dropped asleep.

"The boys aren't back yet, are they?" he said suddenly.

"Not yet. They have cricket this afternoon."

"Do you think Oliver could come up to see me when he gets in?"

"Darling, I do so hate saying 'No,' " she said regretfully, "but you know what a lot of homework he always has to do. And—I really don't think that a sick-room atmosphere is good for a boy. You do understand, don't you, darling?"

He sighed and turned his head on the pillow.

"Yes. . . ."

He was worn out by the pain of the afternoon and sank into a short uneasy sleep.

She came and stood by the bed, looking down at him, every nerve in her body still alive with hatred. It afforded her a curious sensual pleasure to give a rein to her hatred in her thoughts, to let it fill every corner of her being. . . . His grey sunken face looked like the face of a corpse. She thought how frail was the thread of life in him. "I could kill him," she thought, "just by knocking something over, just by startling him. . . ." She looked round the room. That cheap tin clock on the mantelpiece. . . . She went back to her seat by the window and sat there, gazing down at the squalid narrow street over which the grey heat pall still quivered.

A movement on the bed told her that he was awake.

"Biddy's such an old silly," she said with a low laugh. "She talked nonsense all the afternoon. She's always seen me through rose-coloured spectacles. Said that I'd lived all my life for others and a lot of nonsense like that. . . ."

"And it's not true, is it?" said Paul, in a strange far-away voice. He was wandering in that dark place of bewilderment again, but one by one the monstrous shapes were unveiling their faces. "It's not true, is it? You've lived all your life for yourself. You've never loved anyone but yourself—not me or Hugh or even your children. We've never been anything but a sort of background to you. . . . You couldn't bear my being friendly with the boys, because it would have put you just a little out of the picture. . . ."

Stella sprang to her feet. Her face was the colour of clay, her eyes set and glassy.

He looked at her, as if he saw—not her but something beyond her.

"That letter . . ." he went on still in that dull far-away voice. "You hadn't found it then, when you pretended you'd found it, had you? You'd had it for years, but you were keeping it till you needed it, and you needed it to prevent Oliver's going away with me on that holiday. You——"

"*Stop!*" she screamed.

She staggered forward, clung to the mantelpiece as if for support and with a blind movement of her arm swept the cheap tin clock down onto the hearth. It clattered noisily among the fire-irons. There was silence in the room except for a strange rasping sound from the bed and her own quick uneven breathing.

She stood there motionless till the sound from the bed had died away, then picked up the clock, set it back on the mantelpiece and went downstairs to summon the doctor.

Chapter Fourteen

THE cottage was one of the lodges of Neverton Court, but it had not been used as a lodge for some years. It was let or lent at a nominal rent to friends or relations of the Dallases, who owned the Court but seldom spent more than two months in the year there.

Miss Farthing, Stella's old governess, had been governess to the Dallas children, and it was she who had asked them to lend the cottage to Stella for the boys' holidays. It was a charming cottage, its garden cut off from the grounds of the Court by a low hedge, and comprising a miniature lawn, with a gnarled old apple tree in the middle and gay little flower-beds all round.

When she had recovered from the first shock of Paul's death, Stella's courage and resourcefulness had amazed everyone. She had firmly refused all offers of financial help and had set about finding a not too expensive boarding school for the boys, and a post for herself that would enable her to spend the holidays with them. She had finally obtained a post as under-matron at Brookfield Manor, a girls' boarding school in the Midlands.

As her term ended a day later than the boys', Biddy had come over to put the cottage to rights and welcome them home. Mrs. Lytton had died recently and Biddy was very much tied at home, but by dint of some scheming and planning she had arranged to spend the night at the cottage.

Stella had at first seemed very happy in her work, but latterly a note of weariness and disillusionment had crept into her letters.

"It's strange," she had written to Biddy, "how so many people seem to become less likeable the better one knows them. I think this is true of nearly everyone in the world except my dear boys and you, Biddy darling."

Stella, of course, had been accustomed to hard work in her own home, but it must be very different having to work for strangers, thought Biddy compassionately, as she spread fresh lavender-scented covers over the dressing-table and chest of drawers in Stella's bedroom—darling Stella, who had loved her home so dearly and slaved to make it happy and comfortable for Paul and the boys.

To add to the comfort of the cottage, Biddy had brought various things from home which she hoped Stella would think were part of its normal furnishings. Stella was so proud, so nobly independent. She couldn't bear to be under an obligation to anyone, even to a friend—least of all, as she had often said, to a friend.

She glanced at her watch. The boys should arrive in about two hours' time, and Stella about the same time tomorrow. Biddy knew how cheerless the homecoming would be to the boys without Stella, and she had bought lavishly of sweets and games to tide over that first blank evening.

There was a knock at the front door, and she went downstairs to find Miss Farthing standing there. She looked more ghost-like than ever—grey hair, grey face, grey cloak, short-sighted peering eyes and timid deprecative manner. She carried a basket of fruit and a biscuit tin.

"I—I do hope you don't mind my coming," she said anxiously, "but Mrs. Dallas said there was always to be a bedroom for me at the Court, you know, and the children at my present situation have gone away for the week-end with the nurse, so I thought I'd just slip down. I've not seen darling Stella since—since her dear husband died. I have just been round to the head gardener and he's given me this fruit for the boys, and he says he'll send some fruit and vegetables round every day. He said Mrs. Dallas left orders that Mrs. Sanders was to have anything she liked from the garden. And I've brought a few biscuits. Sugar biscuits. I hope they won't think them too babyish."

She entered, put her parcels on the gate-legged table in the middle of the parlour and looked around her.

"I do hope she'll be comfortable here. It doesn't seem good enough for her. When one remembers——" She sighed. "Poor darling Stella! So pretty! So clever! One imagined such a wonderful life for her, full of happiness and success."

"I know," said Biddy tremulously, "I know. . . . She's a saint, Penny. . . . I don't think that Paul ever realised right up to the end what she'd sacrificed for him. Do come in and sit down. He wasn't coarse exactly——"

"All men are coarse," put in Miss Farthing.

Her timid little voice took on a shrill, high-pitched note. Her nebulous little face went suddenly sharp and pointed. She suggested a mouse trying to turn into a lion.

"N-no, not coarse exactly," contended Biddy, "but he was imperceptive. He took everything for granted."

"Selfish," said Miss Farthing. "Selfish. All men are."

"But she loved him in spite of it all. She was heartbroken when he died."

"My darling Stella!" sighed Miss Farthing, turning back into a mouse. "Do tell me about it, Biddy."

"There's nothing to tell," said Biddy. "He died quite suddenly. I'd been there to see Stella that afternoon, but I'd gone when it happened. Stella was alone with him. She'd never have forgiven herself if it had happened when she wasn't there. It was one of those cases, the doctor said, where he might have lived for years or might have died any minute. They weren't surprised . . . and Stella was wonderful. Dazed with grief—but *wonderful*."

They talked about Stella as they laid the tea, recalling incidents of her childhood, examples of her kindness and unselfishness.

"You know, Penny," said Biddy unhappily, "I'm so fond of Doreen, but I wish she understood Stella better. She never has understood her. . . ."

"I expect she's jealous," said Miss Farthing, nodding her grey head and speaking as from a store of deep worldly wisdom. "Small natures are often jealous of characters finer than themselves."

"Doreen isn't small-natured," protested Biddy. "She isn't quite such a fine character as Stella, of course. She hasn't been through adversity like Stella. But——" She sighed. The obstinate refusal of her two best friends to form a friendship together and complete a cosy circle had always been a trouble to her. "Stella's much nicer about Doreen than Doreen is about Stella, but—well, they've never hit it off."

As they talked they piled the little table with the delicacies they had brought—biscuits, cakes, fruit.

Just as everything was ready the boys arrived in the station cab, their luggage strapped onto the top.

The little house was full of chatter and bustle. Biddy and Miss Farthing fussed around them excitedly, helping them off with their things, pouring out streams of questions about the journey and St. Adrian's, exclaiming on how they had grown and how well they looked, exchanging news of Stella.

"She *is* coming tomorrow, isn't she?"

"The blighters might have let her off a day early."

"We'll see she has a real rest."

"We won't let her do anything. I'll cook, and Nollo can be housemaid."

Biddy made the tea, and they took their places round the little table, still chattering excitedly.

It was clear that in the few weeks the boys had been away from home they had developed both in character and physique. Charles seemed older, sturdier, that slight, unconscious hint of arrogance in his manner more marked. He had always been the more practical of the two, with deft clever fingers that could improvise and repair with ease and surety. Stella used to boast that she never needed joiner or carpenter or electrician while Charles was in the house. Oliver's long slender fingers were useless on hammer or chisel. He could not repair even a burnt-out fuse.

The two had never got on well together when they lived at home. Charles had despised Oliver for his timidity and clumsiness, as well as for his habit of day-dreaming and of reading, and, worse still, occasionally writing, poetry. Oliver's championship of their father, half-hearted though it was, had been another offence in Charles's eyes.

Listening to them now, however, discussing school events, recounting school jokes, Biddy realised with joy that the old antagonism was fading.

Oliver was less nervous, more sure of himself. He still looked undersized for his age, but he held himself better, had lost something of his air of timidity and uncertainty.

After tea Oliver went into the little garden that surrounded the lodge, picked a bunch of polyantha, arranged them in a bowl that he found in the china cupboard, and carried it upstairs to Stella's bedroom, while Charles mended the broken handle of the sitting-room door and planed away the sides of a drawer in the kitchen to make it fit more smoothly. He was busy all evening, doing odd jobs about the little cottage, performing, as it seemed to Biddy, miracles of ingenuity. Oliver offered to help, but when Charles quite good-naturedly refused ("No, you old butter-fingers, you buzz off!") was glad to wander down to the lake in the grounds, dreamily watching the play of light and shadow as the sun slowly sank behind the trees.

Inside the cottage Charles was fixing a new wick into an oil lamp at the kitchen dresser and talking to Biddy and Miss Farthing, who were preparing the supper.

"I've decided to have it out with Mother when she comes home tomorrow," he said. "She said that she was going to have us both trained for some profession, but I'm going to get her to promise to let me leave school as soon as I'm sixteen and get work. I'm not going to let her go on wearing herself out to keep me. It ought to be the other way round, and it will be as soon as I can manage it."

"Don't be impatient, Charles," said Biddy. "You must be trained for some sort of career if you're really to help her."

He set his lips.

"I'll make my way in the world all right," he said, "and I'll—I know I can't repay her for all she's done for me, but I'll do my best."

"I'm glad you realise what she's done for you, Charles," said Miss Farthing.

"Of course I do," he said impatiently.

"She's so proud of you . . ." said Biddy.

"Oh, she won't see anything but good in any of us. That's—Mother. We knew that Father let her down all along the line, but she would never admit it even to herself. She always stood up for him."

"I think he meant well," said Biddy feebly.

"I daresay he did," said Charles contemptuously, "but that didn't make things easier for Mother. He'd no staying power. He couldn't stick at anything. He didn't even get his degree. He actually won a scholarship and then chucked the whole thing up out of pure slackness. Mother begged him to finish his time out at college and get his degree before they married, but he wouldn't. He had some quite good jobs after that, but he lost them all. He's never been able to stick at anything. And"—his lips tightened—"there were other things that I can never forgive him for. . . ."

"I know," sighed Biddy. "I'm so glad she's got you, Charles, to make up for it all—you and Oliver," she added hastily.

"There's something of Father in Oliver," said Charles slowly. "He's inherited his lack of staying power but—oh, Nollo's all right."

"How has he settled down at school?"

"Not too badly. I—sort of got to know him better there, and he's not a bad sort. One must make allowances for him, of course. When we were at home I thought he was an absolute muff, but he isn't. He's a sport all right. He sticks things out at school better than I ever thought he would."

Stella arrived the next afternoon. Miss Farthing had had to return to her charges, but Biddy and the two boys were at the station to meet her. She looked very lovely as she stepped down from the train, dressed in deep mourning. She held both the boys to her closely for a moment.

"Oh my darlings! How lovely to see you again!"

Then she turned to Biddy and kissed her.

"How good you are, Biddy! I hope you haven't found these young savages too much."

Her smile embraced them all like a benediction as, arm in arm, they set off to where the station cab awaited them.

She was delighted with the little cottage.

"It's perfect," she said. "How kind everyone is! We shall be so happy here, and the term will soon pass for all of us."

"Mrs. Dallas said that you must ask for anything you want," said Biddy. "The gardener's bringing over fruit and vegetables every day, and she said that one of the maids would come and help with the work in the cottage if you liked."

"Oh no," laughed Stella. "It's sweet of her, but we don't want any help, do we, boys? It'll be fun playing at house again."

The cottage, which seemed to have been empty and waiting without her, seemed now to sing and blossom. . . .

It's like a light shining when she comes, thought Oliver. She was gay and happy, examining the little place with childish delight, going slowly round the garden, an arm in each of her sons', while Biddy went indoors to make the tea.

"Oh, it's so lovely to be back with you," she said. "I'm so happy, I don't know what to do. And now, boys, I must just go and get tidy for tea. I'll be down in a few minutes."

She went up to her bedroom, and, as she sank down on the bed, her face relaxed into lines of weariness. Her position at the school was not too easy, but she had determined to put up with it for a term longer, at any rate, while she looked round for something else. She must not fail her boys. . . . She must carry through the task that lay before her.

She rose from the bed with something of an effort (she was more tired than she had realised in the first delight of meeting the boys again), and, taking out a framed photograph of Paul from her suitcase, put it on the chest of drawers, next the bowl of flowers that Oliver had arranged. She stood for a moment looking at it. . . . Dear Paul. . . . Her thoughts went back over the long years of their married life together. She had fallen short in many ways, she admitted humbly, of the ideal she had set herself, but Paul had seen no fault in her. He had adored her till the end. And with all her faults she had made him happy. In the eyes of the world he had been a failure, but neither her standards nor Paul's were the standards of the world. They had loved each other, they had been happy together, and that was all that mattered. She was glad that her love had prevented his seeing himself as the world saw him. She had saved him that humiliation. He had been dreamy and impractical, and she had from the beginning tried to shoulder his burdens as well as her own. She thought of the last words he had said to her just before that fatal attack had seized him. "I'm not much good at putting things into words, but—you know I'm grateful to you. . . ." The words had been her greatest comfort through the dark months that had followed.

She lifted the photograph and put her lips lightly to the glass. "I'll be brave, darling, for your sake," she whispered.

She changed into one of the black dresses with crisp white collar and cuffs that she had worn ever since her widowhood, combing back the shining hair that, however severely she dressed it, fell always into its soft natural waves, then went down to the three who were awaiting her so eagerly downstairs.

Stella smiled in playful reproach at Biddy over the tea-table.

"How naughty of you, Biddy! We don't budget for this sort of thing, you know."

"Miss Farthing brought the biscuits," explained Biddy, "and I bought the cake. You mustn't be cross with me, Stella. It's a celebration, you know."

There was certainly an atmosphere of celebration about the little party. The boys both chattered eagerly about their school experiences, and Stella listened to them with a tender smile.

"The father of one of the chaps at our school knows Lord Roberts," said Charles. "He's got an absolute bee in his bonnet about Germany, you know. He says they've been preparing for war with us for years, and it'll come any time now."

"Good heavens!" laughed Biddy. "As if the Suffragettes and Ireland weren't enough!"

"Those Zeppelins, you know . . ." said Oliver.

"Oh, they're nothing!" said Charles scornfully. "I heard some of the masters talking about them. They said that Colonel Seely said that there could never be any real danger from the air, and he's Minister for War, so he ought to know."

Then Biddy told them of some people from London who had built a large house just outside Runeham.

"They're simply dreadful," she said. "Ragtime music every night and dances every week-end, with those frightful modern dances."

"Which?" said Oliver.

"Bunny hug and turkey trot and tango."

"Oh, the turkey trot's fun," laughed Charles. "We do it at school, don't we, Nollo?"

After tea they sent the boys into the village to do some household shopping, while Stella and Biddy washed up.

"Stella, darling," said Biddy, "are you really happy at Brookfield?"

"I rather hoped you wouldn't ask me that, Biddy," said Stella slowly.

"Then you're—not happy?" said Biddy, her heart sinking.

"I'm happy, dear," said Stella gravely, "because happiness is something in yourself. It doesn't come from outside. But—I don't know whether I shall stay long at Brookfield. There's a lot about the place that I can't approve of."

"You liked it at first," said Biddy tentatively, remembering the enthusiasm of Stella's earlier letters.

"I don't—dislike it now," said Stella. "I said that there were certain things I couldn't approve of. I don't mind long hours and plain fare, and"—with a little laugh of pure amusement—"I don't mind being treated as a servant. After all, I'm used to hardship and, as you know, Biddy, material things never have mattered to me. But I don't think that one can allow oneself to stay in an atmosphere that jars on one spiritually, among false standards and mental dishonesty."

Biddy looked at her, bewildered but deeply impressed. How wonderful Stella was not to mind being treated as a servant! And how still more wonderful to be affected by spiritual atmospheres that, Biddy humbly suspected, she herself would not have noticed at all!

"Of course," went on Stella, putting cups and saucers carefully into the little china cupboard, "I've never been to a boarding school myself, and I've never before come across that—unhealthy emotionalism that seems to flourish there. I was shocked by it from the first, but when I found that the head mistress herself encouraged it,—well, it *sickened* me."

Biddy, still a little bewildered, thought again of those early letters, in which Stella had playfully described the adoration she seemed to evoke among the pupils of Brookfield.

"Oh, I know," went on Stella carelessly, as if reading her thoughts, "a lot of the girls like me very much—in a perfectly healthy way. I wouldn't put up with the other thing for a second. But Miss Lawless not only expects the whole school to worship her, but also expects me to join in the chorus. Of course, Biddy, she's just a little jealous. I can't help seeing that. The influence she exerts over the girls is not healthy, and I fancy that she resents the more healthy influence that I exert."

"Of course," said Biddy.

The issue was suddenly simplified. Miss Lawless was jealous of Stella. Naturally she would be. Small natures were always jealous of Stella. Even Doreen, who was so wonderful herself in many ways, was jealous of Stella. And, as head mistress, Miss Lawless could make Stella suffer. It was all quite plain now. Biddy's face grew pink and tense with indignation.

"Stella, you must leave at once."

"Oh no, darling," smiled Stella. "I can't do that. I'm the breadwinner, you know. And it's all so petty and futile that it doesn't really worry me. I will leave, but I must have time to look round first and find another job. I'm sure I shall find one. And, Biddy, don't tell the boys about it yet. It might worry them. I won't tell them till everything's settled."

"All right," said Biddy, her eyes alight with adoration. "I won't say a word to them. They're such darlings, aren't they? And, Stella, you know that it used to worry you, their not getting on well together. They really are getting on better now. They've seemed great friends since they got back."

"Have they?" said Stella. She suddenly looked rather tired. "I'm so glad."

Biddy went home that evening, and Stella and the boys spent the next morning working about the cottage and preparing the lunch. The sun poured down with a warmth that was almost summer's, and the little garden was sweet with the scent of wallflowers, gay with tulips and forget-me-nots. Once, when Oliver had gone into the garden to get some parsley, Stella said to Charles,

"How does Oliver get on at school, Charles?"

The usual expression of impatient contempt did not flash into his face at the mention of his brother. Instead, he smiled indulgently, almost tenderly.

"Oh, old Nollo isn't so bad. I thought he was a conceited cowardly little muff, you know, but he isn't. He's—odd, of course, but he's quite a good sport."

"I'm so glad, Charles," she said earnestly.

After lunch Stella went up to her bedroom to rest.

"I'm going to leave you to wash up, and I'm going to lie down till tea-time. It's lovely to get a chance of playing the old lady."

She woke up at three o'clock and looked out of her window. Charles and Oliver were in the garden below. Charles was leaning against the trunk of the apple tree, and Oliver was sitting on the wheelbarrow. They were talking and laughing together. Isolated phrases reached her—"Do you remember when old . . ." "I say, did you know that . . ."—as they exchanged pieces of school news and gossip. There was a suggestion of confidence, almost of affection, between them that she had never seen before. They had forgotten her. . . .

"Let's go down to the village," said Charles, and they set off without even glancing up at her window. She had said that she would lie down till tea-time, but they might have come to see if she were awake, to see if she wanted to go to the village with them.

Charles and Oliver . . . united by a bond of comradeship that would tend more and more to exclude her as time went on. A feeling of icy chill crept over her body. . . .

She went down to the little sitting-room and took out her sewing. She was glad, she told herself, that Charles and Oliver were better friends. .... She wished she felt more sure that it was a friendship that would bring them happiness, but sooner or later Charles's brusqueness would hurt Oliver and Oliver's dreaminess would jar on Charles and things would be worse than they had been before. Oh well, she must just hope for the best and do what she could to help them both. ...

When they came back, she had the tea spread in the garden under the apple tree.

She waved to them as soon as she saw them and smiled a welcome.

"Come along, you old slow-coaches. I thought we'd have a picnic tea in the garden. It's such a lovely day."

"I'm sorry we didn't get back in time to help," said Oliver, feeling, as she meant them to feel, ashamed of having left her to get tea for them alone.

"Surely it's early for tea," said Charles.

"I like an early tea," she smiled, "and I didn't want you to help. You ought to know by now, you old sillies, that there's nothing on earth I love as much as doing things for you."

She looked very lovely and somehow very pathetic sitting there in her black dress under the apple tree, while the sunlight filtered through the branches onto the deep gold waves of her hair. The boys waited on her assiduously, and she kept them busy, dividing her favours between them, excluding by a smile or an inflexion of her voice, sometimes one, sometimes the other, till she became happily aware of the stirring of the old rivalry, the old mutual resentment.

After tea she sent Charles down to the village to get some stamps, and Oliver sat at her feet, while she worked at her embroidery. Suddenly she laid down her work and put her hand caressingly on his head.

"Oliver, darling," she said, "you mustn't let Charles hurt you, you know."

He looked up at her in surprise.

"Charles?" he said.

"He doesn't understand you, darling, as I do."

"But——"

"He's so different himself that he—well, he just doesn't understand. He judges you by standards that don't apply to you. Judged by other standards, *our* standards, he'd fall just as short. When he says that he thinks you're a conceited cowardly little muff, he only——"

"He said—*that*," said Oliver, turning pale.

She glanced at him as if in surprise.

"Surely he's often said it, dear."

"Do you mean since—since——"

Since their new understanding and friendship, he meant, their new drawing together of the past few weeks, which was to Oliver the most wonderful thing that had ever happened to him. "Not since—we came back from school?" he ended.

"He said it this morning, Oliver," said Stella. "Darling, I'm talking to you about it, because I don't want you to let it hurt you. Charles has never understood you, and he never will. You're so different from him. . . . But there's so much of me in you that I understand you almost as if you were myself. All these long weeks at Brookfield, darling—and they *have* been long weeks—the thought of you has comforted and upheld me. I've said to myself: 'Never mind, I've got Oliver. I'm going to be with him again in six—five—three weeks.' Charles is a dear, but he hasn't got quite the same—sense of values that you and I have, Oliver. Always when I've seen something beautiful, I've thought, I wish Oliver were here to share it with me. Beauty means the same to us both, darling. It doesn't mean anything to Charles. You're so near to me that when you let things hurt you they hurt me, too, and—as long as you and I have each other, there's nothing in the whole world that we need worry about."

Oliver snatched her hand and pressed it to his lips with a quick movement. Without her kindness the hurt of what she had told him would have been unbearable. . . .

It was at that moment that Charles returned.

"I say, Oliver——" he began eagerly.

Oliver got up and walked past him into the house without answering or looking at him. Charles stared after him . . . then turned to Stella.

"What on earth's the matter with him?"

Stella shrugged.

"He's feeling moody, I suppose. You know what Oliver is. . . . He's a dear, but just a little—temperamental. At one moment he seems really fond of you and the next treats you as if you didn't exist. He's always been a bit like that. I'm afraid it won't get better as he gets older."

Charles's face was set and stern. He did not readily forgive a rebuff.

"I've no use for that sort of thing," he said shortly.

Stella smiled deprecatingly.

"Oh, darling, don't be hard on him. It's just that he's—made differently. It's lucky that you and I have each other—two sensible, downright people able to face things and tackle them and pull ourselves and others through. It's lucky for Oliver, too, that he's got us. We must always do everything we can to help poor old Nollo along, Charles, but we mustn't expect too much of him and we must try not to rely on him. I'm afraid that if we did, without meaning to, he'd let us down and——"

"Oh, don't talk about him," said Charles impatiently.

She laughed.

"Very well, darling. . . . Come and tell me more about St. Adrian's. . . ."

Chapter Fifteen

It was the first time that Stella had been back to Runeham since her marriage. Biddy was delighted to be able to take her about and show her off proudly to her old friends. Owing to the war, of course, there were fewer festivities than usual (the summer of 1916 was not a time at which to see the social life of England at its best) but Runeham did what it could in honour of Stella. She was nearing forty, but she still wore that look of radiant youth, of shining golden beauty.

"Her outlines are getting just a little blurred," said Miss Templeton to Biddy. "You don't notice it till you're close to her, but they're just a little blurred."

"Oh you're hateful," laughed Biddy. "You've always been hateful about her. I used to mind once, but now I know that it's just your particular kink to be like that. I think that actually it's because you enjoy being different from other people."

"Perhaps," said Miss Templeton, "but—I'm glad that her outlines are getting blurred. She can't do quite so much harm with blurred outlines."

"You're ridiculous," said Biddy. "She's as lovely as ever. Everyone says so."

"Yes," agreed Miss Templeton placidly, "I know she is to the casual eye. Only a very perceptive eye could see the blurred outlines. I have a very perceptive eye."

They went to tea with Doreen at the Hall. Doreen looked pale and worn, for Hugh was in France, and she had not heard from him for several weeks. Each morning she scanned the casualty lists, her heart sick with suspense.

The visit was on the surface a happy reunion of old friends. Beneath the surface currents crossed and re-crossed. . . .

Phyllida, Doreen's little girl, was as radiantly fair as Stella herself. Hugh adored her, and Doreen had more than once wondered if that dazzling fairness sometimes reminded him of the child Stella. But, of course, Pam had been fair, too. . . . And it was of Pam that Stella talked when the child was brought down by her nurse after tea, fresh and dainty in a Liberty smock of pink crêpe-de-chine, the short hair clustering in golden curls over the small well-shaped head.

"How like Pam she is!" she sighed. "When I see her the years seem to roll back. . . ."

And again,

"Doesn't she remind Hugh of Pam? It isn't only her looks, it's her expression, the way she turns her head—everything."

Biddy, watching with a benign smile, was touched by Stella's interest in the child, but Doreen felt the sting beneath the words, and was provoked once into saying, "She isn't like Pam in anything but looks. Everyone says she's advanced for her age," then saw the secret smile in Stella's eyes that told she was glad to have scored a point.

It was arranged that Biddy and Stella should go to the Hall for dinner on the last day of Stella's visit.

The telegram was brought to Doreen that morning as she was having breakfast:

"Home on leave. Arriving 10.30. Hugh."

All her fear and depression dropped from her. She flew round the house, putting everything he might need in readiness, calling Phyllida from the nursery to "help" her arrange flowers in his dressing-room and study.

"Daddy's coming home, darling," she said. "Isn't it lovely!"

"Lovely! Lovely!" echoed Phyllida excitedly, dancing about like a small sprite. "Daddy's coming home."

She was at the station half an hour before the train was due, but at first she hardly recognised the gaunt hollow-cheeked figure that stepped down from the train in the shabby officer's uniform and stood looking around with weary lack-lustre eyes.

"Hugh!"

She clung to him tightly, but there was only a faint response in his tired arms.

"Oh my darling! How thin you are! What's the matter?"

"Nothing," he replied shortly. "The regiment's been a bit cut up and I've not had much rest. . . . Sorry my uniform's in such a mess. I ought to have stopped in London to see about another, but I wanted to get home."

They went to the car, and he leant back with a sigh, closing his eyes.

"I've been so worried, Hugh. I've not heard from you for over a fortnight."

He opened his eyes. They seemed to look through her without seeing her.

"I wrote," he muttered. He passed his hand over his forehead. "I'm sure I wrote. . . ."

They walked round the garden together, and she showed him various alterations she had made, but he seemed bored and indifferent. There was something ghastly in the fixed intensity of his expression. Even Phyllida failed to rouse him from his apathy. He kissed her absently, then seemed to forget that she was there, ignoring her and leaving her questions unanswered. Finally Doreen, fearing that her chatter might worry him, sent her back to the nursery, and Phyllida, ill-at-ease with the stranger who had once been Daddy, went without protest.

It was a nightmare morning to Doreen. The sense of estrangement increased. He seemed to have gone so far away from her that he could not see or hear her. She told him all the local news, but he was patently uninterested. When she questioned him about his life at the front, he turned on her with an irritability she had never seen in him before. "Oh for God's sake, Doreen! I don't want to think about that now."

She searched for something that might interest him.

"Stella Sanders is staying at the Vicarage." He made no comment.

"I asked her and Biddy to dinner tonight, but I can easily put them off."

"Why on earth should you?"

"You ought to rest. . . ."

"I can't," he said curtly. "That's the devil of it."

He couldn't even sit still or stay in one place. He wandered restlessly from room to room, sat down to write a letter, got up before he had finished it, began to read the paper, put it down after reading a few lines, set out to visit the farm but turned back before he had gone half-way, went into the garden and came back into the house almost immediately, once walked out of a room while Doreen was talking to him, obviously unaware that she was speaking. She felt anxious, and bewildered and afraid. It was as if the man she had loved had vanished, leaving this gaunt, curt, indifferent stranger in his place. She shrank from having to entertain visitors and wished that she had, after all, asked Biddy to postpone her visit—Hugh would probably have forgotten that she had mentioned it—but it was too late now. . . .

Stella had obviously taken great pains with her appearance. She wore an evening dress of black filmy lace that made of her porcelain fairness something dazzling and unearthly. As Hugh's eyes rested on her, there came into them the first flicker of interest that Doreen had seen since his return. She felt ashamed of the pain it caused her. She disliked this woman too much to pay her the compliment of jealousy. Biddy, looking outrageous in a violently patterned foulard silk of blue and yellow that did duty for all special occasions, day or evening, her stiff carroty hair escaping as usual in short untidy ends from her "bun," beamed affectionately at her friends, for she was always deceived by the surface friendliness of their greeting into a belief that at last they were beginning to like and appreciate each other. Doreen was pale and silent, worried by the change in Hugh and by the impassable barrier that seemed to have sprung up between them. Sleepless nights of anxiety had drawn dark shadows beneath her eyes, too, and tightened the lines of her mouth.

Stella threw several glances of quiet satisfaction at her during the meal.

It was Stella who saved the occasion from failure. She was gay and animated, breaking determinedly through the heavy depression that overhung the party.

Hugh's face relaxed every now and then into a smile as he listened to her.

"I'm just doing any job that comes my way," she said lightly. "I don't mind what it is as long as it's something useful—something that releases a man for the front. But then I'm used to turning my hand to anything. I've had to ever since Paul died, you know. I've done the oddest things. It makes me laugh sometimes when I think of them. I had to have the holidays free for the boys, you see. I've been matron in schools, mistress in schools, cook in schools. I once had a job as matron in a school, where I had to scrub floors and peel potatoes and clean the head mistress's car, and I once had a job as parlour-maid in a head master's house, which ended in my teaching French and dancing. I've taught Geography and History and Musical Appreciation and History of Art. I once taught Italian, of which I knew nothing at all. I just kept one lesson ahead of the girls, and they never suspected that I wasn't an expert on the subject. Just a matter of bluff, of course. Oh, it's all been fun. . . ." There was something gallant and courageous in her smile. She looked so fragile and exquisite to have battled her way in the world alone. Hugh watched her with undisguised admiration. "And then, of course," she went on, "I've had to look round for a house or cottage or just a couple of rooms for the holidays. I've never cared how hard I had to work in the term, as long as I could be with the boys for their holidays and give them a good time. We've been in the queerest places, but we've always been happy together."

"That cottage of the Dallases was charming, wasn't it?" put in Biddy reminiscently.

"Y-yes," agreed Stella, "but I had to leave it, you know, because I found Mrs. Dallas so impossible. I don't mind being bullied," she went on with her sudden smile. "In fact, I'm used to it. Head mistresses are past mistresses of the art. I don't mind being bullied and I don't mind being ignored, but I can't endure being patronised, and Mrs. Dallas had a way of treating me as if I belonged to the deserving poor. I'm poor, I know, but I hope not deserving."

Hugh smiled.

"Quite right," he said. "And what are you doing now?"

"I've got a secretarial job at present," said Stella. "It's very badly paid, but it releases a man for the army and helps me pay my way. . . . I conducted a bus for a month or two not long ago and quite enjoyed it, but I didn't keep the job on because it would have meant that I couldn't be home with the boys for the holidays."

"It all sounds rather strenuous," said Hugh. "I hope that soon you'll be able to take things a little more easily."

"Well, no," she said. "I've got the stiffest part to come. I want Charles to be an engineer. He's keen and I know he'll do well. . . . It's rather a long and expensive training. He may have to spend some time in the army first, of course. It depends on how long the war goes on. He's sixteen now. But, anyway, I'm going to see that he has the best training he can get if I have to work day and night for it. Then there's Oliver. . . ." She smiled tenderly. "I don't know yet what I can do with Nollo. He's a dreamer. He wants to write, but—well, some way will open for him, I'm sure. The one thing I'm determined on is that they shan't go into blind alleys. . . . They want to leave school and take anything they can get for my sake, but I put my foot down about that. They're dear boys, aren't they, Biddy?"

"Darlings," said Biddy.

"And now let's not talk about my poor little efforts any longer. . . . I'm sure," to Doreen, "that you've done much more important war work."

"I've done nothing," said Doreen.

"Doreen's president or secretary of every sort of war committee for miles around," put in Biddy proudly.

"Oh, but that's wonderful," said Stella. "Now I just couldn't do anything like that, and I do so admire anyone who can. I can buckle to and scrub floors and cook meals and make my own clothes and teach children things I hardly know myself and type and tot up columns of figures and punch bus tickets and do all kinds of dirty work, but I couldn't preside."

She had made Doreen, of course, seem the grand lady playing at work. Doreen said, "You've changed your jobs a good deal, haven't you?" but, as a counter attack, it failed. Stella gave her gay little laugh and said, "I know I have. It's all—adventure. And as long as I'm working for my boys, I don't mind what I'm doing."

"Stella's so clever," said Biddy proudly. "She made that dress she's got on."

"Of course I did," smiled Stella. "I've not worn anything for years that I haven't made myself. I haven't really enough time and I throw them together anyhow. . . . Yours is a lovely dress, Doreen. It's a model, isn't it?"

"Yes," said Doreen shortly.

"It suits you so."

It didn't suit Doreen, and she knew it. The soft grey chiffon had suited her when her pallor had the underlying bloom of health, but it did not suit the dead pallor of exhaustion that her skin wore tonight.

Hugh did not look at his wife. His eyes rested instead on the guest, and Doreen kept her eyes fixed on her plate, because she could not bear to see him watching Stella like that.

"What about your writing, Doreen?" said Stella suddenly. "Are you keeping it up?"

Doreen shrugged.

"On and off," she said. "I've had so little time lately."

She had written less and less since her marriage. Her duties as mistress of the Hall did not leave her much time for writing, and her friends and neighbours were not interested in her work. They treated it, indeed, as though it were a kind of skeleton in the cupboard, never mentioning it themselves, looking embarrassed if she mentioned it, and quickly changing the subject to something safer, such as gardening or the difficulty of keeping maids in the country. She missed the enthusiasm and sympathy of her old Chelsea friends, and she knew that her work had suffered for lack of it.

"I thought I hadn't seen anything of yours lately," said Stella. "I loved your first book."

Doreen said nothing. Odd how this lovely smiling little woman made her feel that she had failed at everything she had undertaken—as Hugh's wife, in her career, even as mistress of the Hall.

And Hugh still watched her with that softening of his drawn features.

"Doreen's books are all wonderful," put in Biddy inanely.

"I suppose you get no time for reading at the front, Hugh?" said Doreen, simply because she had to make him look at her instead of Stella. He turned his eyes to her, but they seemed to look through her as if she were not there.

"Practically none," he answered shortly.

After dinner they fell as if inevitably into two couples—Doreen and Biddy, Stella and Hugh. Biddy chattered desultorily to Doreen about local affairs and local war efforts, and Doreen strained her ears to hear what Hugh and Stella were saying. That dead toneless note had left Hugh's voice. . . . She tried to join in, to make the conversation general, but always Stella managed to bring it back to their childhood's days in which she had no part. "Do you remember . . .?" Once Hugh laughed—the first time Doreen had heard him laugh since his home-coming.

She didn't hear whether it was Hugh or Stella who suggested going out into the garden, but they rose and went out of the french windows, vanishing into the scented dusk. When they had gone, Biddy turned to Doreen.

"Isn't Stella wonderful!" she said. "She's even cheered Hugh up."

Their feet turned by tacit consent to the rose garden . . . to the seat beneath the hedge of climbing roses where he had first asked her to be his wife. . . . They sat down without speaking, and there, in the stillness and fragrance of the dusk, where the first stars showed in a cloudless sky, the tension of Hugh's spirit relaxed, and the nightmare happenings of the last months began to seem far-away and unreal, as if they belonged to a world that no longer existed.

. . . In the half-light Stella might have been the girl of twenty years ago. Time rolled back. He was young once more, full of hope and enthusiasm. . . . The memory of filth and horror and senseless crazy cruelty faded from his mind. The world was clean again.

He took her in his arms and pressed his lips against hers, clinging to her as a drowning man might cling to his rescuer, straining her to him as if to shut out everything else. . . . She bent her head back and lay passive in his arms . . . then he released her with a long sigh and leant back wearily on the seat, his eyes closed. The dim light emphasised the shadows of his face, the sunken temples and hollow cheeks. He opened his eyes suddenly and looked at her. She sat by him, a faint smile on her lips. He dragged his long gaunt body to its feet as if with an effort. She put out a hand to stop him.

"Hugh . . . we must talk things out."

He shook his head.

"There's nothing to say."

The faint smile touched her lips again.

"I suppose there isn't. . . ."

They walked to the house in silence.

Doreen looked up as they entered the drawing-room and noticed that Hugh's face was more grey and haggard than ever . . . that Stella was smiling . . .

When it was time for them to go home, Doreen went upstairs with Stella, while Biddy stayed downstairs describing to Hugh the exact method on which the Runeham Women's War Working Parties were organised. He didn't appear to be listening, but Biddy didn't see how anyone could fail to be interested in the subject.

Upstairs Stella stood for a moment at the bedroom window, her cloak drawn over her shoulders, gazing out dreamily over the dusk-shrouded garden, then turned suddenly to Doreen, who was watching her in silence.

"Doreen," she said slowly, "there's got to be—honesty between you and me. You know that Hugh loves me, don't you?"

Doreen's face seemed to turn to stone. She still looked at Stella without speaking.

"We've got to face it," went on Stella in her grave sweet voice. "You know, of course, that we should have been married years ago. I haven't met him since then till tonight, and—to both of us it's as if all these years between had never existed."

Doreen's throat felt dry and parched. She was relieved to find that she could speak in her normal voice.

"If Hugh wants me to divorce him," she said, "I will, of course, but——"

"No, no," said Stella, with a quick little gesture of repudiation. "I wouldn't. . . . I've made that quite clear to him. We love each other—we've always loved each other—but it won't make any difference to what he feels for you. That's what I wanted to tell you. You need never be afraid that there will be—anything that either of us need be ashamed of. Life's not been easy for me, but I've held on to my sense of values, and I'm not likely to let it go now. Love, to me, doesn't mean—that. To me, love is a union of mind and soul, and Hugh and I will always have that. Something in me belongs to him. We grew up with each other in those years before you met him and——"

"If you're quite ready," said Doreen, "shall we go down?"

Stella shrugged.

"You're foolish to take it like this, Doreen. We might have been friends, you and I. I want to help you. You haven't made Hugh too happy, as far as I can see. . . ."

"Mind the mat on the landing," said Doreen. "It's rather thick. One's apt to trip over it."

They went slowly downstairs to the hall, where Biddy was bundling herself into the large ulster-like overcoat that had been a familiar feature of the landscape for the past six or seven years.

Even Biddy seemed at last to sense the constraint in the atmosphere.

"You neither of you look well," she said, looking from Hugh to Doreen. "If I were you I'd try a tonic."

When they had gone, Doreen went up to her bedroom and, flinging the window wide open, leant out, breathing in the cool night air as if to purify her whole body.

Then she went down to the library, where Hugh sat in his armchair, leaning forward, his head on his hands. She sat down on the wide arm of the chair and waited.

For some moments he did not speak or move, then he raised his head and said,

"I kissed Stella just now. . . ."

"I know," said Doreen quietly.

"When I kissed her," he went on (he seemed almost too tired to speak), "I looked at her and she was smiling, and I knew—I don't know how—but I knew that she did hit Pam. I hadn't told you about that, had I?"

"No. . . . Don't tell me now. Just rest."

He relaxed in his chair with a long quivering breath and laid his head against her shoulder. "God, I'm tired! . . . Don't go, Doreen. Stay with me."

It was the old Hugh who spoke, the old Hugh who looked up at her through the grey tired face. The barrier that had separated them was down. She drew her hand lightly over his forehead.

"Yes . . . I'll stay. . . . Just rest."

Chapter Sixteen

BIDDY scurried, across the platform, dropping her bundles and packages, stooping to pick them up and scrambling into the carriage just as the train was starting.

Wherever Biddy was going she seemed to have innumerable packages, which she dropped at frequent intervals, and, however early she set off, she never seemed to get to the station till the train was on the point of starting.

Her carroty hair, as untidy as ever, was now flecked with grey, her short figure was a little more dumpy and thick-set, her plain kindly face a little broader.

Biddy was a wealthy woman. Her godmother had recently died in Mentone and left her thirty thousand pounds, but she still wore the old shantung coat and faded panama hat that she had worn every summer for the past four or five years. She had retrimmed the panama hat with a new ribbon, but the new ribbon was narrower than the old one had been and left a thin white line just above it. Biddy put away her summer clothes at the end of each summer and took them out again at the beginning of the next. She was extravagantly generous to other people but seldom bought anything new for herself, simply because it never occurred to her to do so. The only thing, in fact, that she had bought herself since she received her legacy was an Austin Seven, which she called Jehu, and in which she drove recklessly but with unfailing pride and delight about the neighbourhood.

Her father had died last year and after his death Biddy had taken a small cottage in the village, where she had settled down quite comfortably with a cat and a canary and the services of a local charwoman. The cottage was generally as untidy as Biddy herself, but there was a pleasant atmosphere of friendliness about it. "Just drop in any time," Biddy would say to people, adding, "if you don't mind a bit of a muddle." She still pottered about the parish, doing quietly and unobtrusively most of the work shirked by other people. The new vicar's wife made fun of her to her friends, but was glad to claim the credit for the work she did, just as Biddy, who hated officialdom and fuss, was glad to let her have it.

The idea of giving her legacy to Stella had occurred to her as soon as she heard about it, but she had put off broaching the matter till the legal formalities were completed. Now everything was settled and she was going to see Stella about it today. She didn't want any of the money herself. She was perfectly happy with her cottage, Pompey (her cat), Dick (her canary) and Jehu. Anything beyond those few possessions would have embarrassed and worried her. Since she heard the news of the legacy, she had never ceased building castles in the air for Stella and the boys . . . a house in the country with a large garden . . . winter sports for the boys . . . holidays abroad for all of them . . . friendships . . . entertainments . . . the full happy lives that such wonderful people ought to have. Stella had always refused to take money from her before, but that was understandable. In those days she had only had her allowance from her father. Now even Stella—so proud and sensitive—would surely not refuse.

She had drafted many letters offering her the money, but none had seemed satisfactory. She was, she knew, clumsy and tactless, and it was so easy to say the wrong thing on paper. Talking to Stella, one could watch her expression and choose one's words. . . .

Stella's invitation to go over and spend this August Bank Holiday with them came most opportunely, just when Biddy had decided that she must offer the money in person.

She settled herself into a corner of her carriage and anxiously checked her parcels to make sure that she had forgotten nothing. She had brought the little presents she usually brought for them—Fullers' sweets, a cake that she had made herself, a silk handkerchief for Charles, a tobacco pouch for Oliver. It was difficult to know what to give the boys now that they were grown up—Charles twenty-two and Oliver twenty.

Charles was at an engineering works, and Oliver had won a scholarship at Oxford and was in his second year. Stella was determined that he should go through with it and get a good degree—not give it up half-way as Paul had done. Stella had fought against Paul's faults in both boys, and they certainly did her credit. They were both doing excellently in their work and both devoted to Stella. Biddy often thought that Stella's marriage was an example of the way good can come out of evil, because, though Paul had been a most unsatisfactory husband, the boys couldn't have turned out better if they had had the most exemplary of fathers. But, of course, that was Stella. . . .

Stella had written that they were going for an expedition into the country today (she generally arranged little expeditions for holidays and Sundays) and that Frances Topham was joining them.

Biddy had met Frances several times at Stella's. She had been a pupil at Brookfield—the first school where Stella had taught—and had adored Stella ever since. She was teaching, herself, now at a school in Eastbourne and often came over to spend the day with Stella and the boys. Stella had hinted in her last letter that she and Charles would probably soon become engaged. It was natural, thought Biddy, with a comfortable sigh. Frances was such a nice girl and Charles such a nice boy. . . .

She took out the morning paper, which was tucked into the string of a parcel, and read it in a desultory fashion. The Coalition seemed to be in disfavour. There was an acrimonious paragraph about Lloyd George's election war-chest and the sale of honours. We didn't seem to be getting on too well with France and there appeared to be some sort of trouble with Turkey. Oh dear, thought Biddy with a sigh, why couldn't the nations live peaceably together and stop all this quarrelling? Everyone had thought that the world would be different when we won the war, but it wasn't. Thank heaven, the Irish question was settled at last, anyway, and there wouldn't be any more trouble in that quarter. Or would there? You could never tell with the Irish, thought Biddy darkly. For comfort she turned to the thought of Stella. It would be lovely to see Stella again. It was a real grief to her that Stella would never come to stay at Runeham. She always made some excuse, but Biddy knew that the real reason was connected with. Hugh Carlswell. Stella had not been to Runeham since that day—five years ago—when (Biddy had gathered from Stella's hints) Hugh had told her that he was still in love with her. That was why she had avoided him all these years. Biddy had been much distressed by the thought of it—especially as Doreen, too, was her friend—but the little tragedy had ended happily, as little tragedies should, for there was no doubt at all that Doreen and Hugh were now devoted to each other and to their children, Phyllida and the boy, Peter, who had been born in the last year of the war. Hugh had won the D.S.O. in the war and was now a J.P. and quite an important person in the county generally. Biddy sighed again—a deep sigh of content—as she reflected how often Things Turn out for the Best.

Stella had moved to the flat in St. John's Wood about three months ago. She seldom stayed more than a year or two in the same place. It wasn't only that sooner or later she came up against "jealousy" and "spitefulness" in her neighbours. It was the old feeling of restlessness and frustration, the sensation of having painted a picture, acted a role to its completion, the longing to start again on a clean canvas . . . before a fresh audience. . . .

She and the boys now occupied half the second story of an eighteenth-century house that had recently been converted into flats.

When Biddy arrived she found Stella, wearing a flowered cretonne overall, cutting sandwiches at the kitchen table, while Charles fiddled with a broken fastening of the picnic basket, and Oliver sat on the dresser, his feet on a kitchen chair, smoking a pipe.

"Look at these lazy boys of mine," laughed Stella, "letting me do all the work."

"She does it so much better than we could,' grinned Oliver. "It would be an insult even to offer to help."

"And she enjoys doing it," said Charles. "She lives for it."

"I believe I almost do," admitted Stella. "I certainly start planning the next picnic as soon as one is over. It's far more of a treat to me than it is to these two sophisticated young men. I'd break my heart when the end of the summer comes if it weren't that there was the winter to look forward to and standing in queues for theatres and concerts. . . . Put the kettle on, Charles, and let's have a cup of tea before we start."

"She even packs picnic baskets for queues," smiled Oliver.

"Well, one needs it some days," said Stella gaily. "We're cheap-seat experts—the boys and I, you know. I think that we know exactly how to get the best seats for the least money in every place of entertainment in London. And we know all the other cheap-seat experts—by sight at any rate—and all their little tricks and subterfuges. Some we hate and some we love. We get far more fun out of the whole thing than people who just pay for the best seats and walk into them. Queues are entertainments in themselves, you know. Do you remember, boys, when . . .?"

The three of them began to recall old jokes and laugh over them. Biddy watched them with a tender smile, thinking that Stella was more like a sister to the boys than a mother. . . .

The kettle boiled, Charles made the tea and Oliver brought out a tin of biscuits from the cupboard.

"Where are we going to?" asked Biddy as she took her cup from Charles and sat down at the kitchen table.

"Bus to Victoria," said Stella, "train to Bromley, bus to Riverhead, picnic on Ide Hill."

"Trust her to have it all mapped out," said Charles. "She arranges a different one each holiday and each better than the last."

"I know I'm ridiculous about it," said Stella with a deprecating, almost shamefaced little smile. "I spend weeks beforehand planning it and thinking out new picnic dishes. I don't mind admitting that I just *live* for the times when I can go on the spree with these two great boys of mine. I don't mind how hard I work in between, as long as I have that to look forward to. They're always talking about the time when I shan't have to work but I tell them that I couldn't be happier than I am now."

"You wait!" said Oliver, smiling affectionately at her. "We'll see that you are."

"What are you doing now, Stella?" said Biddy. "Are you still in that hat shop?"

"No," said Stella, "I gave that up. I didn't mind the long hours and the hard work and the insolence of most of the customers. That sort of thing only amuses me. It was the atmosphere of petty spite and jealousy that I couldn't put up with." Her sweet smile lighted up her face again. "I've got rather an amusing job now. I'm companion-secretary to an old man. It doesn't sound hard work—though actually it is—but he's quite an old pet and does appreciate everything I do for him, and he pays me quite well."

"He tries to get off with her," laughed Oliver.

"Yes," agreed Stella, smiling, "he tries to be amorous, but he's so blind that it's quite safe. He'd be wildly generous if I'd let him be, but I won't let him give me anything beyond my salary."

"He gave her a diamond brooch and she threw it back in his face," said Charles.

"Not quite, darling, but I made it clear that I couldn't take presents from him or anything at all beyond my salary. I had to write it. He was too deaf to hear what I said. Or pretended to be."

"We wrote the letter together," said Charles.

"I wrote it," said Oliver.

"Oliver wrote the most ridiculous letter," laughed Stella.

"I found it in a Victorian Letter Writer," said Oliver. "Part of it, anyway. It said 'My honour, sir, is more valuable to me than any bauble.'"

The three of them laughed at the memory.

"Needless to say," said Charles, "we did not send Oliver's letter. Ma herself concocted a beauty. It did the trick, too. He was as meek as milk afterwards."

"He confines himself to flowers, anyway," said Stella, "which is quite legitimate."

"I still think mine was better," persisted Oliver. "I liked 'Thou pernicious caterpillar, thou fell blight, thou mildew, thou fretting moth, thou canker worm.' Actually that came out of *Clarissa*."

"I don't know what Biddy will think of us," said Stella at last, checking her laughter. "Let's try to be sensible, boys. . . . Biddy, darling, you've not seen this flat before, have you? What do you think of it?"

"I think it's charming," said Biddy. "So nice and bright."

"We like it," said Stella. "We had a lot to do to it, but we enjoyed doing it. We all three buckled to and did it together and it was great fun."

"Are the other people nice?" said Biddy.

Stella made a little face.

"Some are. We don't see much of them. There's a Miss Pattern, who has a room on the top floor, who's rather nice. The boys say she's dull. She may be, of course, but—well, you know, it's character that matters to me and she's one of the kindest, sweetest creatures I've ever met. The others are all nondescript, except the people who have the ground floor, whom I definitely dislike."

There was a short silence, and Biddy was aware of a sudden tension in the atmosphere. Charles took his pipe out of his pocket and lit it with apparent absorption. Oliver looked uncomfortable.

"Oh, they're not bad, Ma," said Oliver.

Stella smiled, serenely, placidly, as if unaware of any constraint.

"The mother and father are all right. It's the girl I object to." She turned to Biddy. "She made up to poor old Charles quite shamelessly when first we came here, but fortunately Charles is capable of dealing with that sort of thing, aren't you, darling?"

Charles got down from the dresser and picked up a spoon that Biddy had dropped.

"I hope you haven't forgotten the cheese straws," said Oliver.

"Of course I haven't," said Stella. "I made them last night. When have I ever forgotten anything?"

"You once forgot the tin-opener," said Oliver.

"You wretch!" laughed Stella. "I wonder you dare mention that. You'd undertaken to bring it."

It was then that Frances arrived, carrying a basket of fruit as her contribution to the picnic. She was a plump, pallid girl, not bad-looking, with ash-coloured springy hair, blue eyes, a blunt nose and slightly negroid lips.

While she was still greeting Stella effusively, praising the picnic arrangements, pouring out news of common acquaintances, Charles went quietly out of the room and made his way to the ground floor flat.

A tall dark-haired girl with a pale oval face and hazel eyes answered his knock and stood looking at him without smiling.

"Well?" she said.

"May I come in a moment?" he said. "Are your father and mother in?"

"No," she said, holding the door open, but not so as to suggest a welcome. "They've gone to Aunt Daisy's for the day."

He followed her into a spacious high-ceilinged room, panelled in white and furnished with a few good pieces of eighteenth-century furniture. Shelves of books filled the recesses on either side of the Adams fireplace. Sewing materials and an open book lay on a small settee, where the girl had evidently been sitting.

"Aren't you going out?" said Charles.

"Yes," she answered, glancing at the clock. "I'm going out with Mark. He's coming for me at eleven."

"Mark?"

"He's the one you don't like," said the girl calmly. "Won't you sit down?"

"No, thanks." He stood for a moment staring at the floor, then burst out, "Look here, Pat. I've felt wretched ever since Tuesday."

"Why should you?" she shrugged. "I thought we were—friends enough for me to suggest that we spent Bank Holiday together, and you said that you'd rather spend it with your mother. That's all there is to it."

"You know that I wouldn't rather spend the day with my mother," he burst out. "Only—she counts on it. Oliver and I always have done. She'd be bitterly hurt and disappointed if I suddenly made other arrangements. You don't understand."

"Yes, I do. That's the trouble. I understand too well. Your mother hates me like poison, doesn't she?"

"If you want to know," he said, "she says you've been abominably rude to her."

"I know I have," she said, "but she asked for it. . . . Oh, I was quite tempted to play her game. I don't mind admitting it. I liked you and I knew you liked me, and I wanted us to be friends. I only had to make up to her and flatter her and pretend I thought her wonderful, and it would have been all right. We'd have been allowed to see as much of each other as we liked. But—the price would have been too high, even for your friendship. We know where we stand, she and I, and I'd rather have it that way."

He flushed hotly. "I don't know how you can speak of my mother like that. If I were to tell you all she's done for Oliver and me ever since we were children——"

She shrugged.

"You have told me," she said, "and Oliver's told me and she's told me. I think I know it by heart. It's not much fun for her, if people don't know, is it?"

He started towards the door, his lips set.

"I'm sorry, Charles," she said with a little helpless gesture.

He turned back and looked at her unhappily.

"Pat—you'll come out with me next Tuesday as usual, won't you?"

She shook her head.

"No. I can't go on like this—just meeting you when you think your mother won't know. . . . Better stop the whole thing. It can't possibly—mean anything to you or you'd have the courage to go through with it."

"It does mean something to me, Pat," he protested doggedly. "It means everything to me. If only you'd try to understand about Mother! She's given up her whole life to Oliver and me. If I talked all day I couldn't make you understand all she's done for us. Father was a rotter—weak and spineless and unfaithful. He led her a dreadful life. She's had to carry the burden of the whole family on her shoulders always, and since he died she's slaved for Oliver and me. We mean such a lot to her. We've always spent these holidays together. It would hurt her terribly if one of us went off on his own. She's so—affectionate and sensitive. I did say I'd suggest to her that you joined in———"

"And I said I didn't want to," flashed Pat. She gave him a long impersonal look. "You're over twenty-one, aren't you, Charles?"

"Yes."

"How much longer is this sort of thing to go on?"

"What sort of thing?"

"You and Oliver kept like a couple of court pages to fetch and carry for her, or rather like a couple of court minstrels to sing her praises. No, don't get angry again. Only—if you ever marry, your wife will have one chance of making a success of things—and only one—and that will be to make you promise never to see or speak to your mother again."

He turned on his heel, his face dark with anger, and went out of the flat without speaking.

She watched him in silence, a little twisted smile on her lips.

When he returned to the kitchen he found that Miss Pattern had arrived. She had insisted on Stella's sitting down and was finishing the packing of the picnic basket herself.

"You're never off your feet," she was saying. "Working for others from morning to night." She smiled at Charles. "If I didn't come in sometimes and make her rest, you know, she'd be worn to a shadow."

Miss Pattern was a shrunken little woman of about fifty, with protruding teeth, scanty grey hair and a fussy restless manner. Her conversation consisted of a stream of platitudes, and she occasionally dropped an aitch.

Oliver, sitting astride a chair and watching them, wondered for the thousandth time at his mother's patience with such people. It seemed inexhaustible. He had often noticed, with a faint sense of disloyalty, that her friends were generally poorer and less well-bred than herself. She had once explained this to him.

"You see, dear, people like that need me. I can help them. I just can't waste my time on people who patronise one or to whom friendship means just entertaining each other in turn. Charles and you laugh at my friends, but I *mean* something to them. I can *give* them something and you know, dear, a relationship in which I can't *give* means nothing to me."

He watched Biddy and Frances and Miss Pattern fussing around her now. There was an undercurrent of rivalry between them as to who could do most for her, who win her sweetest smiles. There was always that sort of rivalry among her friends. There was that sort of rivalry between himself and Charles. On the surface their relations were friendly enough, but beneath was a secret antagonism that neither of them quite understood. It was, he supposed, a tribute to Stella's unconscious charm that they should feel like that. As children each had wanted to come first with her and something of that attitude still lingered.

Charles had come back, glowering furiously. He'd been a bit queer-tempered lately, poor old chap!

Frances and Biddy washed up the tea things, and the four of them studied a map of Kent on the kitchen table.

"How far do we walk?" said Biddy.

"There," pointed Stella. "From Riverhead to Ide Hill. About three miles. Excellent for us all. Especially me. I'm getting fat."

There was a loud disclaimer from everyone. And yet, thought Biddy, looking at her, she *was* getting fat. Not too noticeably, of course, but she was certainly plumper and she had a definite double chin.

"Fat, fair and just over forty," persisted Stella with a gay little laugh.

"You're not a bit fat," said Biddy, then felt slightly ashamed. She prided herself as a rule on not making insincere compliments.

"Time you were off," said Miss Pattern. "Well begun, 'arf done, you know. And, you boys, look after your mother. She's the best mother ever boys had."

Charles and Frances wandered down the slope of Ide Hill. Charles's mind was still full of anger against Pat. He couldn't think how he had imagined himself to be in love with her. The very fact that she could think and talk like that about his mother showed her to be entirely different from what he had thought her to be. It was a good thing that he had found out in time. He could hardly believe that only a few days ago he had dreamed of marrying her. She had seemed perfect . . . but his mother was his standard of perfection in womanhood, and by that standard she fell lamentably short.

His thoughts turned to Frances. His indignation with Pat made Frances seem more attractive than she had ever seemed before. And Frances appreciated his mother—adored his mother, in fact. If he married—and he intended to marry—it would be as well to have a wife who adored his mother. Frances's chief subject of conversation was his mother. She was talking about her now.

"She's always so bright and cheerful, isn't she?" she was saying. "And nothing's ever too much trouble so long as it's for others and not herself. I remember once at Brookfield . . ."

The stream of reminiscences burbled on.

He glanced down at the round pallid face. He remembered that, when first he met her, the small eyes and blunt nose had reminded him of a pig's, and he had nicknamed her Piggy, till he realised that his mother, always intensely loyal to her friends and admirers, was hurt by it. The faint suggestion was still there, but he was so accustomed to it now that it no longer struck him. He had even come to think her pretty, so often had his mother pointed out to him the beauty of her wiry springy hair, and the smoothness of her pallid lifeless skin. And then, of course, there was her disposition. "Such a sweet girl," Stella had said times innumerable. "So kind and good-tempered and utterly unselfish."

He and Oliver had once resented Frances's persistent intrusion into their home circle, but now they accepted it as a matter of course, had even come to depend on her for various small domestic services and were glad to think of her attendance on Stella during their absence.

Yes, thought Charles, looking down at her, she was a dear little thing, kind and helpful and cheerful. Some people would call her dull. He and Oliver used to call her dull. But dullness often meant loyalty and unselfishness and faithfulness. He remembered a talk that he had had with his mother a few nights ago. She had told him that she hoped he would marry and had described the kind of wife that she thought would suit him best. The description had been so like Frances and so unlike Pat that at the time he had resented it. His mind turned to it now, as if for comfort against Pat's unkindness.

"Darling . . . don't trust that feeling of 'being in love,' " his mother had said. "It's so often just infatuation and soon wears off. I've seen it happen over and over agin. When you choose I want you to choose wisely—someone you know well, someone, perhaps, not exciting but whom you've learnt to trust, someone loyal and dependable. It's the solid qualities that wear, you know, darling."

Certainly he knew Frances well (she had been a constant visitor in every house and flat they had had since they were children). Certainly she wasn't exciting. Certainly she was loyal and dependable. She had all the solid virtues. Marriage with her would not mean that plunge into the unknown that marriage with anyone else would mean. It would not jar or disturb his relations with his mother, which were part of the solid background of his life. . . . Last night Stella had said to him,

"Be nice to Frances tomorrow, Charles. She's—fonder of you than you realise."

He glanced down at Frances again. Yes, she *was* quite good-looking. Her hair was pretty, her skin had that thick white opaqueness frequently compared by novelists to a magnolia petal, her eyes, though small, were a deep blue. She wasn't particularly intelligent, but—she wasn't exacting. She chattered on and on about anything and everything and you needn't listen unless you wanted to. . . . She made no demands on you. She would be restful to come back to after a day's hard work. Pat was just the opposite. She had a quick wit and a lively intelligence, and she expected her companion to bestir himself to keep pace with her. With Pat one couldn't sink comfortably into a rut of mental laziness, as one could with Frances. . . . But in any case he wasn't going to think of Pat again. Thank heaven, he had found out in time that she was hard, selfish and jealous, despite her shallow charm.

He wondered what Frances thought of him. He knew that at one time he had been invested with glamour in her eyes simply because he was Stella's son, but he thought that lately she had begun to take a little more interest in him for his own sake.

She still adored Stella, of course, but the more he thought of it the better he thought it would be to have a wife who adored his mother. It would avoid emotional complications that he shrank from facing even in his thoughts. . . . Yes, she was comfortable, familiar, he had a feeling of quiet friendship for her, and his mother had pointed out that it was the feeling of quiet friendship that lasted, not the transitory ecstasy known as "falling in love." Was it friendship or was it simply a sensation of relaxation, a feeling that, so uncritical was she, it didn't matter what he did or said? He gave up the problem with a shrug. It was too complicated. The only thing he was sure of was that he did not want to marry Pat.

"We'd better not sit down on the grass, I suppose," Frances was saying. "It's always a bit damp, and you're inclined to rheumatism, aren't you?"

Her solicitude both touched and irritated him. His mother always fussed over his health, and Frances imitated her attitude to it. Pat, he remembered, had infuriated his mother by laughing at her concern over his occasional catarrh and rheumatism. Both were slight enough, but they had attained a certain importance in the family circle through Stella's insistence on them, and, though Charles himself laughed at her, he, too, secretly resented Pat's ridicule. Frances, of course, had always taken them seriously, had discussed them earnestly with Stella and frequently copied paragraphs from the papers on diet or other cures. Frances was a good cook and a capable housekeeper. Pat boasted that housekeeping bored her. Why on earth did his thoughts keep returning to Pat, he asked himself impatiently. He definitely disliked the girl. As for asking her to marry him, he could hardly believe that he had ever even considered it. . . .

"Here's a seat," said Frances. She inspected it anxiously. "I think it's quite dry. It's difficult to tell, of course. Wood holds the damp so."

"I'm sure it's all right," said Charles.

"I'm thinking of your catarrh," said Frances. "You can't be too careful." They sat down side by side on the narrow backless wooden seat. "How's that new man at your works going on?"

She never forgot anything he had told her about work, and would talk, for hours about it. About his that or about Stella or about herself or himself. What he thought of as "chittering." . . . It demanded no effort or response from the listener. His heart warmed to her suddenly. She was a dear little thing—affectionate, faithful, hard-working and—yes, pretty enough. A man didn't really want a beauty for a wife, didn't want someone who would attract and disturb other men. Pat was too beautiful, too disturbing, too exacting. Again he thanked his stars that he had discovered it in time. Suddenly he decided to take the plunge, to become definitely engaged to Frances. He wanted something to protect him from those pictures of Pat that kept flashing into his mind before he could guard himself against them.

"Frances," he said, "there's something I want to ask you. I——"

He stopped in sudden panic and ended lamely, "I wonder if you know what it is. . . ."

Frances turned and looked at him. Her small blue eyes protruded, and a dull unbecoming flush crept up slowly in patches from her neck, as it always did in moments of emotion. He had often seen her looking at his mother like that.

"Yes," she said. "At least, your mother was talking to me last night. . . ."

Her voice trailed away, and she waited for him to put his offer into words. A sense of outrage seized him, a feeling of suspicion, as if some conspiracy had been hatched between the two of them, a conspiracy from which he was excluded and which was even directed against him. Oliver had breasted the hill and was strolling down towards them. It was a heaven-sent delivery.

"There's Oliver," he said. He rose and waved to him. "Hello, Oliver! Come and watch the view."

Stella and Biddy still sat on the hill where they had had the picnic lunch. Charles and Frances had set off for a walk together, and Oliver had gone alone.

"I shall be glad to have Frances as a daughter-in-law," said Stella suddenly.

"Yes," agreed Biddy. "She's a nice girl."

"I want Charles to marry young," went on Stella. "I think it's good for a man to marry young, before he's got too set in his ways. When two young people marry they have a chance of growing together forming their tastes and habits together. I'm not one of those possessive mothers who want to keep their sons with them. All I care for is my boys' happiness."

"I know . . ." murmured Biddy, and added after a slight pause, "Is he very fond of her?"

"Yes," said Stella. "I had a talk with him about it the other night. He feels for her that quiet sound affection that's the basis of a happy married life . . . He's an attractive boy, you know, and an attractive boy has many temptations. Marriage is a—safe-guard. That girl I told you about in the flat below—Pat Forrester—has been trying hard to entangle him." She wrinkled her smooth brow and sighed. "I've been terribly worried about it. She's a thoroughly fast girl, and has a very bad influence over him. Frances, you know, is a really good woman and I shall be glad to get him safely married to her. I know that he'll be happy with her."

"You'll miss him, won't you, Stella?" said Biddy.

"I've not thought of that part of it," smiled Stella. "I've only thought of Charles's happiness, but, as a matter of fact, they won't be able to set up house for a few years. They'll live with Oliver and me in the flat. The boys have separate bedrooms, and Charles's is quite a fair-sized one. I suppose that really Charles isn't earning enough to marry on at all yet and that worldly-wise people would advise him not to, but"—she shrugged—"I'm not worldly-wise."

Biddy drew a deep breath. She felt that the moment had come for broaching the subject of her legacy.

"Stella," she said, "there's something that I want to ask you. I told you in my letter that Aunt Flora had left me all her money, didn't I?"

Stella nodded.

"I want you to—let me give it to you—all of it. No, don't say anything yet. Let me tell you. I don't need it for myself. I couldn't spend any more money than I do now even if I tried. You know what I mean. . . . I'm in my own little rut and I'm happy in it. I shouldn't know *how* to spend more money even if I wanted to and I don't want to. So, Stella, won't you take it, just to please me and help the boys?"

Stella was silent for so long that Biddy thought she was angry, but when she spoke her voice was reassuringly tender.

"No, darling, I shouldn't dream of taking it. We have all the money we need. I'm—frightened of money, Biddy. It doesn't bring happiness, you know. Too often it brings false values—self-indulgence and ostentation and materialism. Even if I wanted it, my pride wouldn't let me take it, but I don't want it, darling." She smiled—the radiantly sweet smile that had thrilled Biddy ever since she was a little girl. "I've always been afraid of money. I've always disliked moneyed people. I'm happy and the boys are happy. Well, you see us pretty frequently. Do you think that money would make us any happier than we are?"

"N-no, but, Stella, think what you could do for them. I've been thinking of it such a lot. They could go to winter sports and—and—on cruises and things. They could travel and have lovely holidays. And—you said once that you never let them go to stay with school friends because you couldn't afford to repay the hospitality. Well, they could do that sort of thing if you had the money. And think of Charles and Frances. They could have a home of their own, and——"

She stopped. Stella had gone very white.

"Please never speak of this again, Biddy," she said in a low voice. "If you do it will—hurt me very much. I do appreciate your kindness, dear, but you—don't understand. Let's not talk of it any more."

"I'm sorry if I've hurt you, Stella," said Biddy humbly. "I know that I'm very clumsy. But—I shan't use any of it and I shall leave it all to you in my will. You can't stop me doing that."

"Darling," smiled Stella, "I hope that you'll outlive me by many, many years. . . . Here are Charles and Oliver and Frances. Frances looks rather pale. I wonder . . ."

Chapter Seventeen

For the next three years Biddy was a familiar figure driving about the neighbourhood of Runeham in her Austin Seven. In the spring of 1926, as she was returning from a Women's Institute meeting through a thick fog, she ran into the back of a stationary bus and was killed immediately.

It happened that Stella was alone in the flat when she received the solicitor's letter telling her that Biddy had left her thirty thousand pounds. At first she said nothing to Charles and Oliver about it. She tried, in fact, to put it right out of her mind. When she did think about it, she felt angry and afraid. Biddy ought to have known that she didn't want it. She never had wanted money. It meant nothing to her and she had often told Biddy so. She thought of what Biddy had said; "They could go to winter sports and on cruises. They could travel . . ." and her fear and anger deepened. As if she wanted things like that for them! As if they wanted them for themselves! . . . "And Charles could have a home of his own. . . ." As if Charles or even Frances wanted a home of their own! They had been engaged now for a year and were to be married next summer. Charles was still with the same engineering firm and still earning a very small salary. He had heard of several better paid posts abroad and in the North of England and had been inclined to apply for them, but Stella had always dissuaded him from doing so.

She knew how lonely he would be away from her and how many temptations beset a young man removed from a good home influence.

Oliver had got a First Class at Oxford and was now living at home. He had wanted to obtain a post on some newspaper, but

Stella had induced him to take up writing as a free lance instead, and submit his work to editors. She had turned his bedroom into a combined study-bedroom and had taken a good deal of trouble over it, buying a writing-desk, a divan and a deep easy-chair, making new curtains and cushions.

The arrangement, she considered, benefited both of them. It was nice for her to have his company, when he was not working, and her presence helped to keep at bay those moods of depression that so easily assailed him. He had had one or two short stories accepted by good class magazines but was apt to be discouraged by any setback. Often he said that he would prefer to earn a definite salary so that he could contribute his share to housekeeping, but Stella always beat down his arguments, assuring him that she did not need any contribution from him towards housekeeping, and that, in any case, his company was in itself ample repayment for any extra trouble and expense. And certainly she managed excellently. She did all the cooking and housework without help, kept the little flat immaculate, planned, as in the old days, all their jaunts and holidays and was always ready in the evening to entertain the boys and listen to their stories of the day's happenings.

Frances still adored her but was at times somewhat difficult and unreasonable. An engaged girl's nerves, Stella told herself, were notoriously uncertain. Charles and Oliver, too, seemed to irritate each other, and she frequently had to intervene to keep the peace. It needed all her tact and patience, indeed, to guide the little family craft over the shallows and through the hidden currents of their life together.

"That's always been my job," she said once with a rueful, rather weary little smile to Miss Pattern. "Sometimes I feel I'd love to start being moody and touchy myself and let someone else do the soothing down. It would be such a novel experience. . . . They're all darlings and I know they're fond of me, but I don't think that one of them has the faintest idea of all I have to do to keep the wheels running smoothly."

It was Miss Pattern to whom she first confided the news of the legacy, without mentioning the exact sum.

"Do you know," she said slowly, "I've always been frightened of money. I've seen what it's done to people—how it's blurred and blunted their vision, and I'm frightened of it for my boys. I told Biddy that I didn't want it. She was a dear in lots of ways, but she was a materialist at heart. She never understood the things that really mattered to me. I've always believed, not only that money can't bring happiness, but that very very often it destroys it. Now answer me quite honestly. Do you think that I and the boys and Frances could possibly be happier than we are now? Please be quite honest."

"No, dear, certainly you wouldn't," said Miss Pattern, gazing fervently at Stella's pretty flabby pink-and-white face. No doubt at all that Stella was becoming definitely and uncompromisingly fat. She was fond of chocolates and generally kept a box of them in her sewing-drawer downstairs, munching them at intervals throughout the day. The boys and Frances teased her about the weakness and frequently brought her home tins of sweets or boxes of chocolates. She loved cream buns and éclairs and meringues. "I've got a sweet tooth," she would say gaily. "I'm not ashamed of it. Sugar's good for the nerves. That's why I'm so good-tempered."

Miss Pattern, who was herself painfully thin, admired Stella's soft curves and the plumpness of the smooth fair cheeks. She admired everything about Stella.

"I think you're absolutely right, dear," she continued. "Absolutely right. ... You and I feel the same about that sort of thing. Kind hearts are more than coronets." She looked grave, then brightened suddenly. "You could give it all away to a charity."

"Y-yes," agreed Stella without much enthusiasm. "I could do that, of course."

She told the boys quite casually a few days later. "Darlings," she said, "I've got a piece of news for you. I've had a little legacy."

They had finished supper and were in the cosy sitting-room, the curtains drawn, the fire burning brightly. Stella always had a bright fire and a clean hearth.

"A what?" said Oliver, looking up from his evening paper.

"A little legacy, darling," repeated Stella brightly. "Biddy left it to me. Quite a tiny one but definitely a legacy."

"What are you going to do with it?" said Charles. "Or haven't you decided yet?"

"Of course I've decided," smiled Stella. "I decided that at once. I'm not going to do anything with it. I'm going to put it away for your children."

"How much is it?" said Oliver after a pause.

"Well, if you have two children each," said Stella playfully, "they'll each get a nice little nest egg of a hundred pounds."

That fixed the legacy definitely at £400.

"But you ought to spend it on yourself," objected Oliver. "Don't save it. Our children honestly don't want it. Have a maid or buy some new furniture or get yourself some Paris models or something."

"No," said Stella firmly. "There's nothing in the whole world I want. I love this shabby old room and I love my shabby old clothes and I love pottering about and doing the housework."

Oliver looked round the room. It *was* shabby. But Stella was quite firm on the point—a little hurt, indeed, that he should have suggested any improvement.

"I know the loose covers are a bit worn," she said, "but I was going to get some material in the sales and make some new ones. It would be too ridiculous to pay a lot of unnecessary money on having them made now. And you know I love making them myself—apart from its being so much cheaper."

She firmly refused, too, Oliver's suggestion that she should go to a good dress house and get at least one well-designed model.

"Oh, darling!" she laughed ruefully, "I'd hate to be smart."

"I don't want you to be smart," he said, "but I'd love you to have just one really good thing."

"Don't you like my mauve?" said Stella anxiously. "I've only had it about a year."

Oliver often found his fastidiousness revolted by the sight of Stella's now shapeless figure dressed in the cheap clothes that she affected. (She haunted sales and would often bring home dresses or coats much reduced in price but badly fitting or of quite unsuitable style.) He was deeply ashamed of this, remembering how Stella had spent her money on his education, how she had sacrificed herself for him and Charles ever since he could remember.

"Yes, darling," he said hastily. "I think your mauve's lovely."

There was a chance, of course, that they might hear the true facts about her legacy, but it was a remote one. They knew no one in Runeham now and were seldom at home when the post arrived, bringing letters from the solicitor. Stella had always seen to her business herself, and had never confided in them or consulted them. It did not even occur to them to question her suggestion of £400.

"She's just wonderful," said Frances to Charles. "Anyone else I know would have used it to make things easier for herself. She never even thinks of herself. . . . She never has done. . . ."

There were times when Charles was eager to marry Frances, so as to get the thing over and settled. There were times when the thought of marriage to her filled him with panic. ("Every engaged man feels the same, darling," Stella assured him. "It's just nerves. . . . There's nothing to worry about.") As the engagement wore on something of Frances's original meekness vanished and she showed signs of latent shrewishness and ill-temper. She and Charles often quarrelled and made it up, and for some time after the making-up were happy and in love with each other. But always there was an underlying tension that Charles couldn't analyse. He took a perverse delight in proving her wrong over any detail, however small, and frequently found himself, to his shame, drawing attention to her shortcomings, "showing her up," as it were, in public. Oddly, they quarrelled most often about Stella. At any hint of criticism of Stella from one, the other would flare up into quite disproportionate anger.

Stella smiled tenderly over their occasional sulkiness. "The darlings!" she murmured to Miss Pattern. "An engagement's such a trying time when people really love each other as these children do. They'll look back and laugh at it all when they're married."

Charles often felt acutely unhappy, but he had a curious feeling of helplessness, as if he were being carried along by a current so strong that he could not fight against it. Sometimes he played with the idea of breaking off the engagement, but the thought of the distress this would cause both Frances and Stella seemed to put the idea outside the bounds of possibility. And he didn't really want to break it off, even when Frances irritated him most. He honestly thought that he was in love with her (why else should the touch of her soft white cheeks and red mouth stir him so?), and Stella had firmly planted in him the belief that she would make an ideal wife. Also, the fact that she and Stella got on well together still influenced him more than he would have admitted to himself. He shrank from the idea of discord between his wife and mother, and there would be, he was convinced, no question of that between Stella and Frances. He felt that the prospect of coming home to a happy well-run home, a devoted capable wife and a devoted capable mother, should be all that any man could want, and he wondered despairingly why the prospect failed to thrill him as it should. He clung to the conviction that he was in love with Frances. The only other affair he had in his life to compare to his feeling for Frances was the love he had felt for Pat Forrester, and Stella had taught him to look on that as an infatuation, a passion essentially base. . . . He had seen nothing of Pat since they had left the St. John's Wood flat and had tried hard to school himself not to think of her.

Stella herself in these days was unfailingly placid and even-tempered. Plump, serene, smiling, she pottered about the little flat or sallied forth with shopping basket on housekeeping expeditions. Since she had received her legacy her housekeeping had gradually become more and more niggardly.

"It's an 'eating up' meal, boys, I'm afraid," she would say, "but you know how much I hate waste."

Anything that went up in price was immediately crossed off her menu.

"I'm sorry, children," she would say, "but we shall just have to do without it. Honestly we can't afford it at that price."

She was a good cook and would grudge no time or trouble in making appetising inexpensive dishes.

The only thing that hurt or angered her was for Oliver to suggest getting a post with a regular salary, though she secretly encouraged the resentment that Charles felt at the idea of his "loafing about" and "not pulling his weight."

"Of course it complicates housekeeping," she admitted to him. "I'm most particular to spend my own money on Oliver's share and not let any of yours go to it."

"The lazy lout!" Charles growled.

"He isn't lazy, Charles. He works."

"Works! Moons about the place, you mean. He doesn't know what work means. He ought to turn out and earn his living."

"I love having him at home, Charles."

"Oh, you always make excuses for him,"—his face softened,—"and for everyone. But I'm going to have a straight talk with him."

"No, you mustn't, Charles. I shall never forgive you if you mention it to him. Promise, Charles. . . ."

And Charles would promise.

It kept the brothers apart, as something had always kept them apart ever since they were children.

An old pupil of Brookfield School, one of Stella's many admirers, had sent Stella an invitation to her wedding. It happened that the wedding was to take place on a Saturday, when both Charles and Oliver were at home and Frances had come as usual to spend the afternoon. Charles had suggested a taxi, but Stella had been horrified.

"Nonsense, darling! I can't afford luxuries like that. And I'd much rather go by bus in any case."

She went up to her bedroom to get ready, then came down to the others in the sitting-room. She had on a shabby navy-blue suit that she had worn for several years and a faded navy-blue felt hat.

"Well," she said brightly, "here I am! I'll be back as soon as I can. Am I all right?"

They looked at her in silence, secretly dismayed by the dowdiness of her appearance. Somehow they had not noticed it in the ordinary routine of their lives, but for a wedding . . .

Frances, who was feeling sulky because Charles had refused her suggestion of going to the pictures, said suddenly,

"I should have thought you'd have bought something new for a wedding."

The smile faded from Stella's face.

"What?" she said. Her tone was sharply—even shrilly—suspicious. "And have people think I've got money?"

Frances did not falter into retreat and apology as she usually did at the first hint of anger from Stella. Instead she fixed her eyes in sullen defiance on Stella's face and said,

"Well, you *have* got money, haven't you?"

Stella went very white. She did not speak for some time, and when she did speak her voice was low and quiet, though she was trembling.

"I have a little money, Frances, as you all know, but I'm not going to spend any of it on myself. I think I've already told you that I'm keeping it to leave to my grandchildren."

Then she went from the room without looking at them again.

The storm broke as soon as the door had closed on her.

"You blasted little fool!" burst out Charles furiously. "What d'you mean by upsetting her? What business is it of yours, anyway?"

The scene had made him feel sick and ashamed—he couldn't have told why—and it afforded him a vague relief to vent his anger on Frances.

"Leave the girl alone," drawled Oliver. "It wasn't her fault. Good Lord! You'd have thought Mother would have got something decent to wear. She has money, but she won't spend it."

Charles swung round on him savagely. Oliver's quiet drawling voice always infuriated him, and the resentment of years broke its dam.

"Shut up and keep out of it," he snarled. "You're a nice one to talk, aren't you? A lot of help you've been, loafing about and living on her, you——"

Frances broke in with a wailing hysterical cry,

"I hate you! I *hate* the whole lot of you. I wouldn't marry you now if——"

She tore the ring from her finger, flung it across the room, snatched up her hat and ran out, slamming the door.

"Hadn't you better go after her?" said Oliver with a faint sneer.

"Shut up, damn you!" said Charles between his teeth.

He went from the flat and stood staring uncertainly up and down the road. Frances was not in sight. He set off in the opposite direction to the one which she would have taken and strode forward, his face set and scowling. He didn't know where he was going. He only wanted to get as far as possible from the sultry poisonous atmosphere that seemed to have risen from the depths, where it had always lurked, to the surface of their lives. The sudden hatred of both Frances and Oliver (if he had stayed in the room a moment longer he would have knocked the sneer off his face for good and all) that had seized him, filled him with terror. He wanted to go somewhere clean and wholesome . . . somewhere away from it all.

He didn't realise that he had made his way back to the house in St. John's Wood till he found himself at the gate of it—face to face with Pat, who was just going in. They stared at each other in silence.

"What on earth's the matter, Charles?" she said at last. "You look as if you'd seen a ghost."

"So do you," he said.

She gave a twisted smile.

"Perhaps I have. Perhaps we both have."

"Pat . . . is there anywhere we can talk?"

She hesitated.

"You can come in if you like. No one's at home but me."

He followed her up to the sitting-room.

"Well . . .?" she said.

He fixed his eyes on her sombrely.

"Pat, I'm a darned fool."

She shrugged and went over to the window, where she stood looking down at the road.

"I told you that some time ago, didn't I?" she said dryly.

"I've been wretched," he went on, "ever since—ever since——"

"You mean—you've tried to hate me and couldn't?"

"Yes."

"It's been a bit like that with me, too."

She wheeled round as she spoke and found herself in his arms. She let him kiss her, then gently freed herself from his embrace.

"Actually," she said, "I suppose you're still engaged to Frances."

"Actually I'm not. She broke it off about half an hour ago. . . . Pat, you do love me?"

She nodded.

"I've tried hard not to," she said.

"Let's be married soon."

She frowned thoughtfully.

"Surely it's not quite as simple as all that?"

"It is," he persisted. "I know that in the old days Mother didn't—understand, but lately she and Frances haven't been hitting it off too well. I'm sure she'll soon get used to the idea of——"

"Listen, Charles," interrupted Pat. "I meant what I said four years ago. I love you and I'll marry you, but only on one condition—that you never see or speak to your mother again after our marriage."

"*Pat!*" he said aghast. "You can't ask me to do that."

"Even when we have children," she went on inflexibly, "it's to make no difference. It must be as if she were dead. If you agree to that, I'll marry you. If not, I won't."

His face was as white as hers. He was silent for a long time, then said,

"You don't know what you're asking. . . . You don't realise what I mean to her."

"You mean nothing at all to her," she said steadily. "You're—just part of her setting. She sees nothing but herself. You're a sort of stage property to her. You help to display her—to herself and others, but chiefly to herself. I think that if you went it would be quite a long time before she realised you weren't there."

"You don't know her . . ." he burst out.

"I do know her. I know her better than you do. I know that if we didn't cut clean away from the start, she'd wreck our marriage. She doesn't know why she hates me, but I do. It's because I see her as she really is, and she'll never forgive me for that as long as she lives." Her eyes were fixed on his. "Well?"

"I—I can't hurt her as much as that."

"You won't hurt her. She can rearrange the stage quite quickly and effectively. She'll enjoy it in a way. It will give her a new rôle. ... Oh, I'm sorry, Charles. I won't say anything more. I'm not going to quarrel with you again. We quarrelled enough in the old days, didn't we? If it's 'goodbye,' let's say it quickly and not feel bitter. ..."

"I can't let you go, Pat."

"There's only one way to keep me."

He looked at her. Her eyes, in the pale oval of her face, met his levelly, steadfast and searching. Healing and peace shone from them, sending light into the dark places of his soul. He drew a long deep sigh.

"Very well," he said.

Chapter Eighteen

OLIVER opened his eyes, yawned and looked at the clock on the mantelpiece. It was an expensive travelling clock that Stella had given him last Christmas. Half-past seven. . . . He needn't think of getting up yet for another half-hour.

His eyes turned sleepily to the open window, which framed a piece of blue sky, flecked with trailing white clouds. For a moment he felt bewildered. He had expected to see the plane tree, its leaves moving gently in the breeze. But that, of course, had been the Bloomsbury flat. . . . Or the red chimneys of the house opposite. But that, of course, had been in Hampstead. . . . They had "moved" again last week. He was so accustomed to the process now that it no longer worried him. Quite suddenly and unexpectedly Stella would discover all sorts of drawbacks to the flat that had seemed so perfect when first they moved into it, and, before he realised what was happening, she would have found another, and the removing van would be at the door. . . . Always, wherever she went, she quickly made a new circle of friends, and from each sojourn remained a few faithful adherents who visited her regularly in her new quarters and formed the nucleus of the next circle. The types seldom varied. They were the elderly, the second-rate, the very young. Oliver called them "Mother's people" and thought of them sometimes with indulgent amusement, sometimes with angry irritation. . . . One thing they had in common. They adored Stella and were never tired of telling each other how wonderful she was, what a hard life she had had, how shamefully Charles had treated her, and what a splendid mother she had been to both him and Oliver.

He glanced at the calendar that stood on his writing-desk. There was some special connection with the date, and at first he couldn't think what it was. Then he remembered.

It was Charles's birthday. . . . He hadn't seen Charles since that day, seven years ago now, when he had come into the room, his face white and set, to announce that he was going to marry Pat Forrester and to have no further communication of any kind with Stella. Oliver had admired Stella then. She had looked at Charles for a moment in silence, then said quietly,

"If that's the way you feel, Charles, it's no use discussing it."

"I haven't come to discuss it," Charles had said. "I've come to say 'Goodbye' and—I'm sorry."

"You might have had the honesty to omit that," Stella had said.

Altogether she came off the better of the two in the short interview. Charles was embarrassed and shamefaced, Stella calm and dignified. Even when he had gone—carrying his suitcase, walking slowly and unsteadily but without looking back—there had been no reaction. She was pale but dry-eyed, her golden head held high.

"It's outrageous," Oliver had said, starting to the door. "I'm going to fetch him back and——"

She put out a hand to stop him. "No, darling," she had said. "Let him go. He's made his choice. Let's never speak of it again."

When Frances heard what had happened she had wept and raged and flung wild accusations indiscriminately at Charles, Stella and Oliver.

"It's all your fault," she said to Stella, her voice choked by sobs. "We'd have been married by now if it hadn't been for you. . . . I've slaved for you ever since I can remember—done your dirty work and fetched and carried for you and been snubbed by you. . . . Oh, I've seen through you, though I've tried not to for long enough. You didn't want us to get married because you wanted to keep us both dancing attendance on you."

"Don't be such a little idiot," interrupted Stella contemptuously. "And don't blame me because you're too stupid and plain and unattractive to keep a man. I tried to give you your chance, but you were too much of a fool to take it. I don't wonder he threw you over."

Frances covered her face with her hands and burst into a fresh gush of tears, boo-hooing aloud like a child.

"You're cruel. . . . I wish I'd never met you. . . ."

Stella took the girl's wrists and jerked them down from her face. Oliver, sick with revulsion, turned to the window and stood there, hands in pocket, frowning down at the street below.

"Control yourself," Stella was saying. "Do you want to bring the neighbours in?"

For answer Frances freed her hands and, still sobbing convulsively, struck Stella smartly across the check.

"You beast!" she sobbed. "You *beast!*"

Oliver swung round, aghast, but Stella did not seem dismayed. She stood looking at Frances with a faint smile on her lips. The cheek that Frances had struck flamed red. The other was white as paper.

"Now go, please, Frances," she said, "and never come here again."

Blindly Frances had stumbled to the door.

Stella turned to Oliver, still with that little smile on her lips.

"I'm sorry to inflict this scene on you," she said. "How impossible the girl is! It'll be a relief in a way to be rid of her. . . . And now I'll get tea."

Frances wrote a series of letters—abject, apologetic, defiant, unhappy—and Stella flung them into the waste-paper basket without replying to them. She came to the flat, and Stella did not answer the door. She waited till Stella came out, and Stella passed her without looking at her. . . . After that, she gave it up. Oliver, though he had always disliked her, felt a little compunction, but Stella never appeared to give the matter another thought. Frances went out of their life as if she had never been in it. When he had mentioned her by chance a day or two ago Stella had frowned and said,

"Frances? . . . Who's that, dear?"

She remembered almost at once, but he had been amazed to realise that for the moment she really had forgotten.

She had not given up Charles quite so easily. When the birth of a daughter was announced in *The Times* about a year after the marriage, Stella sent the string of pearls that had belonged to Aunt Fanny—the only valuable piece of jewellery she possessed. It was returned in a registered parcel without a letter. About a year after that she went alone to see him . . . and came back the same evening, looking pale and tired, but quite cheerful. She did not mention the result of the visit, and Oliver knew better than to question her. She made no further attempts at reconciliation and began gradually to remove all traces of Charles from the flat till everything connected with him—even the school groups in which he figured—had vanished from it. Last year Oliver happened to meet some people who knew Charles and Pat. They spoke of them quite casually, but what they said showed Oliver a new Charles—happy, confident, with a boyish high spirit and humour that had been lacking in his real boyhood. "Pat's a grand girl and they adore each other. . . . They've got two fine kids." Oliver was conscious both of relief and of an odd lurking resentment. He realised with shame that something in him would have been glad to hear of Charles's un-happiness. Charles had taken his freedom and he should have been made to pay for it. . . . After much deliberation he decided to tell Stella what he had heard. He shrank from causing her pain, but he felt that it would not have been quite honest to withhold the news.

She looked at him blankly for a moment, then said,

"Oh yes . . . thanks, Oliver," and began to talk of something else. He had realised then with amazement that she wasn't acting, that, except as part of the "hard life" story on which she regaled her admirers, Charles no longer existed for her.

There was a tap at his bedroom door, and Stella entered, wearing a dressing-gown and carrying a tray containing a cup of tea, a plate of bread-and-butter and a newspaper. She always made early morning tea in her bedroom and brought a cup for him. She put it down on the table by his bed and stood smiling down at him.

"Here's your tea and the newspaper, darling," she said. "Have you slept well?"

Stella was now over fifty. Her figure was plump and shapeless, but her skin was still unlined, though it had lost its delicacy of colouring, and her hair (she "touched it up" a little nowadays) was still thick and wavy. Oliver thought that she looked like a little girl at this hour in the morning, wearing an old blue pinafore-like dressing-gown, her hair hanging about her shoulders.

"Yes, thanks," he said, sitting up and taking the tray from her. He hadn't slept well. He seldom did sleep well nowadays. . . .

"Drink it while it's hot. I'll fetch mine in and have it with you, shall I?"

"Yes . . . do," he agreed.

She went from the room, and he lay back, slowly sipping his tea. It was made exactly as he liked it, and the bread-and-butter was wafer-thin. She ministered assiduously to his creature comforts, making of them cunning bonds that held him to her. She encouraged his weaknesses, too, catering for his whims and fancies, even inventing them for him and fastening them on him, as it were ("Oliver likes the milk put into his tea-cup first. . . ." "Oliver can't sleep unless he has a cup of something hot just before he goes to bed"), till he came to believe in them himself.

She entered the room now, carrying her tea-cup, and sat down in the small armchair beside his writing-table.

"Going to be a marvellous day, dear," she said. "Did you hear the birds about five?"

"No."

"They were lovely. It might have been right in the country. I do love to hear them. They seem to sing themselves right out quite suddenly and go to sleep again. If I were a musician I'd try to do that . . . to get that wonderful burst of song . . . but I suppose that our clumsy human instruments couldn't reproduce it."

He grunted and looked at her with a certain sardonic envy. The early morning never found Stella moody or silent. She was bright and chatty and cheerful from the moment she got out of bed—proof, too, against the armour of sullenness with which Oliver often tried to ward off her cheerfulness.

She turned to the writing-table and took up a sheet of manuscript that was lying there.

"This is the one about the retired couple, isn't it, dear?" she said. "How are you getting on with it?"

Something in him seemed to curl up and shrivel, as it always did when she asked him about his work. And she asked him incessantly, insisting on knowing every detail of it, dragging from him the plots of the stories he was writing or had in mind. He had tried answering curtly in monosyllables, and she had ignored his rudeness, continuing to probe and cross-examine with undiminished sweetness. He had tried asking her outright not to question him about his work, and immediately there had taken place one of those scenes the memory of which turned him sick with humiliation. Her blue eyes had filled with tears, and she had wept, her fat little body shaking with sobs. "Darling, don't shut me out. I can't bear it. You're all I've got left. You're all I have to live for now. If you leave me I shall die. . . ."

"I'm not going to leave you," said Oliver, gritting his teeth.

"But you are doing. . . . You are leaving me when you try to shut me out. We might as well be miles apart if you won't let me take an interest in your work . . . if you shut me away from everything that matters to you. . . . I've lived for you all these years. It'll kill me if you turn me away like this. . . ."

She clung to him, sobbing, laying her head on his shoulder.

"Darling, don't be so unkind to me. I must share things with you. . . . I can't bear it if you won't let me."

The scene left him shattered. He couldn't face another. He gave in. He had been secretly horrified by the sudden hatred of her that had seized him when she put her arms round him, pressing her wet flabby cheek against his. . . . The memory of it had tormented him for weeks, revealing, as it seemed to him, an unsuspected depth of blackness in his soul. No, he couldn't face another scene like that. Better—just answer the questions she asked him about his work. Better show her his manuscripts (for there had been another scene of the same sort when she found that he had sent off a manuscript to an editor without letting her read it). It couldn't do any harm. But it did harm, and in his heart he knew it. It dried up the clear tenuous stream of his inspiration. It paralysed his sensitiveness of expression. As he wrote, he was always aware of her watching eye, of her inevitable criticisms ("Darling, I don't think a nice girl would say that," "I shouldn't go in for that sort of story, darling. It isn't like my boy," or "Couldn't you alter the ending, darling? It seems so—unsatisfactory"). He found himself compromising as he wrote, putting in things that he knew would please her, simply because he knew they would please her, toning down, sometimes eliminating, what he knew would offend her. It was as if her fingers were on the pen with his as he wrote, fat podgy little fingers rubbing away the delicate evanescent bloom of his talent. When he pandered to her taste, he suffered an abasement of spiritual humiliation, and yet he found himself doing it more and more. He had always been prone to follow the way of least resistance, and beneath Stella's yielding sweetness was something so ruthless and indomitable that he had long ago ceased trying to fight against it. There were times when he managed to see himself as the devoted self-sacrificing son, but more often he knew himself for the poor thing he was, the poor thing that Stella and his own weakness had made of him.

Some years ago he had had some stories for children about animal characters accepted by one of the monthly magazines. Stella had approved of them and kept advising him to write more of the same kind, though he had long since worn out the thin vein of that particular inspiration. She discouraged him from attempting any more ambitious work with an urgency that, he sometimes suspected, hid a secret fear—a fear lest more ambitious work might give him a way of escape from her ("I shouldn't attempt a novel, dear. ... You're so good at short stories and people are seldom good at both. I should keep to the sort of thing that you know you can do"). Her friends frequently heard her boast of the help she gave him in his work ("Oliver and I are collaborators, you know. He discusses all his work with me").

She read through the manuscript and replaced it on his desk.

"I think that's going to be very nice, dear," she said, "very nice indeed. Will you finish it this morning?"

"I don't know," he answered shortly.

She drained her tea-cup and put it down on the tray.

"Don't hurry getting up, dear," she said. "I've got some kidneys for breakfast. I thought they'd be nice fried up with bacon and tomatoes. I had an awful job finding them. Everyone seemed to be out of them. But I said to myself, 'The boy likes kidneys to his breakfast and he shall have them.' You do like them, don't you, darling?"

"Yes," said Oliver. "Thanks."

Titbits, he thought, pushed through the bars of his cage to keep him contented. He used to hate himself for having such thoughts and try to thrust them out of sight, but lately he had encouraged them, taking a malicious pleasure in them, as if in some way they punished her for the subtle tyranny she exercised over his spirit.

"Have a cigarette?" she said, taking a case out of the pocket of her dressing-gown.

"No, thank you."

"I think I'll have one," she said, ignoring his brusqueness. "I like a cigarette first thing in the morning and last thing at night. I don't smoke much in between, do I? Lucky for you," she laughed, "or I'd be smoking the cigarettes instead of giving them to you. . . . Nothing much in the paper, is there?"

He held the paper up in front of him and idly turned over the pages.

"No. . . . Oh, here's a concert on Saturday at the Albert Hall. I think I'll go to it."

He spoke casually enough, but his heart was beating quickly. He had known about the concert for days and had been wondering how he could manage to get to it without her accompanying him.

Something wary and alert came into her face. Her plump features seemed to sharpen.

"I'll come with you, shall I?" she said.

"It's modern music," he said, "Stravinsky and Ravel. I don't think you'd enjoy it."

"I would with you, Oliver," she said. "I always enjoy things with you."

There was a pleading in voice and eyes that broke down his defences. Like most over-sensitive people, he attributed his own sensitiveness to others and was incapable of deliberately saying or doing anything that he thought could cause pain. Despite the irritation she caused him, despite those sudden flashes of hatred for her that terrified him so ("It's just that I'm neurotic," he would excuse himself. "It's not me. It doesn't mean anything"), he was fond of her and suffered acutely when he thought he had hurt her by his ungraciousness.

He was silent for a moment, then said feebly,

"Oh well . . . let's go to the pictures instead."

She had little real appreciation of music, despite her youthful virtuosity at the piano, and he couldn't endure the thought of sitting through the concert with her beside him—fidgeting, looking round, obviously bored. . . .

("Oliver doesn't enjoy anything without me," he had often heard her say to her friends. "He likes me to go everywhere he goes just to keep him company.")

"Yes, that would be nice," she said. "Well, I'll take the tray down now, shall I? Won't you have your breakfast in bed, dear, just for a treat?"

"No, thanks."

She put his cup on the tray, smiling down at him, and went towards the door. He watched her go from the room. Her slippers were down-at-heel, her dressing-gown faded and threadbare. She had had them both as long as he could remember. She hated buying new clothes. . . .

Oliver had discovered the truth about her legacy quite by accident. He had met someone from Runeham in the tube, who had mentioned the sum casually, taking for granted that Oliver knew it. Oliver went home and taxed Stella with it. She had shown no embarrassment or dismay, had only laughed and said,

"Of course I was going to tell you about it sooner or later, dear. I wanted it to be a little surprise."

It was, she told him, all to come to him when she died. Charles and Charles's children were not to have any of it. She remained adamant to all his suggestions of using part of the money now. She didn't want to travel or move into a larger house or employ maids.

"We're so happy, darling," she said. "Let's go on as we are. . . . You can do what you like with it when I'm dead."

He took courage at last to ask her to advance him a sum so that he could take a holiday abroad.

She refused sweetly, but very firmly.

"I don't want you to leave me, dear. I couldn't bear to be without you. You probably won't have me for long now, and when I'm gone you can do what you like."

Though she spent little money on herself, she spent a good deal on Oliver's comfort, buying him expensive food and presents and paying all expenses when they went out together. She doled out pocket-money to him, however, very sparingly. . . .

Oliver threw back the bed clothes, got out of bed and went to the bathroom. Stella always saw to it that the water was warm for his morning bath and that everything he needed was at hand. As he took off dressing-gown and pyjamas, the mirror showed his body, gaunt and angular, his face lined and haggard, set in a mould of moodiness and indifference, if Stella looked young for her fifty-two years, Oliver certainly looked old for his thirty-one.

Though he had not thought of Charles for months, the memory of him kept returning now. He felt again that bitter envy, that unreasoning resentment. . . . Charles had escaped into the normal life of men and women. He himself had long ago given up the hope of escape. Without quite realising why, he knew that Stella would not let him go as easily as she had let Charles go. He was more important to her. He provided, in all probability, the last scene left to her in which she could play an effective lead. And it wasn't only that. The rot had seized upon his own soul. Though one part of him longed for freedom, the other part shrank from facing life without the comfort she provided, dreaded the plunge into the unknown, knew with soul-sick certainty that he had lost that enthusiasm and faith in himself that alone might have carried him to success.

As soon as he reached the dining-room and saw her sitting cheerful and smiling at the well-appointed breakfast-table, he knew that it was one of his bad days, days when everything about her—the sound of her voice, the touch of her hand, the sight of her round flabby face—filled him with revulsion. There were days when he enjoyed being with her, when she gave him that happy sheltered feeling that he had always had with her when he was a child, almost justifying the nickname of "Darby and Joan" that she laughingly gave them . . . but this was not one of them.

The table-cloth was spotless, the cutlery shining, the kidneys, which she served at once from an electrically heated dish, perfectly cooked, his coffee hot and just the strength he liked.

He was glad that no long envelope lay beside his plate, containing a returned MS. He felt that he couldn't have endured her questioning and sympathy. . . .

She had her own picture newspaper and read out pieces of news across the table as she ate.

"This Hitler man's been made Chancellor in Germany," she said. "Oh well, I don't suppose he can do much harm. . . ."

He answered in monosyllables, trying not to look at her. . . . As he raised his cup of coffee to his lips, his hand shook so that he almost spilt it. If only he could get away from her, he thought despairingly, just for a few weeks—away from her, among fresh people. But if he suggested a holiday she would take for granted that she should come too. It would mean pottering about some holiday resort with her, and she would become more on his nerves than ever because he would not have his work as an escape.

He leant back in his seat, his long thin nervous fingers drumming the table, his brows drawn together in a frown.

"You're not looking well, dear," she said suddenly. "How would you like to take a holiday this morning and come shopping with me?"

"No, thanks," he muttered. "I—I think I'll go straight up and work now."

He sat at his desk, with a half-filled sheet of foolscap in front of him, and rested his chin on his hands, gazing unseeingly into the distance ... while his mind slipped along the forbidden track to her money. He thought of the time when it would be his. He would travel ... get to know people ... young people ... literary people. Stella disapproved of what she called "modern youth" and he knew no young people of his own class. At intervals he indulged in furtive and unsavoury little love affairs that revolted his fastidiousness and left him sick with misery and remorse. Each time it happened he decided that it should be the last, but always he returned after an ever-lessening interval. ... When he had her money he would marry, have a home of his own, know people of his own sort. At present he was confined to the ever-changing but ever the same circle that surrounded Stella. ... He would form the literary and artistic contacts he had always longed to form, and they would stimulate his dulled mind and revivify that thread of vital talent that must still be there beneath the heavy discouragement and despondency. ... At first he had not allowed himself to think of her money, but of late he had thought about it more and more frequently. He tried to fix his attention on the story he was writing, but his thoughts persisted in returning to her money.

Familiar pictures passed and repassed before his eyes. He saw himself free—visiting Paris, Rome, Vienna, meeting people with the same tastes as himself, being received by other writers—if not as an equal, at least as a congenial companion ... saw the shadowy woman who would be his wife. ...

A cold fear gripped him. He was over thirty now. He couldn't wait for it indefinitely. It mustn't come too late. ... He thought of Stella without affection or hatred, but coldly, dispassionately. Her heart was quite strong, but she had had bronchitis badly last winter. The doctor said that she had narrowly escaped pneumonia, and pneumonia, of course, was often fatal in elderly people. Another cold winter ...

He dropped his thin face into his hands with a shudder of self-loathing. He seemed to be standing on the edge of an abyss looking down into the blackness. . . .

When the luncheon bell rang he had not written a word. He rose from his desk with relief. The sound seemed to break some evil spell and bring the world back to normality. . . . He would go downstairs and find Stella her most pleasant self; he would feel that surge of grateful affection for her that he so often felt; they would discuss trivialities in a happy intimacy as they so often did; his "mood" would vanish. . . . He had often had these "moods" before and they had always vanished—but, he knew despairingly, they returned more and more frequently, his hatred of her more bitter, the picture of what he could do with her money more vivid.

And today it didn't vanish. He sat opposite her at the luncheon-table, silently pleading with her to become the attractive lovable woman she so often became even now in his eyes, but she remained fat, vapid-looking, slug-like. . . .

He fought against it with agonised vehemence, but his hatred for her grew, till it seemed to fill the room like a monstrous tangible presence. Usually these sudden gusts of hatred of her made him shrink from looking at her, but it seemed now to take on a new terrifying quality. He fixed his eyes on her, gloating in secret over every imperfection, noticing the loose flesh that sagged beneath her chin, the pouches under her eyes, the coarseness of her once flawless complexion. Monstrous insults, obscene taunts came into his mind and he repeated them silently to himself, exulting in them.

He was making a pretence of eating, but his throat seemed to have lost the power of swallowing. He played with the food on his plate, trying to control the shaking of his hands.

"You're eating nothing, dear," she said. "Don't you like it?"

"Yes, thank you, but I don't feel very hungry."

"You're not looking well," she said. "If I were you I'd take a day or two off. We could go into the country." She looked at him anxiously. "No, you really *don't* look well. . . ."

He threw a quick glance at his reflection in the mirror on the wall near him. It showed his thin face, white and drawn, dark circles round his eyes, his long mouth set and tense. He could feel a nerve throbbing in his temple. He was suddenly afraid—of her, of himself, of everything. He must get away from her, if only for a few hours.

"I'm all right," he muttered. "I think I'll just run down to the Public Library on my bike. I've got one or two things to look up, and it'll give me a breath of fresh air."

The Public Library was one of his ways of escape from her. She could not very well accompany him there and sit in the reference room while he looked up references for his work.

"I'll come with you," she said. "We'll go by bus and I can pop in and see Miss Harwood while you——"

But he had gone from the room.

Chapter Nineteen

HE pedalled past the Public Library, and on through the streets of the suburb. He didn't notice how quickly he was riding, didn't notice even the thumping of his heart or the trickling of the sweat down his brow as he rode, with undiminished speed, up a steep winding hill. . . .

A mist had arisen since he set out, and a thin drizzle of rain began to fall.

The idea of escape had first occurred to him as he was passing the Public Library. It came with the force of a blow. He need never go back to her again. . . . He could go right away . . . now, at once . . . live his own life, fulfil himself, give outlet to the talent that had been frustrated for so long. He had on him a gold cigarette-case and a gold watch which Stella had given him. He would pawn them for his immediate needs. He would live sparingly, half starving if necessary. . . . Heady excitement swept through him. He felt as if he were being released from prison, as if he breathed the fresh air, saw the world of free men, for the first time. Then gradually his exultation faded, and depression took its place. It was too late. Once he could have stood on his own feet, have faced life and made his way in it by his own exertions, but now—it was too late. She had stultified his talent, made him dependent on her, body and soul, sapped his initiative, dulled his inspiration. He could have done it once but—it was too late. He knew that what he had earned in the past year would not have kept him for a month.

He fought against the depression as he pedalled on through the mist, his face grey with exhaustion, wet with rain and sweat. . . . It would need an effort, he told himself, but he could make it, he *must* make it. His salvation depended on it. He would go to—He realised suddenly that there was no one he could go to. He had not a friend in the world. For one wild moment he even thought of going to Charles, but realised almost at once that that would be impossible. She had set barriers between him and Charles that nothing could break down. But he must escape. . . . He must escape. . . . He redoubled his pace, his thin body bent low over the handlebars. He was trying to escape not only from Stella but from himself, from what he had glimpsed in the depth of the abyss over which his mind had hovered. . . . You didn't rest at wishing someone dead. . . . You didn't rest at hating them. . . .

He rode on through the mist and rain as if pursued; pursued by the ghosts of what he might have been—an artist with an artist's birthright of freedom; of what he was—his talent rusted, his will power rotted; and of what he might become . . . of what he might become. . . .

At first he couldn't think what the odd sound was that accompanied him . . . then he realised that it was the sound of the hammering of his heart. He was ridden out. He couldn't go on any longer. . . . He dropped from his bicycle and, propping it against a wall, stood gasping for breath. He had been riding too quickly, of course. He must take it more easy.

A woman, passing by, looked at his ashen face as he stood there panting, hesitated, then said, "Are you all right?"

He nodded, and she went on, glancing back uncertainly.

He became aware that he was drenched to the skin. Dusk was falling. Pictures of Stella's cosy sitting-room came to him—the bright fire, clean hearth, the shining tea things. . . . Instinctively he turned to go back (he could easily pretend that he had been so busy at the Library that he had forgotten the time), then he pulled himself up. He couldn't go back. But, despairingly, he knew that he would go back. If not today, tomorrow—if not tomorrow, next week—if not next week, next year. He would go back to her in the end. He couldn't stand on his own feet. She had deliberately unfitted him for it. . . . He would go back—back to the hatred, the shame, the humiliation . . . the blackness of the abyss.

"No, *no!*" he said aloud, and, mounting his bicycle, continued his way along the wet mist-shrouded road. But his strength—physical and moral—was ebbing from him. He was trapped. There was no way out... no way out. His breath came in dry rasping sobs. His feet had barely power to push down the pedals. The rhythm of the bicycle seemed to take on a refrain of its own. No way out ... no way out... no way out.... And suddenly in a flash it came to him. There was one way out ... only one. ...

A lorry appeared at the bend of the road coming towards him. Setting his teeth, lowering his head, he rode straight into it.

Chapter Twenty

DOREEN walked slowly down the road, looking at the numbers of each house.

She had had considerable trouble in finding where Stella lived. Everyone in Runeham had lost touch with her long ago, and she seemed to have changed her address frequently even in the last year. The address had been given to her by a boarding-house keeper in Bayswater. It had been a dingy enough place, but this, to judge by the neighbourhood, would be yet dingier. ... Stella, she had heard, had only moved in last month, so she should still be there. ... Odd how Stella had completely vanished from the life and memory of Runeham. Doreen had read in the paper of Oliver's death in a motor accident about eight years ago. The bicycle he had been riding had skidded on a greasy road and run into a lorry.

She remembered the shy handsome boy, with the sensitive mouth and deep-set dark eyes. He had been, even that one meeting had told her, talented and artistic and highly strung, and his death seemed a tragic cutting-short of promise. She had written a letter of sympathy to Stella but had received no reply.

She tried to picture Stella as she must be now—a woman of sixty—but could only see the girl of forty years ago, slender and graceful, exquisitely lovely. She thought of the time she had seen her presiding over the family luncheon at the kitchen table in the little house at Peckham. Even then she had been as lovely as ever—neat, efficient, gravely absorbed in her task, hovering about the family like some tender angel of domesticity.

Perhaps it was the confusion of the present—a world plunged headlong into a war whose end no one could foresee—that threw such a glamour over the past, giving it a beauty and serenity that it probably had not had in reality.

More and more, of late, Doreen had wondered whether she had misjudged Stella. From the beginning, of course, she had been jealous—jealous of her charm and beauty, of Hugh's love for her. It had been Hugh's love for which she had not been able to forgive her. Her mind went back over the years of her own marriage to Hugh . . . those years of mutual understanding, of quiet friendship. The first love of his manhood had been given to Stella, but she no longer grudged it to her. What she, Doreen, had had was different but infinitely more worth the having. There had been something rocklike in her own relations with Hugh, his love for Stella had been built on shifting sands. Both Doreen and Hugh were reserved and inarticulate, and the steady deepening of the passion that united them into something firmer and more secure than passion itself, the uniting of their interests and outlook till everything either of them did or said or felt seemed to spring from the same root, was so gradual that neither realised it till the process was complete. Their absorption in their children helped to unite them, of course. Hugh was restless and ill-at-ease away from his family, and Doreen, immersed in the duties of her home, would snatch at any excuse to avoid leaving it. On either side the feeling was centred in the other, and after Phyllida's wedding last year (Peter now had a commission in the Guards) they had settled down to a quiet life of joint home interests. Then came the war, crashing into their lives like the bomb that was its sign and symbol. . . . Their happy enclosed life vanished. Doreen turned the Hall into a military hospital, but no casualties arrived, for the two armies remained entrenched behind their lines through the long winter months. Peter went out to France, came home on leave, went out again. . . . Men in the village were called up. On the sea and in the air relentless war continued, but the men of the land forces stayed immobile, watching each other. . . . There was a sinister terrifying feeling of suspense. . . .

Hugh was restless and unhappy. It irked him intolerably that his country had no need of his services.

"I'm as fit as ever I was," he said. "I'm as fit as Peter any day. And I've got the experience of the last war as well."

Then came the staggering blow of the invasion of Holland and Belgium, and beneath the dismay was a faint sense of relief because the ghastly inaction was over at last. The piercing of the French line, the cutting off of the British Expeditionary Force . . . the seizure of the Channel ports. . . .

Hugh slept hardly at all. He was worrying about Peter, who was out with the British Expeditionary Force, brooding on his own forced inaction, his spirit haunted by a sense of shame because of it.

That May was the loveliest within memory. Lilac, laburnum, horse chestnut, pink and red hawthorn, cherry blossom and rhododendrons flamed against a cloudless sky. The orchards were starred with daffodils, the gardens gay with wallflowers and ranks of tulips. The new green of the grass and of the trees was like a song of praise. The whole earth seemed to blossom exultantly. And Hugh, who knew and loved every tree and flower and blade of grass around his home, saw none of it. . . .

The lines on his face deepened. He became irritable for the first time in his life.

Doreen's heart turned over in sick suspense when she saw Hugh standing in the hall opening the orange slip.

"Tell me quickly if it's Peter," she whispered with white lips.

He read it, and the years seemed to drop from him. . . . He handed it to her. It was from an old friend with whom he had once spent a yachting holiday. "Am going to Dunkirk. Will you come with me?"

At once he was a young man again—eager and excited as Doreen had seldom seen him even in his youth. He sprang upstairs three steps at a time to collect his belongings, calling directions in a quick vibrant tone she hardly recognized.

She did not dare voice her fears.

"Au revoir, dearest," he said as he kissed her. "I'll be back soon. . . ."

He drove off at breakneck speed in the ramshackle old car he kept for his own use. She watched him turn out of the gates through a sudden mist of tears.

He was wounded by fragments of a German bomb that burst on the beach just as he was starting on his third return voyage across the Channel. Doreen arrived at the hospital just in time to see him before he died. His face was as white as the pillow it rested on, but it still wore that eager boyish look.

"You've come," he breathed. "I knew you would."

Then for a moment he was back in his youth pleading with Stella to marry him.

"Stella . . ." he said brokenly, "Stella . . ."

After that he knew her again and fixed his eyes on her with a look of such utter love and serenity that there was no need of words. He only spoke once more and that was to say her name.

Her children rallied round her to comfort her, but she could not feel any excessive grief. She loved him too much for that. He had died in doing that which of all things he had most longed to do. The world he knew and in which he was at home was crumbling. He was a man of routine, a man whose pride it was to live as his fathers had lived before him. He would have felt bewildered and unhappy in the new world that was shaping, too old, too uncompromising in thought and outlook to adapt himself to it. Moreover, all her memories were of comradeship and unity, of joys and sorrows shared, of help given and received, of trust and happiness. The sting of death is remorse, the victory of the grave the memory of strife and bitterness. Her memories of him were so real that they seemed to form a tangible presence, accompanying her, comforting her, shutting out desolation. . . . There were times, of course, when she missed him poignantly, when life seemed unbearably black and empty without him, but she had almost unconsciously absorbed something of his simple unquestioning faith, and she looked forward with sure hope to reunion after death. In the nature of things she could not have so very long to wait now. . . .

It was not till some weeks after his death that it occurred to her that she owed it to Stella to tell her how Hugh's thought had turned to her at the end. For some time she put the idea away from her. She had a strange repugnance to renewing contact with Stella. . . . But once she had faced the necessity, as she saw it, of doing so, her memories of Stella became stronger, invested with the glamour that generally invests memories of one's youth. Stella, young, radiant, lovely . . . when all the world was young, radiant, lovely . . . before ugliness and cruelty had lifted their heads to trample down all beauty.

She felt vaguely surprised as she went down the street, with its dirty brickwork, scaling paint and dingy lace curtains. . . . The strips of brown paper pasted across the windows and the various "blackout" makeshifts deepened the atmosphere of squalor. She thought of the small fortune that Stella had inherited from Biddy. Surely she could afford to live in better surroundings than these. . . .

At last she came to the number she was looking for. The house was just like the others—strips of brown paper already peeling off the glass, discoloured lace curtains, a drooping fern in one window, a vase of tarnished metal, filled with artificial flowers, in the other.

She knocked at the door. A girl in a greasy overall, with bare legs and once-white canvas shoes, through which the big toe protruded on each foot, answered the door.

"Is Mrs. Sanders staying here?" asked Doreen. The girl stared. She wasn't used to callers like Doreen.

"Yeah," she said. "But she's not in now. You can wait in the drawing-room if you like. She'll be in for lunch."

She threw open a door just inside the hall.

Doreen entered. It was the room one would have expected from such a house—cheerless, musty, haunted by a faintly unsavoury smell. The furniture consisted of numerous occasional tables and a heterogeneous collection of chairs in various stages of shabbiness, with apparently no attempt at arrangement. The carpet was threadbare and ingrained with dirt. There was a dusty fan of faded coloured paper in the empty grate.

An old lady was sitting by the fireplace knitting. She looked up questioningly as Doreen entered.

"I've come to see a friend of mine," explained Doreen. "The maid said I could wait in here."

"What's your friend's name?" said the old lady.

"Mrs. Sanders."

The old lady beamed.

"Oh, yes. . . . She's only been here a month but she's *quite* an acquisition. So sweet, isn't she?"

Pictures of Stella came to Doreen across the years. She saw a golden-haired child playing in the garden of East Lodge, saw a slender girl in a white dress walking with Hugh beneath the cedars of the Hall. . . .

"And such a sad life she's had," went on the old lady.

"I suppose she has," agreed Doreen.

"Left a young widow, you know, with two little children to support. Worked her fingers to the bone to give them a good education. Her whole life, you know, has just been one long sacrifice for others. Have you seen her recently?"

"No . . . not for years."

"You know how badly her elder son treated her?"

"I—heard something about it."

"Not a word or a line since his marriage. And never a word of blame from her. All sweetness and forgiveness. 'When they need me,' she said, 'they'll turn to me. All I've ever wanted to do is to help them.' And her other son, you know, was killed in a motor accident. He was different to the other one. Him and her were all in all to each other."

Doreen glanced at her watch. There was something curiously oppressive in the frowzy little room and the garrulous old lady.

"She'll be in to lunch," the old lady assured her. "She's always in to lunch. The food is dreadful but not a word of complaint from her, though she's not been used to this sort of thing no more than I have. She's shown me photographs of the house she was brought up in and photographs of herself on horseback and in a ball dress." Her voice sank to a note of reverence. "Carriage folk, they were, you know, in those days."

A wave of almost personal humiliation swept over Doreen. Could Stella really have stooped to this sort of thing?

"So bright and kind and cheerful always," prattled on the old lady. "It's made such a difference having her here. A ray of sunshine, I call her. . . . And so brave. She's lost all her money through this dreadful war, you know."

Doreen wondered how Stella could have lost Biddy's legacy, safely invested in trust funds, through the war. . . .

"Oh yes, she's very poor," went on the old lady, "but so kind and generous. Can't do enough for people. . . . Had a little tea-party for us the other day in her room and gave us all little presents. . . . You know her well, I suppose?"

"No . . . I don't think I ever knew her well," said Doreen slowly.

"She's very sensitive," said the old lady. "Very sensitive indeed. She was very hurt the other day. Mrs. Price interrupted her when she was telling us about her old home and began talking about something else. I've never liked Mrs. Price myself, but in a place like this you've got to put up with all sorts."

Doreen rose abruptly and went to the window. The feeling of oppression was growing stronger. The memory of Stella's grace and loveliness was fading. . . .

"Sweet, that's what she is," said the old lady. "How anyone could be unkind to her! But they can. Some people at the last place where she stayed treated her most unkind. She was telling me about it last night."

She paused as if waiting for Doreen to ask for details.

Doreen stood at the window, her back to the room, silent.

The old lady began to gather up her knitting and hand-bag.

"Well, I'd better go. It's nearly lunch-time." Suddenly Doreen saw a woman pass the window, carrying a confectioner's cardboard box. She was repellently fat, and she waddled along on a pair of down-at-heel shoes. The hair, beneath the shabby hat, had a harsh metallic gleam, the flabby pendulous cheeks were rouged a crude pink. The lips were curved into a fixed complacent smirk.

For some moments Doreen looked at her without recognition; then with a sudden stab of horror she realised that it was Stella. She watched the figure, feeling as if in the grip of a nightmare. It couldn't be . . . but it was. Beyond all possibility of doubt it was. For the ghost of the old Stella was still there, her slenderness haunting the monstrous bulk, her sweet faint smile the empty smirk.

"There she is," said the old lady suddenly. "Such a dear! Well, well. . . . Cold meat it'll be, I expect. It's never anything else. The food gets worse and worse."

She went out of the room, leaving the door ajar.

After a few moments the woman Doreen had seen through the window crossed the hall and began to mount the stairs without looking into the drawing-room. Evidently she had not been told that a visitor was waiting for her. Doreen stood there uncertainly. She felt that she could hardly breathe. She must get away at once—away from this dreadful house and the hideous caricature of the loveliness that had been Stella. She went into the hall. It was empty. She opened the front door and stepped out into the street. She stood there for a moment drawing in the fresh keen air. A strange exhilarating sense of freedom swept through her, as if the last link that had bound her life to Stella's were broken. Then she walked quickly away without looking back.

Stella waddled upstairs to her top-floor bedroom breathing noisily and clasping the bag of cream buns, her lips still wearing that set fatuous smirk. . . .

Printed in Great Britain
by Amazon

50045814R00138